SHATTERED TO PIECES

SHEVAUN DELUCIA

Words Written, LLC New York

www.shevaundelucia.com

Publisher's Note: This is a work of fiction. Names, characters, places, and incidents are a product of the author's imagination. Locales and public names are sometimes used for atmospheric purposes. Any resemblance to actual people, living or dead, or to businesses, companies, events, institutions, or locales is completely coincidental.

Shattered To Pieces/ Shevaun DeLucia/ Print ISBN 979-8-9985764-1-6

Shattered To Pieces / Shevaun DeLucia/ eBook ISBN 979-8-9985764-2-3

To the women who are shattered, never give up on the possibility of love.

PROLOGUE

"*M*iss, is everything okay? Is there someone you would like me to call?" I ask the frightened woman in front of me. Her son clutches his little hands around his mother's neck with his life. The little boy is scared and not quite sure what is going on; he's not aware of the magnitude of this situation but, how can he be? He can't be any more than two or three years old.

The woman gazes at the pebble stones in front of her, never looking directly at me. I see she's in shock from the terror that has just been sprung upon her. No woman should ever have to go through what she's just encountered. I hate this part of my job. The things I must witness can sometimes stay with me for long periods of time. This may be one of them.

"No, I don't have any family," she replies. "My son is all I have."

I look around my surroundings, giving myself a moment before I can speak again. "There are shelters for battered and abused women with children. You would be safe there until you can figure out your next move," I explain to her. I just hate the thought of walking away when she seems so fragile and vulnerable.

She finally looks up at me with these big brown eyes. These are eyes that will haunt me for years to come. The hurt, defeat, and vacancy I see in them is gut-wrenching, and though I want to ask her how she got in this situation, I keep my question to myself.

"Should I be worried about him being released tonight?" she asks.

I watch as my colleagues take off with the man in custody. "I already looked at his prior convictions, and it looks like he's gone and violated his parole. He won't be getting out tonight that's for sure and I'm assuming once his parole officer gets wind of this, he may not be getting out anytime soon," I answer.

She looks relieved. "Okay, then I should be fine here. How will I know if he gets bailed out?" she asks. She kisses the top of her son's head and rocks him a bit to calm him.

I give her the police report and write the number to the county jail on it. "Here, call this number and they should be able to confirm his court date or if he's being released on bail."

She smiles timidly. "Thank you." She looks back down to her son and kisses the top of his head again.

"Caruso, you about ready to wrap it up?" my colleague yells over to me. I nod.

I turn back to the woman. "Now, are you sure you're going to be okay?" She nods without looking back up at me. I take out my business card and write my cell number down. I don't normally do this, but in this case, she has no one else to contact if trouble comes back around. I go to hand her the card. She looks at it, then looks back up at me unsure. "Please, take this card. It has my cell number on it. If anything should happen again, please call me."

She agrees and takes it. "Thank you."

I know I must walk away but looking down at them so vulnerable and shaken is killing me. This is always the hardest part of my job, but for some reason, tonight seems to be affecting me even harder. I nod to her and walk to my car leaving with an unsettling feeling deep down in my gut. I wish the best for them as I take one last look at the two of them sitting on the front porch, then drive off.

CHAPTER 1

SKYLAR

"Wow, Mom! This place looks pretty cool!" my son yells out right before running inside our new home.

I pause, putting my hands on my hips just taking it all in. This place feels right. This is our third house in two years. I don't think I can handle another move. I never felt at home as a kid, I was shuffled from foster home to foster home during my young years. Some of the places I had to endure were just a step up from being on the streets; cockroaches, rats, floors so dirty I didn't even want my shoes to touch them. But as long as there was a bed to sleep on, clothes on my back, and food in the refrigerator, the state said that was good enough; we just needed the bare necessities to live, anything else was a privilege.

I take a deep breath and exhale. I'm sick of moving around and I'll be damned if I fuck up my little boy's life. It just never fails, though, the moment we seem to get settled in a place, *he* finds us, and we're forced to grab what we can and leave everything else behind.

It's not the ideal situation, but it's the only way I know how to protect my son. I was young, naïve, and needed a quick escape from my hell when I met him—*Antonio Castro*—the father of my son, Drake. He was older and charming, and at the time he was exactly what I needed to take me away from the hellhole that was my life.

Antonio Castro was protective and demanding at first; like a father would be with his daughter. I guess I needed that; I craved that at that time due to the lack of my biological parents' presence in my life. My mother was a crackhead, and my father was her pimp—so I was told. I was dropped off in a box and left on someone's porch. So, when Antonio gave me attention, I closed my eyes and grabbed a hold tightly to him. He was my breath of fresh air at the time, and he was my only way out. It wasn't until I was too deeply involved that I found out what type of man he really was. By then I was already pregnant with Drake.

"Mom! Come inside!" Drake calls out with excitement from his new bedroom window.

I shake my head and laugh. "*Ok*, I'm coming!" I yell back.

As I'm walking toward the door, I hear a car door slam. I look to my left. A man walks around to the passenger door of his SUV to let his dog out. He watches me intently as I enter the house while calling for his dog to follow. Weird. There's a familiarity about him, but that can't possibly be right. I haven't been back here in years.

I shake my head, and I chalk it up to paranoia. Knowing my luck, he'll know Antonio and I'll have to pick up and leave again in the middle of the night. This thought gives me that burning acidy feel in the pit of my stomach making me swallow hard. I force myself to shake it off before the panic sweats begin to erupt throwing me into another spiraling meltdown.

I jog through the front door and up the stairs to the right. Drake wears a huge smile when I enter his room, and it makes my eyes tear up to see him so happy. That look, *that* smile is what I want to prevent from being tainted. This beautiful sweet little boy should never have to experience the wretched horribleness that life can bestow upon us, but because of my stupid decisions, he has. The guilt I hold just eats away at me day by day. Somehow, I must make this right. Drake deserves a normal life. *We* deserve a normal life.

"I love my room, Mom!" he says, running up to me and wrapping his arms around my legs. "Did you see how big my closet is? We can put a tent in there and go camping!" he yells excitedly. I chuckle.

He pulls me over to the closet and opens the door. I look in and *wow*, it really is impressive. "You're right, bud. We probably can fit a tent in here. Maybe that might be something we can get for your birthday that's coming up," I tell him.

His eyes grow wide as he begins to jump up and down with excitement. "That would be *awesome!*"

A dog barks in the distance, and it sounds as though it's coming from our front yard. Drake has been begging me for a dog for over a year now, but we can't take care of one with our lifestyle. His eyes grow big as he runs to the window, smiling and jumping ecstatically. "A doggy!" he yells. "It's a *big* doggy, too!" He turns and takes off down the stairs out the front door. Shit! I run after him, calling his name.

"*Drake!* Stop! You don't know if that dog bites or not!" I screech from behind him.

By the time I make it to the front door he is already kneeling petting the dog with slobber all over his face. I put my hands on my hips, shake my head, and laugh. He's like the dog whisperer; every time. I don't know how he does it.

"Benny, you just don't listen, do you?" the man from next door scolds as he walks over.

Every muscle in my body locks up. Not only is he a stranger, but he's a fucking *hot* stranger at that. "I'm sorry, ma'am. For some reason, he just loves your yard and kids. He just can't help himself," he tries to explain. I'm holding my breath in, devouring it, like it's the last breath I will ever breathe. Fear courses through my blood, licking and coating every drop, as I stand here wishing that Drake and I could magically become invisible.

It takes everything I've got not to turn my head and look at him. If I do, would he recognize me? Will he know Drake and I have just barely escaped my past from trying to rip us apart? I just don't think I have the strength to pick up and run again, but as soon as I look at my incredible little boy, I know that's just not true. So, I do it. I look up to meet the eyes staring back at me and wow—*those* eyes. Just fucking wow!

They immediately feel familiar. Those penetrating smoky blue eyes cause me to instantly rack my brain for a memory. My eyebrows furrow as I squint trying to study them more intensely. They're kind, yet stern. They're actually sorta beautiful right along with his godly body. He's of medium build—not much taller than me, biceps full of peaks and chest full of curvy muscle that could lift me up and ravage me like a rag doll if he chose, and a sharp chiseled jaw with lips I could kiss for days. I can almost picture them gliding down the nape of my neck as I squirm in pleasure.

He clears his throat with a smirk trying to get my attention clearly entertained. My cheeks heat up as I snap myself out of the trance. I'm a fucking idiot.

I clear my now dry throat. "Oh no, it's completely fine. Benny is in luck because he found a kid that absolutely loves dogs," I respond back attempting to hide my embarrassment.

Now it is him that is examining me closely as his eyes sweep over my body inch by inch causing my cheeks to now burn under his extreme scrutiny. I want to shrivel up and vanish into thin air. This is totally awkward.

"What is he, Shepherd?" I ask, trying to put his attention on something else besides me. I can't risk being noticed. God only knows, with my luck he may know Drake's father somehow.

He looks over toward Drake and Benny. "Yup, he's a Shepherd. He's my K-9 dog. My partner. He just finished his last level of training," he tells me, proudly.

Shit. A cop. This guy is a cop. I just recently learned that Antonio has a couple of cops on his payroll. That's how Drake and I were discovered this last time. I inwardly scold myself – I knew moving here wasn't far enough. Antonio has a reach as far as Timbuktu. I should have run far away across the country because I can't trust a single soul on this side of the map. I don't know what I was thinking. It's time to draw the line now. I have no choice but to put the wall up and make sure he gets the point. I don't need anyone to get too friendly with me or my son. Friends can't exist in our lives.

"Drake, it's time to go start some unpacking," I say, hoping this man will get the hint to retreat. Drake whines but gets up. Benny comes over to sniff me out. I pet the top of his head, then turn to his owner. "It was nice to meet you—" I just realized I never got his name.

He jumps in. "It's Neal. Neal Caruso."

I nod my head. "It was nice to meet you, Neal Caruso," I say, grabbing Drake's hand quickly heading inside before he can ask me mine. I shut the door quickly then lean my head against it for a moment to gather my thoughts. I take a deep breath in and then exhale slowly. I need to be more careful. I can't trust a single soul. Which means no small talk. No new friends.

"MOM, are we going to stay here for a while?" Drake asks me as I pull up the covers over his chest.

I take a deep breath as sadness engulfs me. I feel as though I have failed as a mother. It's my job to keep him from worry and fear. "Yes, baby. We'll stay here for as long as possible," I give him the best answer I can without lying to him as I kiss him on the forehead.

"Will the bad guys find us here?" he asks, eyes wide with wonder dripped with a little fear. My heart shatters even more. *God damn, Antonio!* Why can't he just leave us alone? I know he gets released soon. I'm just not sure how soon. He wants our son and will go to any lengths for this to happen, even if that means eliminating me.

I always told myself no matter how hard it is, I will always tell Drake the truth. The good, bad, and the ugly, only I may sweeten it a bit until he's old enough. "I hope not, little one. That's why we have to stick together, okay? We need to look out for each other always."

"Don't worry, Mom. I'll protect you," he says in his sweet munchkin voice.

God, I love this little boy. What would I do without him?

I lean down giving him a tight squeeze. "Thank you, my strong sweet boy. Now, get some sleep. We have to be up early to check out your new school in the morning."

I turn off his light and keep the door cracked just a bit. My room is directly across from his, which makes me feel much more at ease. I didn't sleep much at our last apartment because his room was too far down the hall, with a closet and bathroom between us. I went to sleep anxiously, afraid that I wouldn't hear if someone came into the house to take him and woke up in panic attacks with the angst that he would already be gone. I was constantly getting up in the middle of the night to check on him. The thought of finding him gone terrifies me to no end.

I look around my empty room, only 3 boxes to unpack. I'm now almost twenty-five and this is all I have to show for myself. I need to figure out a way to get my life back; to gain control and be free from Antonio. I just don't know how to do this. He's still in prison and still has full control over my life. How does this happen? Who the hell does he have behind him? And now I can't even think about going to the police. I can't trust a single person. We are utterly alone in this.

Last month two men dressed in police uniforms came to my door. It was late, probably just after 11pm. The hairs on the back of my neck stood up; my pulse raced as if my body knew something I did not. Finally, I opened the door, I mean they're cops, so I should have been safe, right? Wrong. They told me they were looking for a man by the name of Eric and when I told them there was no such person, they asked if they could come in. Something about them was off, and I knew I should have listened to my initial gut reaction. I slammed the door in their face before they could stop me. After that, all I remember is pure panic—life flashing before my eyes type of horror. The kind that I felt when Antonio held a gun to my head in front of Drake years ago threatening to pull the trigger while Drake watched in terror.

They broke down my door, but before they could search for me and Drake the neighbors all came out to see what was going on. The action caused a scene that in turn scared them away long enough for Drake and me to pack what we could grab and leave. I don't know how we did it, but by God's grace we managed to escape. We've been staying in low budget motels using cash over the last couple of weeks as we made our way here.

I shut the bathroom light off after completing my nightly regimen, climb in my bed, and close my eyes. It's been a long and stressful week, now my next hurdle to jump over is finding my ass a job. I loved my last job. I worked as a receptionist at an insurance agency. They paid decently, and I really liked the people who worked there.

I felt bad for just not showing up after they were so nice to me, but it's not the first job I've had to do this to.

I'm just hoping it will be my last. I take a deep breath out as I look around my room and smile before turning off the light. Night one in this place and I can breathe. I mean really let my body relax feeling safe. This place is already feeling like home.

Today's a big day for Drake and me. He doesn't even give me a moment to sleep in a bit. I see the excited twinkle in his eyes as he tugs on my blanket to wake me up. The sun bursts through my sheer curtains warming the room with its cheerful brightness. I can already tell that today's going to be a good day.

"Mom, Mom, it's time to get up! I have to go to school today," he tells me loudly. I wipe the crusties from my eyes, then look down at him smiling.

"I see you've gotten yourself dressed," I say surprised, trying to hold back the laughter. God bless his little soul. He has on his favorite play jeans with the rip in one knee and grass stain on the other, his Batman night shirt, and his sneakers; thank God they are Velcro.

He twirls around. "Do you like it?" he asks, glowing, proud of himself. These are the moments I need my camera, but I left it in our first apartment we ran from two years ago.

I sit up and swing my legs off my bed. "I do very much, but I picked out a special outfit for you just for today. Maybe you can put this one on when you get home?"

"Yay! Okay!"

"How about we go downstairs and get some breakfast?

I got you your favorite Cap'n Crunch cereal and mama is in dire need of some coffee," I tell him.

He races downstairs before me. I go downstairs and I look out the living room window to get a peek of outside; to see what neighbors I might have to fend off when leaving, but mostly because I hear a car door slam and my heartbeat picks up a knot. It's Neal and his dog, Benny, backing out of their driveway in his SUV. I exhale releasing the jitters that just compiled in my gut. The last thing I need right now is a run-in. Even though he's extremely easy on the eyes, I'm just not up to putting on a facade at the moment.

We finish breakfast, get dressed, and head out the garage door. I really need to look for a new car. This Buick no longer blends in; I feel as though the gold is now a sore thumb. These guys that Antonio has hired are probably searching for the car as we speak. I can't help but watch my back every turn I make. My hands are always shaking just a bit. My nerves are going to be the death of me. I left this town a couple of years ago and I haven't been back since. Maybe I should have uprooted to a whole different state, but I love New York. It's what I know, and since I have no family, being where I know is comforting to me. I need to hold on to something, so this is what I choose. Probably not the smartest, but I promised myself if we have to run again, it won't be anywhere near here.

"Mom? What if my teacher doesn't like me?" Drake asks as we're stopped at a stoplight. I turn to look at him and see the worry in his eyes.

I rub my hand over his head. My heart melts. "Your

teacher is going to *love* you!" I assure him, because I know this is true. How can you not look at this face and not love him? He's so precious and pure.

I see him squeeze his stuffed turtle just a little tighter. This seems to be his coping mechanism. This is the one thing we make sure never to leave behind. Especially during new unknown moments like these. Last year I had to pay for daycare. I felt as though I was working solely for that, but this year he's old enough for pre-school. It's only half a day, but it's some help even if I have to pay for part-time care after school. My new landlord was nice enough to wave my deposit. I had just enough for rent and some groceries, and the house was already furnished. I'd like to think my luck may be changing, but every time I attempt to think positive, I get my hopes up.

We pull up to school, and I can see Drake's eyes widen. To me it looks like a small brick building; one story with windows lining the outside. To him, it must look like the Empire State building. I rub my hand over his newly buzzed head again to gain his attention.

"Hey, everything is going to be okay. You're going to meet lots of other kids and you're going to love it so much you won't want to come home," I tell him, trying to erase his fears away.

He looks over at me with his big brown eyes. "I don't want to live here, Mom. I like my new room," he tells me, as serious as can be. I chuckle.

"I would miss you if you lived here," I tell him with a smile. I unbuckle my seat belt. "Come on, let's go inside." I wait for him to unbuckle his as well, then we head out of the car together.

I meet him at his car door and hold my hand out to him. He places his tiny hand into mine and holds on tight as we walk to the front doors. I press the little red button outside the entrance and wait to be let in after I explain who we are. This makes my tension ease just a bit. Security is always a good thing, especially in our case.

This place is alive and welcoming. Children's talented drawings cover the walls, the lights have a warm glow, and children walk by in a single line as the teacher reminds them to use their inside voices. Drake looks up at me with a huge smile. The receptionist smiles brightly at me as she asks if she can help me. She's a plump older woman with rosy cheeks and a kind smile. She throws off the comforting motherly vibe. I immediately feel at ease in her presence.

"Hello. I'm here to register my son, Drake, into preschool. We just moved into town," I explain to her.

"Well, that's great! Welcome," she says as she stands up to gather some paperwork. She hands me some forms and a clipboard. "Okay, you can sit down in those seats behind you to fill these out. Bring them back up when you're done and we can get Drake settled in Mrs. Turner's room."

"Thank you."

I grab the clipboard and direct Drake to take a seat. I complete the forms, and the receptionist walks us down to his new classroom. Drake has a death grip on my hand. We enter the classroom and it's drawing time.

I look down at Drake. "We came at the perfect time," I whisper to him.

Mrs. Turner comes right over to greet us; she's young

and vibrant. Her hair is fiery red with speckles of freckles dotting her face. I'm guessing she may be in her twenties just as I am, but she, unlike me, walks with a confidence and purpose that I wished I portrayed. The receptionist exits.

"Hello, welcome, Drake!" she says excitedly. "It's so great to meet you. If you like, you can go have a seat next to Tabitha right there and she can show you where the coloring tools are."

"Okay." He then looks to me. I nod my head for approval.

Mrs. Turner turns her attention to me. "Mrs. Kramer—"

"Please, call me Skylar," I advise her.

She smiles. "Skylar, I can assure you Drake will adjust just fine. If anything should come up, I will be more than happy to give you a call. Sometimes it takes a kid a couple of days to adjust," she says. We both look over toward Drake and he's already coloring away. "But I can see he's going to do just fine."

"Thank you. Drake's father isn't involved in our lives. Can you please call me if you should hear from him?" I ask her without giving her too much detail.

"Of course. I'm sorry to hear that."

I thank her and head over to Drake's table. He looks content. "Hey buddy, I'm taking off. If you need anything, let Mrs. Turner know, okay?"

He nods, gives me a big hug, and then gets back to his coloring. I sniffle trying to stop the waterworks from coming. My baby boy is getting too big. Where did the time go? I head out passing the front desk. A bright yellow flyer catches my attention saying a job opening is available. I immediately walk over to speak to the sweet older lady who brought Drake and I to class.

"Hello, I noticed that you had an opening available. What exactly does the job entail?" I ask the receptionist.

"We need help here in the reception area. One of the girls just went out on maternity leave. Have you any reception experience or worked for a school?" she asks.

"I was working as a receptionist at an insurance agency before we moved into town. The commute was just too far so I had to resign," I explain to her.

The phone rings. "Excuse me one moment."

I look around, smiling as some of the staff walks by me. These are people that I could possibly be working with if I get a job here. The thought of getting to know a new group of people stresses me out a bit; the continuous questions about where I'm from, what made me move here, and whether I'm married or not gets tiring every time. I'll have to come up with a new storyline; something believable and simple. Something that won't be too complex to remember when telling lies.

This job would be perfect for me. It's almost too good to be true. I could keep an eye on Drake while working. That would give me so much relief just knowing he's down the hall. She hangs up the phone. "I'm Jess by the way—" she says, holding out her hand.

I place my hand in hers. "I'm Skylar."

"Let me speak with Mrs. Conner, the principal, to see how the interview process is. I know I had to apply through the district, but we need someone asap. Maybe she can interview you now," she tells me.

This woman is amazing! "Oh, that would be great!"

She heads off into the principal's office and comes

back five minutes later. I meet with Mrs. Conner, and she tells me that after a background check comes back she will call me. This is the perfect job. I need this job. God, please give me this job I pray silently to myself.

AFTER DOING some running around and grabbing Drake from school we head home. The street is quiet at this time of day, not much action at all, except for Neal playing catch in his front yard with his dog, Benny. *Shit*. Ok, if I pull into the garage quickly, I can close the door right away to avoid any conversation, and to keep Drake from running over there.

"Benny!" Drake yells. He looks back over to me. "Look, Mom. Benny is out!" Damn.

I pull into the driveway, press my garage door opener above my head, wait for it to open, and pull in. I hit the button a second time for the door to close, but nothing happens. I press it again and look over my shoulder and nothing. What the? Drake gets out and screams Benny's name to get his attention. *Damn*, this plan didn't go very well.

I get out of the car and yell after Drake. "Drake! We need to get dinner started—" but it's no use. He's a goner. I take a deep breath and head out of the garage. Drake is kneeled in our front lawn *again* getting slobbered by Benny. I just shake my head and chuckle. I just wish I could get him a dog. This kid is too much.

Neal comes over and stands next to me with his hands in his pockets. He seems a bit nervous or maybe a little unsure. He's wearing ripped faded blue jeans and a black

V-neck formfitting T-shirt. His upper arms bulge with strength as his veins paint his forearms. The sex appeal is undeniable; my body is extremely aware of his. I see nothing but power and beauty; the kind of strength that could make me feel safe and protected. But his eyes are what gets me; they lock me in a trance just like before. I just can't turn away. The way his eyes penetrate me, reaching right through me, and coaxing me to relish in them is insane. They're beautiful. *He's* beautiful. If only we could stay this way forever. *Shit.* What's wrong with me?

Again, he clears his throat slapping me back into reality. My reality where strangers and men are to be avoided at all costs. My reality where no one is to be trusted. Of course, maybe not being with a man in over three years is affecting me in some way. I miss the smell and the touch of a man. I miss the sweet whispers at night while lying in bed wrapped in each other's arms. Antonio did this the first couple of months we were together. I had thought heaven had answered my prayers; but boy was I wrong. I will never allow myself to be wrong again, but it sure does get lonely not having someone to talk to or even rely on. It's exhausting constantly being on guard and always having to be strong. I've given up on love and desire. The only love I want is my son's, and the only desire I have is to protect my son at all costs. Everything else no longer exists in my world. *This* is my world; scary, undependable, and utterly alone.

"So how is the unpacking going?" Neal asks.

I rip my eyes from his finally and watch Drake and Benny play. "It's going good. We still have a couple more boxes to empty," I answer, keeping things short.

Drake is now rolling around on the ground with Benny. Great.

"Drake, you're going to get your clothes dirty!" I yell. He doesn't even hear me. Figures.

Neal chuckles at the two of them on the ground. "I didn't catch your name the other day—"

"That's because I didn't give it," I snap.

He jerks his head toward me caught off guard. Good. But I do feel a bit bad. He's been nothing but nice to me so far. "I'm sorry. I didn't mean to be rude. It's been a long day. My name is Skylar," I tell him, giving in just a bit. I mean, we are going to be neighbors for a while, hopefully. He may find me more suspicious if I act too guarded.

He smiles. "Skylar, huh? Nice name. Where you from, Skylar?"

These are exactly the questions I was hoping to avoid. "That's kind of a loaded question, don't you think?" I snap back.

His eyebrows furrow. "You think? It's just a common question people ask to get to know one another. I was just asking because you look familiar," he states.

This is not good. My heart is now beating in sprints. I'm beginning to panic a bit; my air constricting from my lungs. It's time to abort. "Well, I doubt we've meet before. I'm sorry, if you'll excuse me, I need to get dinner started," I lie. "Drake come on. It's time to go in."

He's in mid-roll with Benny. "Aww, *Mom!* Do I have to?" he questions hoping I will say no.

"Yes," I tell him so matter of factly.

Before I say anything else, a white car pulls up with a woman in the driver's seat. This must be the same girl I saw the other day. I'm assuming a girlfriend by the way he calls Benny and heads toward his house so quickly.

Drake and I walk through the garage. I attempt the door opener one more time as we open the door to the house and it works! *Phew.* I almost feel like it didn't work just a minute ago on purpose. Like God's playing a little evil trick on me.

CHAPTER 2

NEAL

"Hey, baby," I say, giving my girl a kiss.

I step aside so she can enter the house first, then Benny pushes his way through before me. My eyes drift over to Skylar's house before I enter my own. I can't help but wonder why she's so damn guarded. I mean, I only asked her name, and she almost ripped my head off. I shake my thoughts off. I guess it really doesn't matter. She's just someone who lives next door to me.

I follow Missy as she walks through the hallway toward the kitchen. "Who was that you were talking to?" she asks.

I grab Benny's bowl to dish out some of his food. "That's my new neighbor, Skylar, and her son, Drake," I answer. I feel a bit of tension and jealousy in her voice.

She puts her purse on the counter and grabs a wine glass out of the cupboard. "And there's no father or husband?"

I can tell she's trying to hide her jealousy. Skylar is a beautiful girl. Her curves are to die for. Most girls would feel inferior to them, and I can see Missy may be feeling this way as well. But I don't think she has anything to worry about. Skylar doesn't even seem to like me already. Her son is a cool little dude, though.

"Nope, none of the above. Is somebody *jealous?*" I tease while walking up behind her and pulling her into me.

She giggles. "*No*. Of course not!" Then she turns around to face me. "Why, should I be concerned?" she questions with a raised brow.

Ah, there it is. The question without really questioning. "Why would you ask such a silly question? Have I ever given you reason to doubt me?"

She exhales. "No."

I kiss the tip of her nose. "Okay, then. What should we do about dinner?"

THE REST of the night is relaxing. We do our normal cooking together, clean up, and watch some TV. She has her own place but sleeps over a couple of times a week. Missy and I have been dating on and off for the past two years. We met through my friend, Johnny Triano, on the force. It was his birthday night, and we were all throwing back some beers at a local bar. I'd never seen Missy before, so I was intrigued when she walked in.

She's a California blonde with light blue eyes, extremely petite, with very seductive body language—the tempting girl next store package. She has this pout that made me drop to my knees when I first met her; now it's getting a little old. She's been hinting around about wanting a ring, and that all her friends are now settling down and getting engaged, but it doesn't interest me at the moment. It just doesn't feel right. I take our relationship one day at a time. Some days I'm all in and some days I have to push through.

Missy and I still have a lot of issues, and we don't see eye to eye on a lot of things, but it's the sex that has brought us back together time after time. But how long can that go on? It's okay—*for now*. It satisfies my urges—*for now*. But I still feel as though something is missing. There's a void that she just cannot fill. Sometimes I think it may just be me, but there's other times, deep down in the depths of my gut, that I know it is not; it's us.

We head up to bed. By the time I brush my teeth and come back into the room, she is sound asleep on her side of the bed. I crawl into my side, put my hands behind my neck, and rack my brain on where I've seen Skylar before.

Those eyes are ice cold—almost removed like she has a fortress built up around her. But why? How is a girl like that so blocked off? What has she gone through to make her so closed up? Her son seems happy and carefree, trusting, unlike her. But what is her story? And most of all, why do I even care so much?

I have no idea why this is bothering me. The last thing that bothered me this bad was the girl I left on the front steps. It took me forever to get that vision from my mind every time I closed my eyes and still, I think of her from time to time—and then it hits me like a wrecking ball. My stomach sinks into my balls. *Oh shit!* It was *her*. She is the woman I met years ago that I haven't been able to forget or let go of. She was the woman holding the little boy, devastated and scared, as I tried to comfort her when answering to a domestic dispute. Her son's father almost killed her. He held a gun to her head in front of her son. If it wasn't for the window being open and her neighbor hearing her cries, she could be dead right now, and that little boy could be motherless and forever traumatized.

I knew I knew that face. I just *knew* it! And those big brown eyes, I couldn't forget them then and I sure as hell can't forget them now. There's just something about the haunted darkness that draws me in. But now it makes sense why she's so closed off. I would be too if I had to endure that. She probably has no trust for men, and she probably is trying her hardest to protect her son from witnessing that ever again. And who could blame her?

Should I tell her I know? Would she be grateful to see me again? I wonder if she's thought of me over the years like I've thought about her. God, I'm just being ridiculous. Of course, she hasn't thought about me. I mean, why would she? I'm just a man in a uniform that she met momentarily during probably the worst time of her life and I wouldn't blame her if she never wanted to think of that moment ever again.

I just can't believe she now lives next door to me. Out of every person in this world that could have moved there, she did. It's so weird how the ways of this world work. Maybe I have a bigger job ahead of me. Maybe we were brought together so I can be her protector. *God, get a grip, Neal.* Now that I have figured out who this familiar woman is, maybe I can get some sleep. I take a deep breath, close my eyes, and drift back to that very first moment I saw her.

THE SHRIEK of the alarm clock rips me from my sleep and when I open my eyes, I see that Missy has already left for work. We used to cuddle throughout the night and wake up to some good sex in the mornings. Now, we do neither. It honestly sucks. I feel like we're already that cliché married couple.

I don't have to be at work for another two hours, but I must get my morning jog in. Being on the police force requires me to stay fit so I don't get winded on the job. My agility becomes important when raiding a house and the perpetrator goes on the run. Things can get crazy in a matter of minutes, so my guard is usually up at all times by habit. Even when I'm off the clock.

I throw my workout clothes on and head downstairs to grab some orange juice before I head off. It's a beautiful September morning. Summer's coming to an end, but fall has always been my favorite. The smell of fireplaces and the colors of the autumn leaves get me hyped every year, it's hands down my favorite season.

I step out the front door and begin my stretches on the front porch. Benny runs off the porch over to the neighbors. I hear Skylar swearing in frustration. I smile. She didn't seem like she had it in her.

I walk over to see if everything is okay. Benny has already found Drake.

"Hey, Drake," I yell over to him. He waves and continues running around the front yard with Benny chasing behind him. Skylar runs her hands through her hair clearly irritated. "Hey, you okay?" I ask.

She exhales violently clearly stressed. "No, this damn garage door won't go down. I have to get Drake to school and now he's going to be late," she explains.

It's a good thing I'm handy. "Hey, listen, take him to school and I will work on fixing this for you," I offer.

She looks at me unsure, and it takes her a moment to respond. "*So,* you can fix this? Are you sure? I don't have any money to pay you right now. I can always call my landlord—" she says all in one breath.

I chuckle. "Yes, I can fix it. And no, I don't need any money for it. I'm your neighbor just being neighborly," I attempt a joke. "I'll close up when I'm finished."

She calls for Drake. "I won't be long. His school is right up the street," she says, heading for her car. She gets Drake in the car, then turns to me relieved. "Thank you, Neal." I think this is the first genuine niceness I have received from her so far.

I nod and wave her off. I go inside to my garage to grab my tools and head back over. The problem wasn't too hard to find; there was a wire that was frayed which could have caused a fire, so I'm glad I offered to check it out. I tape it up with electrical tape and test the door. It works perfectly. It didn't even take me more than fifteen minutes. I make sure the door to her house is locked and close the garage door behind me.

Benny and I get back from my jog. I look to see if Skylar came back, but I can't tell because the house is how I left it. She didn't mention having a job. Maybe she just went shopping or had some errands to do. Part of me wants to check on her, but that might throw her off a bit. I don't want to make her nervous, I mean I've finally just gotten her to speak with me.

I get in the house and have a text from Missy waiting for me. I wipe my face with the towel from around my neck and open it. She tells me she won't be over tonight.

That she's going to dinner with a friend, but the weird thing is—she doesn't mention the friend's name like she usually does. I text her back, "ok." I've never really been the jealous type. I guess with my job I've seen some of the horrific outcomes jealousy can cause. It's just not in my blood, or maybe it's because I'm with the wrong girl.

I hop in the shower and head off to work. I have a long day ahead of me. With my job I never know what kind of day I'm going to get. It's my job as head of my SWAT team to guide and train my men so no one gets hurt. These guys are like family to me. We all protect and have each other's backs on *and* off the field.

I get into the office and say hello to the officers passing by. A couple of my guys are huddled around looking at some new evidence.

"What's going on, guys?" I ask as I walk toward their desks.

Jacob Smalls, a short stocky Italian dude with thick black hair, speaks up first. "We just got a tip on another load getting dropped at a warehouse off Cut Street in a few days."

Man, this is some good news. "Yeah, Caruso, the informant is saying we're looking at at least a six figure drop," Cam Tully says.

Cam is the human version of Ken from Barbie, but on steroids. He's ridiculously huge and ridiculously ballzy, so we like to let him lead the raids. He's like a bull. Once someone sees him, they run. I've seen it hundreds of times. Never fails. Happens every time.

"Ok, let's meet up in the training room in thirty so we can go over our game plan," I tell them all. "By the way, when does Johnny come in?" I ask Cam.

Johnny is my second-in-command. He's my go-to man. If I need something done, he's the man to go to. I need him by my side because we work off each other. He was in my same boot camp, too. We were bunk buddies for months. So, if I trust anyone with my life, it's him without a doubt.

"He'll be in at ten," Cam answers. I nod and head to my office.

IT's NOW 10pm as I pull into my driveway. I see a white box at my front stoop. I park and head up to look. It's a semi-small box, warm, and it's light when I pick it up. I look around quickly. I usually don't get presents left at my door. This is odd. I open the box and there sits a warm apple pie inside. The note on the top says:

Thank you for this morning.
~ Skylar

I smile and take a big whiff. It smells mouthwatering. If it wasn't so late, I'd make her and Drake join me. I step into the house and Benny is overly excited to see me. He's ready for a bathroom break. I lock up behind me and head to the back-sliding glass door to let him out. I had the backyard fenced in as soon as I got him just for these occasions. I tend to get home late and walking him at this time of night is not something I enjoy.

I immediately grab a plate from the cupboard and cut myself a piece of the pie. The first bite is delicious. French vanilla ice cream would go perfect with this. Store-bought is the closest I ever get to homemade apple pie. I need to help her more often if this is the thanks I will get.

I pour myself a glass of milk and sit back down at the table. I scroll through my phone to see if there's any text messages from Missy I missed—but nothing. This is very unusual. Either she stops by to see me, or she messages or calls me before I head to bed. I throw her a quick message to see if everything's ok, let Benny back in, and then head upstairs to jump into the shower.

I grab the towel and begin drying myself off. I walk into my room and head over to close my blinds. I can see Skylar's room from mine. I see her walk across her room in only her bra and underwear to also close her curtains. My dick is now hard as a rod. Her silhouette through the sheer curtains is exquisite. What I wouldn't give to run my hands along the contours of her body. My hands would fit perfectly over those hips as I pumped deep inside of her. My dick salutes her just thinking about it. *Fuck.* I quickly draw my blinds down and step away before she catches me watching her. I shake my head. What the hell am I thinking? I'm acting like a creeper. Cops aren't supposed to creep. We arrest Peeping Toms, but I just couldn't help myself.

I look at my phone again to see if Missy has responded to my text—and still there is nothing. Maybe she ended up going to bed early; I mean, it's a possibility after all. As soon as my head hits the pillow exhaustion sets in, but my mind doesn't seem to get the memo. I wish I didn't just peep Skylar out because thoughts of that curvy body are now flooding my head. Those hips, those perfectly thick legs, and that smooth kissable stomach I would love to rub my lips across, are now stuck in my brain giving me a major boner. Great. Just what I need, blue balls.

It's been a couple of days since Missy and I had sex therefore my mind must be going overboard with the first woman I see undressed. Skylar seems to bring out the teenage boy in me. I roll over and will myself to sleep. Of course, this does me no good. I rarely have moments of obsession, but something about her just does it for me.

BENNY WHINES as he nudges my hand. I crack my eyes open only to see his tongue lick my face. I shove him away from my face. "Come on, Benny! Just give me a minute to wake up," I complain like he can understand me. He's demanding just like a kid. I stretch, then toss my covers off me, and get my ass out of bed.

Benny barks at me to hurry me up. "Okay, okay! I'm coming," I snap at him.

I feel as though I haven't slept. I had some vivid dreams last night; Skylar seemed to be in most of them. I'm guessing this is because she was the last thing on my mind before I fell asleep last night. Now that I've opened her up a bit and she's being receptive to me, maybe I can get to know her a little bit more.

I open the sliding glass door to let Benny out. I pull open the refrigerator to grab the orange juice, but what I really could use is a nice strong cup of coffee instead. I put my empty glass in the sink and head upstairs to get my jogging clothes on. I head back downstairs, put on my sneakers, and let Benny back in only to put his leash on. He loves our runs; he prances in excitement.

It's seven. Most of the neighborhood is heading to work or getting ready to head to work. Over the years I've studied and learned the tiny details of my neighbor's lives. I guess paying attention to detail is just engrained in me. Mrs. Ortega, the elderly woman across the street to my left, lets her cat out every morning at five am. Mr. and Mrs. Tilla live on the other side of her to my right; he leaves for work in his white 2020 Town and Country van every morning at 8:15am, and Mrs. Tilla walks her two twin boys, Keith and Kurt, to the bus stop every morning at 8:20am, then leaves for her yoga class that she teaches in town. Jack Sullivan, who lives to my right, is recently divorced and is now on the prowl. Women come in and out of his house like a convenience store. I must admit, he has some good taste, but nothing seems to interest me like Skylar does.

I must know who I'm surrounded by at all times. It's important to pay attention to detail. Being on the force can create enemies. The type of people I deal with aren't happy when we raid their livelihoods. It leaves a lot of angry people in our wake and that's when the thoughts of revenge take place.

It happened to my last partner, Simon Kates, just as we joined SWAT. We raided a house for dope, confiscated 400k worth, and arrested three men. Unfortunately, they were only minnows in the whole scheme of things. Millions of dollars are passed through drug dealers' hands, and we only touched a crumb. A week after that my partner was hunted down and killed coming out of a grocery store. He left behind a wife and two kids. It was horrific. All I could think was, why not me? I didn't have a family. It should have been me. But I knew that I was going to be next. It was only a matter of time. I was transferred to another precinct and was relocated back to this area. There's not a day that goes by that I don't run the risk of being hunted down like Simon was. But that's the chance one runs into when choosing this type of career.

Benny tears me from my thoughts as he forges ahead tugging on his leash to hurry me up. He's so impatient. I look over toward Skylar's house, and it seems quiet and still. If Drake were awake, he would be already out here with Benny.

I feel like I need to learn more about Skylar and her ex. I wonder if he's been released since that night. A small part of me feels like it's my duty to make sure she's looked after and protected. I mean after all I am her neighbor who just happens to be a cop. I want to know more. I want to know she and Drake are ok. Just because I'm off the clock doesn't mean I stop being a cop.

I finish with my run and daylight has now broken through the sky. I love watching the sun peek up as I run while clearing my mind. I swear you can hear it as it's birthed from the horizon while the rays of the sun burst through the sky. It's so peaceful being out here alone while the rest of the world is just waking up. Some of my best thinking has been done during these moments. The sky looks painted as it is melded with light blues and oranges looking picturesque and calming.

Benny and I head inside. I freshen up his water bowl and fill his food bowl before heading upstairs to shower. I do something I know I shouldn't do—I peep out of my bedroom window toward Skylar's, but there's no movement. Man, what the hell is *wrong* with me?

I head over to the bathroom and hear the chime of a

text notification going off on my phone. It's a text from Missy. She says she drank a little too much at dinner last night and went straight to bed after dinner. Then tells me she will be by when I get off work tonight. I was hoping to stop by Skylar's to thank her for the pie when I got home, but maybe I shouldn't push it.

I HEAD INTO WORK, straight to my office before I meet with the team. Johnny said there was some intel that was passed along from the informant, so we have a meeting set up to go over tactics with the captain. There has been a major epidemic happening in and around our surrounding areas; young girls are vanishing into thin air and cocaine is now on the rise more than ever. This particular strand that is going around is being cut with fentanyl. It's cheaper and they can get more use out of their product which in turn has led to more deaths caused by overdose. There's been some talk of possible connections to the cartel which goes hand in hand with the human trafficking as well.

One takedown at a time is what we aim for in hopes to just make a dent in the big fight, but unfortunately, when one piece of crap dealer is eliminated, two more pop up in its place. Patience in this type of takedown is a must. We have undercover officers involved with years of evidence and hard work put into these investigations. We're the last line of defense that's called upon once all that hard work has come to a head and needs elimination. So, it's important that we're all up to speed and on the same page.

"Hey, what's up, man?" Johnny says, closing the door

behind him and taking a seat in the chair in front of my desk.

I'm going through all the files on my desk of each perpetrator we think is connected to this drug deal. We've been staking out the place ever since we got the tip yesterday. It seems this drug deal might be the mother-load; bigger than we expected. So, we need to make sure we have our asses completely covered. If one thing is amiss that could be detrimental in the safety of my men.

"Not much. Just going through these files before our meeting," I tell him. "Listen, can I ask you for a favor?"

"Sure. Name it."

"Three years ago, we arrested a man regarding a domestic dispute over in East Spencer on Cambridge Drive. There was a girl named Jennifer with a young child involving a gun and a parole violation. Can you narrow down some more information and bring me the file on it?" I ask.

He looks at me a little confused. "Is this related to the case?"

"No, it's personal." This is the only thing I answer.

He nods, understanding. A knowing look between us means it stays between us.

"Thanks, man."

CHAPTER 3

SKYLAR

"Mom, Mom, look what I made for you!" Drake screams across the room. He runs up giving me a beautiful painted picture of our new house, me, and him. I squat down to give him a big hug. My little man is so thoughtful.

"I absolutely love it! Did you paint this all by yourself?" I ask, already knowing the answer.

He nods his head eagerly up and down with a humongous smile. "I did!"

Mrs. Turner walks up to us. I stand back up to greet her. "Can I talk to you for a moment in private?" she asks.

My heart begins to pump vigorously. I'm completely freaking out inside. My stomach is doing somersaults in a vat filled with acid. Did Drake's father contact her? Did one of his goons already find us? What could she possibly want to know?

I follow her to the back corner of the room. She turns to me with a look of pity or could it possibly be sadness.

"I'm sorry, but what is this about? Is everything okay with Drake?" I question becoming extremely antsy.

"Yes, he is an amazing little kid, but I am a little concerned," she admits. I don't say anything. I wait for her to continue. "I asked the kids to draw their favorite super-heroes and to tell us why they choose that particular one. When he was finished, he drew you. He said that you have special powers because you keep the bad guys from hurting you both," she finishes.

Oh, wow. Okay. It's now time to go into recovery mode. "Drake has an incredible imagination. The thing is that his father is in prison, and he associates prison with bad guys. So naturally he has come up with this elaborate idea. I really don't tell too many people this because most seem to judge, but I just want Drake to grow up with a normal life. I'm doing my best to not let any of this affect him," I respond honestly, holding back all details.

I feel a small bit of relief telling someone this even though it's uncomfortable. But if anyone should know, it should be the person who spends a good amount of time with him each day. The pit in the bottom of my stomach is praying she might understand; praying that she doesn't think of me as a horrible mother for choosing a monster as a father for my child.

I can't tell what she's about to say to all of this and it's driving me crazy. "Mrs. Kramer, there is no way I would ever judge you based on what someone else has done. You didn't choose this for Drake and I'm truly sorry you've had to deal with this. I may understand more than you know. I would like to suggest one thing, though," she adds. "It may benefit Drake to visit with our school counselor, Mrs. Jackson. You don't necessarily have to reveal all the details to her, but she has ways of teaching the kids coping mechanisms that can help throughout their lives starting at a young age."

I think about this for a moment, fiddling with my purse zipper, before answering. "Can I take some time to think about this?"

"Yes, of course. The offer is always here. I just want to tell you again what an amazing little boy you have. He's just so sweet," she compliments.

Her eyes are a calming golden brown; tiny wrinkles flare out from the corner of her eyes when she smiles. I feel that what she is saying is coming from a good place and this makes me feel at ease.

She almost brings tears to my eyes. "Thank you so much for your kind words."

"You're very welcome," she tells me.

Drake comes over and tugs on my coat. I look down at him. "Are you ready to go, buddy? Come on, let's go home." We say our goodbyes and head out of the classroom.

As we're heading out the front door, Jess, the receptionist, calls me over. She takes me into the principal's, Mrs. Conner's office. Mrs. Conner kindly offers me the job as assistant receptionist. I immediately jump up, accepting without even taking a moment to think and give her a hug. Jess and her both laugh. This feels so surreal! I can't believe I got the job. I'm ecstatic and completely on a euphoric high. This couldn't have come at a better time. Maybe my luck is turning around finally.

"Thank you, thank you so much!" I tell them. Drake is giddy with excitement watching me jump around like a nutcase. He follows along doing the same thing.

Mrs. Conner told me I can start training tomorrow with Jess. I need to be there an hour before school starts every day. They have a school program held in the gym, and she advised me I can bring Drake in for that with no charge. Now, I just need to figure out the afternoon situation, but I finally feel like the heavens are opening and shining down a bright warm light on me.

Drake and I head to the grocery store to grab some things to cook for dinner. I tell him he can choose whatever he wants because tonight we're celebrating. His little eyes grow with excitement as he thinks about what to get. He finally decides on sloppy joes and French fries—his favorite.

I take a right down my street. It's now about two in the afternoon; the sky is baby blue with only a few clouds lingering. I have my window halfway down letting the warm fall breeze graze my face. Today is a good day. I haven't felt this happy in a long time, but now I'm wondering when the floor underneath me is going to crack open and suck me down to my normal hell. There's always the tiny nagging reality that slams me back down just as I'm having a little joy in life.

Most of my neighbors seem to have daytime jobs, so it's quiet and still. I pull up to my driveway, push the garage door opener, and head in. I push it again and the door closes with ease. Thank God for Neal. I wonder if he liked my pie. I almost didn't leave it because that would mean another conversation owed, but I must admit, a tiny part of me is hoping for that because human contact was so nice.

Drake helps me bring some of the groceries in like a little gentleman. After he drops them on the floor, he runs upstairs to play. I chuckle to myself, at least I got him to help me with the bags. It's a start for now, I'm just hoping we're here long enough so I can begin to teach him about chores before he enters teenage hood.

Dinners finally ready after a couple of hours of cleaning. The house is finally feeling like my home. I hear a knock on the door, and I freeze. Drake looks at me with wide eyes. I pause, and I smile, exhaling softly so I don't scare him. But that doesn't stop the knot of fear from forming in my throat as I try to swallow it down. Who could this possibly be? We could quickly get into the car and be off before whoever is at the door has time to follow. But what if there's someone else waiting in the car just for that reason? I'm sure I won't be as lucky as last time.

I tell Drake to stay put as I slowly get up from the kitchen table. I inch my way to the door quietly. The knock happens again, and I jump out of my skin a little. My blood is rushing furiously through my ears, pounding and beating like a drum that's about to explode. My hands shake as I lay them against the door and peek out of the peephole.

I immediately close my eyes taking a deep forceful breath trying to calm my nerves. God, I am such a disaster. I catch my breath before I open the door and stand there waiting for him to speak.

He has a nervous uncertain grin plastered on his face while holding my pie. "Hey, I didn't mean to disturb you, but I wanted to thank you for this *amazing* pie. I didn't want to eat the whole thing alone, so I thought maybe you and Drake would like to have some with me," he explains.

My brows furrow as he speaks and I'm just now realizing that I have not yet taken another breath. "I'm sorry, did I come at a bad time?" he asks.

God dammit. Get yourself together, Skylar. I can only imagine what my face is betraying. I snap myself out of my thoughts long enough to answer. "No, no. I'm sorry. Please come in. We were just having some dinner. Would you like to join us?" I ask. No! Why the hell did I just invite him in? I'm just asking for trouble.

He grins and accepts. He follows me down the hall to the kitchen. As soon as Drake sees Neal he asks for Benny.

I take the pie from him. "Hey, Drake. Benny's at home relaxing. But I brought over your mom's delicious apple pie to share with you both."

Drake's face brightens up. He loves my pie. "Me and my mom are celebrating. Do you want some sloppy joes? My mom makes the best!" Drake informs him proudly.

Neal looks over at me then back to Drake. "And what are you guys celebrating?"

"My mom got a new job at my school!" he answers with his little munchkin voice, ecstatic.

I can't help but laugh. Neal also laughs, then looks at me. "That's great!" he says. "Congratulations. What will you be doing there?"

I dish out a plate of food for Neal and hand it to him. "Thank you. I will be the assistant receptionist. The job just kind of fell into my lap. It's nice I'll get to check on Drake, and he won't be too far away from me," I tell him.

"Man, I haven't had a sloppy joe in *forever!*" he says, looking at Drake with sauce all over his face and his napkin tucked into his shirt.

Drake laughs. "Well, you better put on a bib because

they are messy!" he tells Neal as his voice squeaks at the end.

Neal opens his napkin and tucks it into his shirt. He absolutely looks adorable like that, but what's turning me on more is the way he's interacting with Drake. Drake seems to soak up the male attention like a sponge. His eyes sparkle as he watches Neal's every movement.

"How's this?" he asks Drake. Then looks over toward me.

I laugh. "Looks great," I tell him still giggling. I haven't laughed this carefree in a long time. It feels light and freeing.

Neal takes a huge bite of his sandwich and moans as he chews. This sound awakens the hidden beast right between my thighs. The nervous pit in the depths of my belly now awakens a hunger that has been starved for so long. My body begins to slowly defrost as the burning heat arouses me straight between my legs. I cross my legs to control the throbbing. It's been a very long time since my body has reacted to anyone, but never to this magnitude.

I swear my face must be flushed. I quickly turn around, so I am away from his scrutiny before I give myself and my needs away. "This is really good, Skylar," he tells me in between chews. Then he changes his attention to Drake. "How do you like school, Drake?"

Drake lights up as he tells him about his whole day all the way down to the color of crayon he colored with. Neal seems very patient as he listens to his whole spiel. I clean up and do the dishes as they talk. I take out three little plates and cut the pie.

"Would you like some coffee?" I ask Neal.

He tears his attention away from Drake to answer. "Yes, I would love some. Are you sure you don't need any help?"

"Nope, I got it all covered over here."

After the coffee is made, I sit down at the table with them and join in the conversation. The way Neal listens and responds to Drake is just so natural. You would think he has kids of his own. After dessert, I send Drake upstairs to play and it's just Neal, me, and the silence that's sitting between us.

"Drake is a really cool little kid. Is his dad in the picture?" he questions. I freeze for a moment, then try to relax.

"No, he hasn't been in the picture for a while. It's just been Drake and I over the last couple of years," I tell, him trying not to say too much. "Do you have any children?" I ask, changing the conversation to him.

"No, no children. With my line of work, it just isn't feasible or make any sense for now. My hours are pretty crazy, and I guess I'm a little old school; I'd like to be married before starting a family," he answers.

My cheeks burn with embarrassment. He must think I'm some type of whore that got pregnant out of wedlock. "Oh, yes, that's what most people hope for. Have you been on the force long?" I ask, attempting to change the subject, again.

He must have seen the hesitation in my face because he looks at me more intensely when he speaks this time. "Skylar, marriage is just a sacred thing to me. I refuse to make that jump unless I know with every inch of my soul that she's the one. Coming into a relationship with a child would never be a deal breaker for me, either. It just means more to love," he explains as if he knew exactly what was going through my mind. "My mother was young when she had me. She struggled as you could understand. Raising me alone wasn't an easy task. My father was a dead-beat dad who was in and out of jail my whole life. I swore when I was old enough, I was going to join the force and be nothing like him. So, that's what I did."

"Your father not being around must have been hard for you when you were younger. I'm afraid it will eventually take a toll on Drake in the years to come. I know I can't replace his father, but I'm hoping I will be enough for him," I tell him honestly. I haven't spoken this way with someone ever. It feels good, but I know I need to tread carefully on what I reveal.

He reaches over and places his hand over mine. I suck my breath in freezing from the human touch. The warmth of his hand feels so amazing. There's a current of pure power that runs through my skin to his. It's unmistakable and I know he feels it just as much as I do. "Drake seems to be doing just fine. It's his father's loss for not being involved. He'll thank you once he's old enough for all that you've done for him. I can promise you that."

I nod my head but remove my hand from underneath his. This isn't something I can get used to. It's hard enough doing this on my own, but it will be even harder keeping myself from something I want so badly. I remind myself that I can't allow anyone in. I remind myself that I need to protect my little boy at all costs even if that means depriving myself of companionship. I just can't put my trust in anyone and for all I know, Neal could be on Antonio's payroll as well. I immediately stand up and start clearing the table.

Neal looks confused. "Did I say something to offend you?" he asks.

I keep myself busy with the dishes. "No, you're fine. I just need to get to bed early. I have my first day of work tomorrow," I tell him so he will get the hint.

He stands up. "Ok, I understand. Thank you for dinner, Skylar, and tell Drake I said goodbye. I'll let myself out," he finishes. By the time I turn around he is gone and the front door clicks closed.

I stop doing the dishes and put my hands against the sink with my head down. Something about him just makes me want to lose control. I want to put all fear aside and just get lost in him. I crave those strong arms around me, praying they can protect me from the world. But what I want most is him buried deep inside of me, so we become one; not knowing where we begin or where we end. *Fuck.* What the hell is wrong with me? I barely even know him, but there's just something so familiar about him, too. I just can't place it. It just doesn't make sense.

I finish cleaning up, go upstairs to get Drake in the bath, get him to bed, then jump in the shower so I'm ready for tomorrow. Mornings have never been my favorite, so it's going to take some time to get used to this new schedule. I put my warm PJ's on, then walk over to my window to close the curtains. I see Neal walking through his room shirtless. My body flashes with heat, stirring awake by just the mere sight of him, and then I see her. My heart twinges with a slice of pain and sinks down to the pit of my stomach. He's hers and I need to remember that. I quickly close my curtains before they can see me and climb into bed.

I almost forgot about her—*his girlfriend.*

CHAPTER 4

NEAL

*M*issy ended up coming over last night at around eight. My mind was still swirling with thoughts of Skylar, and I almost felt as though I was mentally cheating on her. A swarm of guilt consumed me because I didn't want to stop. I thought of her while I kissed Missy. I thought of her when I was having sex with Missy, and I thought of her when I laid my head down on my pillow before falling asleep next to Missy.

I don't know what it is about this girl, but she just has a hold on me without even knowing. I see the strength in Skylar that she doesn't see in herself. Anyone that can come out of what she went through is amazingly strong and the fact that she is raising her son on her own just as my mother had; I have that much more respect for her. If only she could see herself the way I do.

I saw her freeze on me and shut down when I touched her. I shouldn't have put my hand over hers, but I couldn't help it. She almost recoiled from me. It made me aware of how much damage her ex had caused. But it also feels as though she's keeping something big inside; something that's eating away at her.

What she doesn't know is that I looked into her old case file from that night years ago. Only she has changed her name. It used to be Jennifer Bishop. Drake's father is named Antonio Castro. After some digging I discovered Antonio Castro is the brother of Ray Castro; one of the biggest and most notorious drug lords on the East Coast. I'm not sure if Skylar realizes this, but this is not good at all. I know she must be scared about something, or she would never have changed her name. Either she was involved in something or she's running from something – or from *someone*. Whatever it is, I'm going to find out. She needs me whether she knows it or not.

Antonio's release date is set for June of next year, but his early release date is set for next month. I'm not sure she's even aware of this, but a part of me thinks I should tell her. Antonio's family has money and connections. She may think she's safe now, but she's really a sitting duck when it comes to Ray and his family. I feel as though God speaks to us in mysterious ways, and in this case, we've crossed paths again for a reason—she's here for me to protect. She's been a passing thought every single day from the first moment I laid eyes on her. She's been in my dreams night after night; there's no way to count how many. But the craziest thing is, I feel as though she's already a part of me.

Today's supposed to be my day off, but I need to go into the office to do more digging. I feel like there's something I'm missing. Something important that I need to know. What has she done to make her change her name? Or more like what has *he* done to her to make her change her name? Antonio could possibly be getting out in a month, and I need to know exactly what I'm up against. It's only a matter of time before he finds her and Drake and I want to be there when he does. No one, I mean no one, will be touching them. I put my life on that.

I pull up to work with Benny. His tail is wagging furiously with excitement as I let him out of the truck. He loves his job, and he loves all the attention that my co-workers give him.

"Hey, Caruso," Jacob says to me as he walks by. Jacob Smalls is considered our cyber geek of the squad. You need to get past the passcodes and through the barriers, then he's the man we go to. There's nothing that he can't crack. Jacob bends down to pet Benny. "Hey, Benny!" Then looks back up to me. "We just got some new leads. You might want to come check them out."

This is the news that I love hearing. "You should have called me then," I tell him. "Where is everyone?"

Jacob nods his head toward the conference room. This is where the information is pinned across the bulletin board. If someone was to walk into this room, it would look like a scene from a movie. There are pictures of faces and names, locations, and information linked with tacks and string. This operation that's been going on over the last couple of months has been massive.

Every raid and takedown over the last couple of months has one person as the common denominator – Ray.

Ray Castro is who we're gunning for. He's huge in being connected to the cartel. We've been trying to go after him for years, but nothing ever stuck. If we take him down, we may be able to stop the human trafficking and the widespread of drugs that's been happening throughout this area.

Unfortunately, this isn't as easy as it may sound. He's very well-connected and has friends in every aspect you can think of, including the police force. I'm not sure if any of our guys have been tampered with, but it's always a possibility. That's why this room is locked down; only secured access is allowed.

I work with a very small team of men I would die for; men I am sure would also die for me. I trust these men and I believe in these men. I've worked and trained with them for years; I know their families. These are men of honor, men who live by the code, men who would never trade their souls for a paycheck. I can't say this for the men or women in other departments.

I've seen what money and threats can do to people. The right bribes or the right type of threat can cause someone to make a choice they normally wouldn't make. This is what causes people to deter from their morals and choose the wrong fighting sides. This is what causes traders, moles, and rats. With this type of work and the type of people we are going after, you can never be too careful and vigilant.

I close the door behind me with a big thud. Everyone looks up. "Hey, Caruso," Cam greets. Cam's the ladies' man of the group. He's always telling us these crazy stories that most guys dream of. Woman after woman, night after night. I call him the walking STD, then he pulls a condom out of his pocket every time just to prove me wrong. I should tell him about the offer I received the other week. He would kill me for turning down such an amazing opportunity.

"What's going on, guys? I just saw Jacob in the hallway, he said there's a new lead—" I question.

Cam steps up. "Yes, a house was just raided a couple towns over. Just on the outskirts of Buffalo. There were fifteen women, and about eight teen girls found tied up and drugged. Also, cocaine and heroin were confiscated with two hundred thousand in cash. But here's the best part—they arrested Ray Castro's nephew, Jose. He was the man who oversaw this operation. What we're not understanding is why he planted his nephew so far away from him though. It's just not adding up."

This is amazing news. There's no way he won't come for his nephew; Jose is his sister, Helen's, only son, but Cam is right. Why would he risk having his family so far away from him?

"Do we know where his sister is?" I ask.

"It looks as though Castro has also moved Helen to New York as well. Why they chose Upstate New York beats the hell out of me," Jacob chimes in.

Jacob is right, why would he choose to relocate his core family here when most of Castro's operations come through Miami. But then it hits me – *Drake*. That is why they are here close by.

They must be preparing for Antonio's release. He's going to need somewhere to be paroled to, so my guess is, he will be assigned to his sister's house. I'm not sure if I'm ready to mention this to the guys, because then, that's putting Skylar and Drake right in the middle of the investigation. But someone beat me to it, because Antonio's name and picture are now tacked to the board with a direct line to Ray Castro. It's only a matter of time before they figure out who Skylar is—or should I say, Jennifer?

If my guys can find her, then Antonio Castro can find her as well. I need to speak with her. I need to somehow warn her, but if I do, I know she will take off again. I just got her back. I can't risk losing her again. God, I sound so damn selfish, but if I can't protect her, then nobody can. So, it's gotta be me.

I STOP at the pet store on my way home to grab some dog food. They all love Benny here. All the clerks go gaga over him, and he just soaks it all in. "You're such a stud muffin," I tell him as we walk to the truck.

I notice a black Suburban parked a couple of rows down; a 2024 with black tinted windows. This truck was a couple of cars behind me when I left the station. I can't see the driver's face because of the windows, but my gut tells me something is a little off.

I hurry Benny in the truck through my side. I try to spot the license plate so I can have it run, but the angle of the truck doesn't allow me to see. I've always found the best form of action is to confront the problem head on. So, I drive my truck toward theirs to get a better look. As soon as they see me coming, they speed off and enter traffic without stopping. I'm fuming. My blood boils, overflowing, as the wave of anger takes me over. This is not good. I call Johnny to give him the rundown; to see if we have any links to that kind of SUV.

I take the long route to my house. The route I have planned for in these types of scenarios; though I've never needed to use it before I had to take precautions after my partner, Simon, was murdered. I have a garage set up with an alternate car to switch out before heading home. I can't take any chances with someone following me, especially now with having Skylar and Drake next door to me.

I pull down a side street that leads to a dead end. There are no houses and no reason for anyone to be behind me. The road is secluded, hidden by a sea of trees. I turn my truck off when reaching the dead end and sit for a moment. I look for any signs of movement—but nothing. It seems to be safe. No one has followed. I turn the truck back on heading down the small gravel road in front of me.

I slowly travel down the road; rocks crackling and snapping beneath my tires until I reach the garage. I open my secret compartment in my dashboard to grab the garage door opener. I park and close the door behind me. This garage could fit about three big Suburban's if it had to. I have monitors set up for the five camcorders I have around the perimeter. So, if I happened to make the mistake of thinking no one was following, I would catch them on these. Any movement is recorded and sent to my phone.

I have a couch, and a fridge filled with necessities in case I need to wait anything out. After Simon's death, I couldn't take any chances. I had to protect myself and now, I feel in my gut that things are going to get sticky. That SUV smelled of money, of power, and there's something that just feels downright dark and dangerous.

I have surveillance surrounding my house as well, but I haven't been actively checking it. This all changes after tonight. I call Johnny again and some of the men on my team to give them a heads-up. I give them the lowdown on the SUV and the last three numbers of the license plate I was able to catch. It's not much to go by, but at least they can keep their eyes open in case that SUV decides to come around again.

I take some time to run through the recorded video; there's not much to see but some deer and racoons. It records only on movement. I've always known the danger and risk this job entails, but it never hit me until things became personal, and I had to relocate years ago. I was young when I entered the police force; proud and hotheaded. I wanted to step into the opposite footsteps of my father. He hated the badges. I made sure when I grad-uated from the academy and received my first police badge, I visited him in prison.

I wanted him to know that I've become what he hated the most. I never went to visit him again after that. As far as I know he has another five years to go. I decided after that that nothing was going to get in my way of getting the bad guys—even if it killed me. I think that's why I've never intentionally gotten too serious in a relationship. I've always kept myself at an arm's distance. Then there would be no need to be afraid. The fear of someone I loved getting hurt because of me crippled me and after Simon, I just couldn't take the chance.

Missy's been a great distraction, but we ultimately live different lives. She talks about moving in together, but I won't entertain the idea. It just doesn't feel right. Skylar is what feels right. But is it selfish to want her in my life with danger always following close behind? And then there's Drake; I couldn't risk his safety. I won't risk his safety, which means my desires should just stay as that—desires.

Benny and I have been here for a little over an hour. I think it's safe enough to head home. I hop into my black Dodge Charger and head out. Only this time I take the stone road behind the garage that leads me out to another side road. My eyes are glued to the rearview mirror and side mirrors. My mind's in overdrive as I make my way across town. If someone is following, I will know. I've trained for this. Every little detail and movement could be a clue to something bigger.

I drive through my neighborhood, pass Skylar's house, and head up my driveway. It's quiet during the late afternoon, most are still at work and as the night quickly creeps upon us earlier that leaves this place motionless and somber currently.

Drake is outside playing with a basketball. Benny's ears immediately perk up with his nose smashed against the passenger window. He whines as he watches Drake while shifting paw to paw excitedly. As soon as I open my car door, he is right behind me ready to jump out. I laugh as I watch Benny jump on Drake, knock him down, and slobber all over his face.

I wave at Mrs. Ortega from across the street as she lets her cat out, then closes her screen door. I turn my attention to the scene unfolding in front of me. "Hey, Drake. How was school today?" I ask him.

He breaks away from Benny for just a moment. "School was great! I got to play with Adam and Jake at recess!" I chuckle. If only I could go back to those times when life was simple and the goal for the day was to play outside for as long as possible.

"Man, that's awesome!" I tell him. "How about any girls? Did you get yourself a girlfriend?" I ask, teasing.

He looks at me and crinkles his nose. "Eww! I don't like girls. They have cooties. My mom even told me so," he informs me extremely serious.

I can agree with him there, but as I grew up, I learned that girl cooties made you hot and feverish, and I got addicted to this highly deadly virus real fast. "Well, your mom is a very smart woman," I tell him. "Is your mom busy inside?"

My stomach becomes instantly wrapped in excited knots thinking about seeing her face again. There are things about her past I want to know, things that I can't learn from a file like the why's and how's. She has nobody but Drake. No one to lean on or to trust, and I want to be that person for her. I want her to feel safe when she's around me. But how can I do this without seeming too bold or pushy? How can I possibly earn the trust of someone who's shattered to pieces?

"No! She's just getting dinner ready," he yells, now trying to get Benny to chase him.

I knock on the front screen and wait for Skylar to come to the door. I almost want to walk in, but I decide against it, we're just not there yet.

She looks a little confused when she sees me. She opens the screen door just enough to speak. "Neal, hey. What can I do for you?" she asks very guarded.

I put both my hands in my pockets. She looks sexy and domestic with her hair in a messy bun, small strands fallen, outlining her face, and a dish towel in her hands. I almost forgot why I even stopped by. She looks incredibly eatable, and I do my best to hold my dick at bay. She waits patiently as I think of a response to her question needing to jumpstart my brain again.

"I just came by to ask you how the garage door was doing," I lie. She eyes me carefully, almost stripping me bear with her eyes as she tries to decipher whether I'm telling the truth or not.

She finally answers. "It's working great. Again, thank you for saving me from having to call my landlord," she says politely. She then pauses for a moment as if she's battling something internally. "Would you like to come in for some late afternoon coffee? I just made a pot. I was just coming to call Drake in; I'm not a fan of leaving him outside unattended."

I feel the weight of relief lifted off my shoulders. "Yes, I would love that. I could totally go for some coffee right about now, and Benny will keep an eye on him," I reply with a boyish grin. What I could really go for is a drink of her. I bet she tastes amazing, every part of her as sweet as honeysuckle.

She opens the door wider for me, allowing me in. I walk past her close enough that my arm brushes hers. My skin lights on fire from the touch and my dick immediately twitches in response. I feel her tense up from the contact, but I don't lead on to the fact of seeing it. I don't want her self-conscious around me. The house smells delicious; of butterscotch and something else I do not recognize.

I take in a big inhale. "What is that smell? It smells amazing," I say now entering the kitchen. I've been in the kitchen many times before. The previous renter was an older man who I would help out from time to time; fixing his sink or helping him bring in groceries. He lived on his own with only one son who lived outside town. So, anything I could do to help make his life a little easier, I would do. Besides, I liked his company. But this kitchen never smelled *this* good.

"I just made butterscotch caramel macaroons. It's a new recipe I'm trying. They smell good, but I'm not so sure how they taste," she says as she pulls down the oven door to check on them. My eyes drift to her ass. It's plump and would be a perfect padding against my hips as I pump deep inside of her. Fuck. This is not the greatest time to get an erection. She closes the oven door, then turns to me. I shift my eyes away onto something else. "I'm not really a baker. Never had the chance to learn, so I figure why not start now?" she says, shrugging her shoulders.

She pours me a cup of coffee and sets it in front of me along with the cream and sugar. "No baking in your household growing up I take it then?" I ask. She's talking so I might as well take full advantage of it.

She sits down across from me and grabs the sugar. A little strand of hair falls onto her face, and it takes everything I've got not to lean over and brush it away. "No, I never knew my mother or father. I was an orphan raised in the foster care system. If you can believe, none of my foster care mothers really cared about cooking let alone baking," she states so matter-of-factly with little emotion.

She puts on a hard exterior, and my guess is that's she learned to lock this part of her life up very tightly. "Yeah, unfortunately, the foster system isn't too particular where they place the kids. Pretty much anyone can be a foster parent as long as they have no felonies or have been deemed unfit by CPS's standards," I say, agreeing.

She stirs her coffee after pouring the French vanilla

creamer in. "There was one couple who wanted to adopt me when I was younger, but I ruined that. I guess it was self-destruction. I was too scared to belong to anyone. What if I didn't like them? How would I ever be able to leave if they owned me? So, I got myself into some criminal mischief. I was fifteen at the time. After that, they decided against adopting me since I clearly had some issues, and then I was moved to another home," she reveals.

This woman in front of me has strength that I don't see in many. She's had the odds against her from the beginning, and she still managed to beat them. Yes, she may be running from something or someone, but she still manages to keep a smile on her face even if it's only a façade for her son. But I can see right through it. She may be damaged, but she's not irreparable.

Drake comes running in with Benny right behind him before I can even reply to her. "No, Benny. Outside." I point. He whines and puts his head down before he turns to walk out.

Skylar stops me. "No, it's fine. He can stay. I really don't mind," she tells me.

I snap and Benny turns to come next to me. "Can he come in my room, Mom?" Drake asks, then looks to me as well. I don't answer though. I let her make that decision.

She smiles and gives Drake a pinch on the cheek. "Yes, I'm okay with it as long as Neal is."

Now they're both looking at me waiting for an answer. I chuckle and nod. The oven timer goes off; Skylar gets up to remove the cookies and place them on top of the stove. She now throws a small pan in the oven and sets the timer again.

I feel this underlying energy between us. The longer we're in each other's presence, the stronger it seems to get. Every time our eyes connect, it's straight fire I feel. I see hesitation when I watch her. I know she feels the same because she quickly disconnects from me when her cheeks highlight pink.

She breaks the quietness. "Would you like to stay for dinner? I made lasagna. There's enough for all of us."

It's now four thirty when I look at my cell. No calls or texts from Missy, so I'm assuming she may not come by tonight. "I would love that. Do you need me to make a salad or something? I can run over to my house. I have to go over to feed Benny his dinner anyways," I tell her.

"Sure. It won't be ready for another hour though. Do you mind if we go into the living room? This chair is killing my back," she says, rubbing her lower back.

I leave my empty coffee cup on the table and follow her sitting down on the opposite couch. I want to be able to see her face. The top of her breasts poke out of her tank top looking full and kissable. I have to force myself not to stare for too long or she might catch me.

"So, tell me about yourself, Neal. What made you want to join the police force?" she questions. She turns on the TV but turns down the volume so it's now a low thrum in the background.

"My father has been in and out of jail my whole life. I guess I grew up wanting to be nothing like him. This is the one choice of mine he despises, which is perfect since I despise everything about him. He hates knowing that my job is to put people like him away. My mother was hoping I would choose another career path; she hates worrying about me," I explain to her.

She fiddles with a string on her pillow. "How bad did it affect you growing up with him being away for so long?"

"He got into some big trouble when he was in his early twenties. He finally violated his parole and ended up getting a pretty long sentence. My mother found out she was pregnant with me after the fact. It's always been just my mom and me. I was an only kid growing up. It kinda sucked. But I survived. The whole situation takes a toll on kids. Some harder than others, but my mother was my savior. She gave me enough love for the both of them. So, I try my best to take time out each week to go visit her, so she doesn't get lonely. I owe her that."

She smirks one sexy little smile. "You're such a good son. I hope Drake's like that when he gets older. I couldn't imagine going weeks without seeing him. Though, I'm so sorry about your father. That must have been hard on you. I just pray Drake sees things the way you do in the future."

I nod. This is always a hard subject for me to speak about, but if I want her to open up to me, then I need to open up to her, so she gains trust with me. I want her to feel completely safe about being open and honest with me, too. "Yeah, it definitely affected me as a teen. I took it hard every time he got into trouble. I took some of my anger out on my mom and I have a lot of regrets about that. I should have been better toward her because none of it was her fault. I did blame her for continuously going back to him though," I admit.

She softens her expression toward me. "I bet she understood. Don't be so hard on yourself," she tells me.

I feel like we've opened up enough for me to ask

what's on my mind. So, I'm just going to ask it. "Does Drake see his father?"

She goes rigid and her face turns stone cold. I see I have misinterpreted our situation and I'm afraid I've just asked the one thing that can shut her down. I want to rewind and go back to a minute ago, when things were going smoothly. I shouldn't have pushed so early; she needs more time. I am such an ass!

"He's no longer in the picture. Never has been. He's not a good man, and he definitely is not a good role-model for my son," she tells me without saying another word.

I take a deep breath and think of something to say so I can rectify this situation. "I'm sorry. I didn't mean to pry. If he's a bad man, then I'm glad he's not in Drake's life. Some men shouldn't get the privilege of being a father. It's his loss, not Drake's," I finish.

I see her shoulders lift as she takes a deep breath and relaxes. Good. I have her back. "Does Drake like football?" I ask her.

Her eyebrows furrow unsure of why I'm asking this. "I'm not too sure. I do know that he's loves basketball though," she answers.

"There will be some high school football games coming up and maybe you guys would like to go to one with me some time," I ask. What's the worst that can happen, she says no?

She takes a moment to think before she gives me an answer. "Ok, yeah, that would be fun. I think Drake would love that."

I didn't realize I was holding my breath this whole

time while waiting for her to answer. "Cool," I finally say cracking a grin like an idiot.

The stove timer goes off, and we both jump. We look at each other and laugh. I get up and start heading out of the living room. "I'm going to go make the salad. I won't be too long," I say, walking toward the hallway. I call up for Benny, and he comes running down with Drake right behind him.

"Neal! Neal! Can Benny come back and play?" he asks in his tiny voice. His eyes sparkle with hope as he sways back and forth against the railing of the stairs.

"Benny needs to go eat his dinner right now. But how about this, he'll come over another day this week and hang as long as it's ok with your mom. How does that sound?" I ask.

I look back to Skylar for confirmation. Maybe I should have asked her first. But she nods her head yes with a smile. My eyes stay locked on her. She's so beautiful it takes my breath away. I want nothing more than to touch, smell, and taste every part of her. I crave her; I *want* to nuzzle deep inside of her until the craving dissipates, and even then I don't want to stop, but I quickly look away before she gets uncomfortable.

I turn back to Drake. He's jumping up and down like a little jumping bean. "That would be awesome!"

"Ok, it's a deal!" I tell him, laughing.

I head out of the house with Benny. I take a step onto her porch and smile to myself. I feel happy, I'm floating on cloud nine, but as soon as I turn for my house I freeze. My stomach drops to the pit of my gut as if I'm on the tip top of a roller-coaster ride about to roll down to my death.

Missy's here. I pull out my phone to see if I missed her call or text, but no—nothing. *Fuck*.

Dread swarms through me soaking me all the way down to my toes. This isn't going to be good. Missy isn't going to like the fact that I've been over here this whole time and she sure as hell isn't going to be ok with me coming back to Skylar's for dinner. I almost want to turn back around to explain to Skylar that I may have to pass tonight, but Benny has already made his way to the front door. If I'm not right behind him there is going to be hell to pay and I'm just not in the mood to argue tonight.

I hustle home. I open the screen door and Benny rushes in. He immediately heads for Missy. She leans down to pet him, then pushes him away. Dogs really aren't her favorite, but she tolerates Benny because of me.

She already has a glass of wine poured and her arms folded over her chest while sitting at the counter—she looks tense, readying for a fight. This is a clear sign that she is pissed. I slap a smile on my face and lean down to give her a kiss. She turns her cheek to me. I end up kissing her ear. Perfect.

"Hey, babe. When did you get here?" I ask, not letting her attitude affect mine.

She glares at me. "Where have you been?" she sneers.

It's obvious not very far since my car has been parked in the driveway. "I took Benny over to play with the little boy, Drake." I walk over to Benny's food bowl and fill it. "Why didn't you tell me you were coming?"

She takes another sip of her wine and puts it back down gently on the table. She's being too precise and too quiet. This is not a good thing. "I didn't realize I had to. Do I need an invite next time I plan on coming here?

Anyways, I thought I mentioned I was coming by tonight." Clearly, that was the wrong question to ask.

I put Benny's filled bowl down, then lean against the counter facing her. "No, it's just I would have been here waiting if I knew you were heading over. I forgot you mentioned you would be coming by."

"So, what were you doing while Benny was playing with the boy?" she questions, brow arched accusingly.

I run my hand through my hair. I know exactly where she's going with this. "I was just having some coffee with Skylar. I was getting to know her. I mean, she is my neighbor," I remind her, but I know none of my words are putting her at ease. "Come on, Missy, there's no need to be jealous."

"*Jealous?* Is that what you think this is?" she asks, raising her voice.

"Yes, that's exactly what I think." I can't hold back anymore. She knows how I absolutely *hate* the jealous act.

She pushes her chair back to stand. "I *think* it's nice to be friendly, but it's inappropriate to hang out with her alone when you have a girlfriend! What if I had done this? Would you feel ok about me having *coffee* with my hot neighbor?"

Ok, I can totally see her point, but she also knows I'm not really the jealous type either. So, if she told me I had nothing to worry about, then I would believe her. I just wish she could do the same for me. I walk over to her and reach for her, but she backs away. "I don't want to fight. We had a good night last night. Let's not ruin tonight. You have no reason to be upset. Can we just start over? How about I cook you your favorite—fettucine alfredo?"

I bend down just a tad to get her to look me in the

eyes. I see a hint of a smile which means she is warming back up. A small wave of guilt rolls over me as Skylar passes through my mind, and then it hits me. She's over there waiting for me to bring a salad. I don't have her number to text her, and I know if I leave Missy here to go speak with her, she will leave. Damn it!

Missy wraps her arms around my neck bringing me back to her. "Ok, sounds like a deal," and then my mind drifts back to Skylar.

CHAPTER 5

SKYLAR

"Mom, I thought Neal was coming back?" Drake asks me. I look at the clock over the stove, and it's been twenty minutes since he left. It can't take that long to feed Benny and make a salad. I go to grab my phone, then realize I don't even have his phone number.

"I don't know what happened, baby. Maybe we should pop over there to see if he needs some help," I tell him.

He jumps off his chair immediately. "Yes! Let go see!" he yells excitedly. I can't help but laugh. He's never been this excited to see anyone. It's adorable, but it also worries me. What if he gets too attached and then we must leave abruptly again without saying goodbye? Will Drake recover as he did the last couple of times?

Something just tells me to check out the side window next to the door before opening it. I see a white Honda Civic parked in Neal's driveway. He has company and I'm guessing it's his girlfriend. That's the same car she was driving the other day when she pulled up, and my guess is that he had no idea she was coming. I feel a bit disappointed. I was enjoying our conversation. It's not very often that I have adult one on one time. I would only speak to others where I would work in the past, but never outside of the job. I was always included in the invites for meeting up outside of work by my co-workers, but I always had to turn them down. I'd rather spend my nights with my son than go on a social outing any day.

It was hard though, everyone else seemed to have a bond or shared a secret that I just wasn't privy to because I always missed out. So, I always felt like the outsider looking in no matter where I was. That's kind of how I've felt my entire life. Some of my foster parents had biological children, and no matter what, I just never felt at home. Most of those kids made it known to me that it would never be my home. They could be cruel and got extreme gratification making me feel that way. A tough exterior is something I had to form at a very young age.

I feel a tug on my arm. "Come on, Mom. Let's go!"

"It looks like Neal has some unexpected company. We should probably start without him," I say to Drake, leading him back to the kitchen. He seems a little bummed. I know he craves male company. I mean, all boys I believe need a father, and if one's not available, I think a male friend or role model can be just as beneficial.

I get dinner cleaned up, Drake bathed and in bed, then get myself ready for bed. I hear a quiet knock on my door as I attempt to hop into bed. I freeze. My heart speeds up pumping blood to my ears in record time. I hear the knock again. I quietly and slowly creep down my stairs and peek over my railing just enough to get a glimpse through the sheer curtains on the side window. It's Neal. I blow the breath I'm holding out relieved. What is he doing here so late?

I open the door. He's standing in front of me with his hands in his pockets looking badass in his black V-neck T-shirt and pajama bottoms. He gives me a crooked smirk that jump starts my heart again pumping blood furiously to all parts of my body, zeroing in straight between my legs. *Oh lord, get it together, Skylar.*

"Hey, Neal. What's up? Is everything ok?" I ask a little confused.

A crease forms between his eyebrows before he speaks. "Can I come in?" he asks quietly.

I'm intrigued as to what he wants, so I open the door wider. "Sure." I should really tell him to go home.

His shoulder brushes mine again as he walks by which heightens my awareness of him even that much more. I hold my breath, secretly praying to myself for him to hurry by me, it's just too tempting to close my eyes and inhale his tangy manly aroma that follows him. The last thing I want is for him to turn around as I'm sniffing the air behind him looking like a complete crazed woman. My body seems to sing to life when he's in my presence. I not only crave the touch of skin on skin, but I crave the emotional connection as well. And though he's never touched me, I can only imagine the imprinted burn he would leave behind.

I follow him to the kitchen and wait for him to speak. He turns to me unexpectedly, making me take in a fast breath. "Skylar, I wanted to say I'm sorry for not showing up. I wasn't expecting Missy to show up like that unannounced. Usually, she calls to give me a heads-up," he explains.

I see the desperation of truth in his eyes. I believe him, but I'm not sure why he feels the need to explain this to me. "Neal, it's ok. I kind of figured something like that happened when I saw her car in the driveway."

He walks closer to me, his eyes smoldering with something I do not recognize. I may be very inexperienced, but he almost looks like a hungry lion on the prowl. This is dangerous. I'm cornered, I know this is wrong, but the worst part is I have no desire to get away.

My breath exhilarates and I unconsciously back up. "No, it's not ok. I wanted her to leave so badly so I could come back over here. I don't usually tell someone I'm going to do something and not follow through. That's not me. I like talking with you. I've been thinking about these moments since the first moment I laid eyes on you years ago."

Before he can say another word, I jump in as anger swarms me. "You son of a *bitch!* How much did he pay you?" I growl.

Oh God! I don't know why I thought I might be able to trust this man. I let my guard down for one second and this is what happens. I should have known he is working for Antonio. What good am I if I can't even protect my own son?

I back up enough to grab a knife out of the holder. He's not taking my son. He'll have to kill me first. I won't go down without a fight. Neal holds up his hands. "Skylar, please put down the knife and let me explain," he says very calmly.

My eyes dart between him and my garage door. If I run out, then I can call for help, but that's means leaving Drake alone in the house with him. No, never. That's not even a possibility. What do I do? Come on Skylar, think fast. I only have seconds to decide my next move. "You're not getting my son. You'll have to kill me first," I spit out. Neal moves closer to me. I put the knife further in front of me as a warning. My hand is shaking. I try my best to control it. "Don't you dare move any closer!"

He stops dead in his tracks. "I don't work for Antonio. Skylar, I was there the night Drake's father almost killed you. I was the cop on duty. I was the one who was speaking with you and Drake that night," he tells me.

My mind quickly tries to flip through the memories of that night, but it's blurry. I've tried my hardest to bury that night deep away and to now trudge back through that muckiness makes me break into a panic.

I back up to lean against the counter, so I don't fall down from the thoughts of that night years ago. Remembering that night brings back all the terror and helplessness I've tried so hard to forget. I was so weak back then, and I've vowed to myself I would never be that girl again. I would fight for me and for Drake no matter what the cost is.

I look back up toward him, and I can't believe I didn't put those pieces together earlier. I knew he looked familiar, but I've locked that night up so tightly that Neal was locked away with those memories as well.

I drop the knife in front of me. "Why didn't you tell me?" I question him accusingly. This still doesn't make any sense as to why he wouldn't have mentioned this.

He now walks carefully toward me, picks up the knife dropping it into the sink, and stands before me. "At first it didn't register, but then it hit me a couple of days ago when those memories came back to me. That night changed me, Skylar. I've seen a million tragedies throughout my career, but that night I've never been able to fully get out of my mind. You've haunted my dreams for years and I always wondered what had happened to you. I wanted to tell you the moment I figured it out, but I didn't want to have to bring that night back up to you," he explains calmly.

His eyes flare with life as he speaks; it penetrates right through me down to my core. "I want to be here for you and Drake. Anything you need, just say the word," he says, standing directly in front of me, intimately, and heavenly close. He reaches his hand up to my face and slowly trails down my cheek with the back of his hand. I immediately close my eyes, lean into him, and take in his touch. He feels so comforting and safe. I'm not used to this. "Skylar, look at me," he whispers.

I open my eyes and look up at him. Our eyes lock and my breathing halts. He has me completely breathless. He slowly leans down and gently touches his lips to mine, a featherlight kiss. It's so perfect and tender, and just what I need right now.

Before I know it, his lips are no longer on mine and my eyes are still closed. I open them and see him staring at me with such ferocity and such a wild hunger it immediately drives every part of me insane. I've never felt the hot heat between my legs like this up until this moment. This is all new to me. My skin is scorching as the burning within me tries to claw its way out. I've only seen this kind of frenzy in the romance movies I watch. I've never known the feeling of pure sexual desire. I'm literally melting like hot lava in his arms. Everything in my being has jolted to life. It's like my body and inner sexual goddess have been hibernating all these years and is now *finally* seeing the light.

"Don't stop—*please?*" I beg him. I want more. I *need* more.

And that is all I needed to say. He smashes his lips against mine as I run my hand around his neck pulling him closer to me. God, I need this like I need air to breathe. With just his touch my body has sparked alive. I am consumed by the absolute need of him. I swear, I can't seem to get close enough. My lips part just enough for him to delve his tongue deep with mine. We dance together in such a beautiful rhythm, matching each other stroke for stroke. His kiss is full of power and strength; something I have secretly craved for so many years.

I moan softly. He then reaches under my thighs, lifts me up, and places me on top of the counter behind us. "Shit, Skylar. You're so fucking gorgeous and sexy. You don't know how many times I've pictured this moment in my head. *This* moment is everything to me and I want nothing more than to be your everything too," he tells me.

Those words slam me into reality and before he can kiss me again, I place my palms on his chest as a barrier. What the hell am I doing? His brows furrow as he looks at me questioningly. "Neal, you have a girlfriend. I'm sorry. I should never have allowed this to happen. I just got caught up in the moment," I tell him, he backs up allowing me room to hop down off the counter to gain some space. As much as it kills me inside, I have to stop this. It just isn't right.

He looks disappointed, but what does he expect. I've never wanted to be the type of girl to get involved with a taken man. I just won't do that. Shoot, I'm not the girl that gets involved with any man, so this step was big for me. But there's a big problem—I *really* like this taken man. And I *really* like kissing this taken man, too. But I have to be fair. Fair to him, fair to me, and fair to Drake.

"Okay, maybe you're right. But I'm not sorry, Skylar. I just couldn't help myself. I've never done this sort of thing before," he admits, running his hand over his hair. He looks torn. I'll believe him considering I don't really know him. I'll give him the benefit of doubt.

"I just got carried away, but to be honest, I don't regret a minute of it. You've been on my mind almost every day for years now and when I realized it was you, that you are now living right next door to me, I feel like it's all for a reason. Even if it's just me being here for you. Us just being friends if that's what you need," he claims.

I grab a glass out of the cupboard, with my back to him, and pour some cold water in it from the sink. I just need to grasp on to reality. This is some heavy stuff he is bringing on me, and fast. I need a moment to gather my thoughts, to wrap my head around all of this. I need to keep my back to him, because the only thing I can seem to concentrate on is his lips—those soft pink lips. *Damn it!* I'm acting insane. Is this what I missed out on as a teenager? These crazy uncontrollable emotions that throw all sanity aside? How the hell did we go from neighbors to this in just a matter of hours?

He's waiting for me to say something—*anything*. I'm almost afraid to speak. My words might betray me, but I find my voice. "Neal, I think you should leave," I finally say with my back still facing him.

It takes everything I have just to say those words, because goddamnit, the last thing I want is for him to leave. I want him to wrap his arms around me and kiss me like there's no one else but him and I in this world. I want him to fuck me like I've never been fucked before, because if he can fuck like he can kiss, I'm a goner. But most of all, I want him to whisper sweet nothings into my ear until we fall asleep wrapped up in each other's arms. And now I'm afraid if I turn and look into those beautiful smokey blue eyes, I'm not sure I can be strong enough to follow through with this. Every neuron in my body is screaming no and the liquid heat between my legs is screaming fuck me—*now!*

I've only had sexual relations with Drake's father, Antonio. I've never been with anyone else, and I've never kissed anyone else, until now. I have a whirlwind of emotions rushing through me, and I think the best thing for me right now is to get clear of the sexual haze and get my grounding back.

Neal is now behind me. The electricity that is burning between us is at full force and the only thing I can do right now is hold my breath, no sudden movements. If I move, I might give in to my body's heavenly desires. I must stay in control.

"I'll leave because you asked me to, but next time I promise you, you will be begging me to stay," he whispers in my ear before he walks away and lets himself out. I release my breath as soon as I hear the door shut, my shoulders sag, and I prop myself up against the sink because my knees are now weak and about to buckle beneath me. What the hell just happened here? How did I let it get this far?

My body completely betrayed me. I am always in full control; always careful who I allow around me, which is no one. I just had a moment of weakness, I tell myself. Everyone is allowed one free pass to weakness. The only difference is, I have another little helpless human to consider, and I can't let these moments happen ever again. Drake needs me, he depends on me, and I must think of him before I give in to temptation again. I would never forgive myself if I subjected him to danger because of my weaknesses.

I don't believe Neal is a danger himself, but I do believe his line of work is dangerous, and that's what scares me the most. Regardless, I'm not sure how he thinks he's able to protect us when he knows nothing about us.

I'M EXHAUSTED. I tossed and turned all night. I sit up wiping the sleepies from my eyes, then look over toward my window confused. The sun is barely up. What time is it? I look over at my alarm clock on my nightstand and it's only 6am. I slam my head back onto my pillow. I don't have to wake up for at least another hour.

Parts of last night with Neal feel like a dream, then I place my hands on my lips and remember how his lips felt against mine. I was completely consumed by him. My body sinking by the second into his quicksand. But the reality is, he has a girlfriend. It doesn't matter that he wants me because he is taken—plain and simple.

I've never been the other woman and I'm not about to start now. Maybe if I meet Missy in person, put a face to the name, this will keep me from dabbling into temptation. I wonder what she's like, and how long they've been together. He must love her to still be with her. But if he's been thinking about me all these years, then he's not giving her a fair chance. There's a piece of him that belongs to me and not her. I'm not quite sure how I feel about this, but I'd be lying if this thought didn't put a small smile on my face.

I decide to get up and throw a load of laundry in, then wake up Drake after I make us some breakfast. There's no way I'm falling back asleep, so I might as well get up. I head downstairs to put the coffee on. I take a peek outside and notice that Neal's car is gone. I wonder what happened to his truck. Maybe this is part of his job— swapping out vehicles. This reminds me. I need to trade in mine.

Breakfast is made so I head upstairs to get Drake up. I can't help but stare at him as he peacefully sleeps. My sweet boy. I want him to always sleep this serenely without a care in the world. I rub his back to ease him out of sleep.

His eyes crack open. "Hey sleepyhead, breakfast is ready."

He smiles at me. "Morning, Mom. I smell bacon. Did you make bacon for breakfast?" he asks. Bacon is his ultimate favorite along with a dab of syrup.

"I did." I grab his clothes that I placed at the end of his bed last night. "Put these on and come downstairs." Drake jumps up like a jack-in-the-box. I love his enthusiasm in the morning. I wish I could think of life as exciting and blissful as he does.

TODAY'S my second day at work. Jess, so far, made my first day extremely comfortable. She introduced me to all the teachers we crossed paths with and all the parents that came through the front doors. She knows everyone by first name and flows easily into conversations with them all. I'm not so sure how to do that. The thought of taking the time to get to know everyone when I might have to possibly pick up and leave at any moment seems like a waste of time to me. The less relationships I incur, the easier it is to walk away.

"Good morning, Skylar," Jess says with a chipper smile.

I already walked Drake to the cafeteria where they hold the before school program. I put my purse under my desk and begin to clock in. "Morning," I respond with a smile.

"Are you ready for day two?" Jess asks, her chair now facing mine.

"I am," I tell her honestly. There's just something about her that's so calming and nurturing. I feel at ease and comfortable around her. "I can't thank you enough for reaching out to Mrs. Conner for me right away. I feel so much better working all day knowing Drake's so close by."

"Of course, dear. I am happy to help a mother in need. I know it's hard when moving to a new town and not knowing a single soul. I was there once upon a time," she tells me with a kind smile.

She turns to buzz in a parent, greets her, then continues with our conversation. "I still have to introduce you to our gym teacher, Mr. Brody, and to a couple more teachers. We have a staff meeting tomorrow morning, so you will need to get here thirty minutes earlier. We have this meeting once a month so all staff can all be on the same page. Things are constantly changing around here, so it's important to keep up," she advises me.

"I'm a fast learner," I inform her.

She smiles and the lines around her eyes crease deeper. "How are you and Drake holding up? I know a move can be difficult with getting used to a new place and all," Jess asks.

I place my things in the desk storage she provided me with. "Actually, it hasn't been that bad. I've met a couple of my neighbors, one is a cop, so I feel safe where I am. And Drake does well anywhere. He's really just a blessing. I couldn't have asked for a better kid," I answer.

"Good morning, ladies!" A man walks by with a huge bag over his shoulders.

He's young, maybe in his early to mid-twenties. The first thing that catches my attention is his bright blue eyes. They're magnificent. The color of crystal blue waters of the sea. His dimples are flirty, his hair is a bit longer than I normally like, but it seems to fit him well. He wears a hoody and sweats, and my first thought is— gym teacher.

"Oh, Mr. Brody, I wanted to introduce you to Skylar Kramer. She's the new assistant here. She just started yesterday," Jess tells him. She has a devious twinkle in her eye and I'm beginning to smell a hint of a set up in the air.

He looks over at me with his dazzling smile. My cheeks betray me as the heat creeps through them. "Hey Skylar, it's very nice to meet you," he tells me. I fear if I speak back right now, I might croak like a toad. I'm not normally this dumbstruck when meeting people but lately this seems to be a pattern, but he's just so damn pretty.

I return the smile and realize if I don't say something in this moment than I'm going to look like an ass. "Great meeting you, too, Mr. Brody. My son, Drake, just started as well. He had you yesterday and thinks very highly of you already," I inform him doing my best to keep the eye contact to a minimum.

"Please, call me Richie," he tells me. Then he racks his brain for a moment. "Ah, yes, I remember him. He was totally into our lesson on kickball. Seems like a good kid. Were you working at a different school around here?" he questions, now hanging against the counter.

Jess lets in another parent. Richie moves to the side of the counter to continue our conversation. "No, actually, I worked for an insurance agency a couple of towns over," I answer. God, I hope he doesn't ask me anymore more personal questions.

He takes his bag off his shoulder and holds it by his side. "Well, I'm sure we will be crossing paths a lot since the gym is right across the way here," he says, pointing to the door right across from the office. Wow. He is right. There's going to be no way to avoid any run-ins with him in the future. He's closer to me than the restrooms are.

I smile and nod. "And us older ladies absolutely *love* the view!" Jess interjects with a wink to him. We all laugh. Jess is old enough to be his mother, so there's no harm done when flirting. She's only saying what most woman are thinking.

Richie Brody exits into the gym and Jess turns to me. I'm confused by the look on her face. "What?" I ask.

"I think someone was a little smitten by you," Jess informs with a wink.

My brows furrow. "What do you mean?"

She shakes her head in disapproval. "Richie, silly! He was smiling from ear to ear. I've never seen that glimmer in his eyes until he saw you. He's a good catch you know," she says. I exhale loudly not meaning to. She laughs.

"Well, unfortunately, I'm not looking for anything. I have Drake, and that's enough."

She frowns. "Everybody needs somebody, honey."

Boy, she is right, but I'm not going to admit that out loud.

The rest of the day goes by with ease. I ate lunch in the facility room; Richie came and sat with me. We chatted about the weather and the kids. I kept the conversation simple and when it seemed to get too personal, I redirected it. I think from now on, though, I will be eating at my desk or maybe in the cafeteria with Drake. I'd hate to give Richie the wrong impression or get too comfortable so the personal questions will no longer be able to be avoided.

None of this helps when flashbacks of last night come front and center. Perspiration forms on the back of my neck with just the thought of Neal's kiss. I feel like a cat in heat when this happens. There's no controlling my body when it comes to him. One moment I can be completely fine and then when he pops into my head, that's it, I'm a goner! This is so extremely annoying that the mere thought of him completely undoes me. How the hell am I supposed to keep it together around him if I can't even keep it together away from him? My body is completely desperate and in need of a repeat of last night until my brain finally kicks in. No—*freaking*—way!

I shake the excess thoughts from my mind and head to the classroom to pick up Drake. I see Mrs. Turner first.

"Hey, Skylar. How's the new job going so far?" she asks me.

"Good. I just need to get down everyone's names. That's always the hardest part." I chuckle.

"Maybe we can grab a bite to eat. I get sick of bringing my lunch, so I try to get out at least once a week. Oh, and please, call me Emily," she offers.

"Yes, I would love that. Let me know when and I'll make sure not to pack my lunch that day," I agree. Usually, I would never agree to something like this, but she seems sweet, genuine, and the fact that it's not taking out of my time with Drake works for me.

"How does tomorrow sound?" she asks.

"Sounds perfect," I respond. "How was Drake today?"

She tells the kids to line up in a single file line so they can walk out to the bus. Then she turns her attention back to me. "He is just amazing. I've never seen a kid adjust so well, and he's so helpful with the other students. I just adore him already," she boasts.

This is a proud mom moment. "That's so awesome to hear. I'm gonna grab Drake and let you get to the students. Just come get me tomorrow when you're ready," I tell her. She nods and then turns back to the kids.

I call Drake over. He grabs his book bag and runs to me. I rub his head. "Hey buddy, how was school today?" I ask him.

"Good, Mom! I was Mrs. Turners' teacher's helper today. I got to pass out all of the crayons," he tells me excitedly. I chuckle. His enthusiasm makes my day.

I grab his book bag from him as we walk out into the hallway. "Wow! That is *so* cool! I told you that you were going to love it here. What should we cook for dinner tonight?"

"Can we make a pizza?"

I chuckle. "Yes, that's a great idea!"

We hop into the car and head home. I make sure to watch all my mirrors and surroundings just in case I see anyone following us. It's been quiet over the past couple of weeks, and I know things are always too good to be true for us. Just when a place starts feeling like home, that's when the awakening hits and the reality of never being safe comes flooding back full force. I decide to make a stop at a used car dealer before we head home. I need to see how much I can get on a trade in for this Buick.

"Why are we here, Mom?" Drake questions, looking at all the cars in the parking lot.

"It's time mama gets a new car," I tell him.

I get out and walk around to Drake's side to grab his hand. A salesman wastes no time in greeting us. I tell him I'm looking to trade in my car for another as he's giving me a once-over like an easy target.

"Okay, let's see what we can do for you. Go ahead a take a look at what we have and let me know if there is anything that catches your eye," the salesman, Bert, tells me.

Drake and I walk around looking at the prices, year, and mileage on these cars. I see a couple that are nice but they're a little pricey. I'm not looking to get a loan, that's a sure way for Antonio and his goons to find me. I need an even trade.

Bert comes back with an extremely low number for my car, and I can't help but wonder if it's because I'm a woman. If I were a man, would he have given me a decent price? This gives me little hope. Sometimes I think I'll forever be stuck living in a man's world.

I tell him I'll think about it. Drake and I head home. I pull up to my driveway, and I see Neal doing some work on his car in the garage. I look over at Drake, and he has his face plastered to the window. I know there's no way of getting him inside the house right away, so I don't even say anything. I decide to be a big girl and speak to Neal about what happened last night. I need to tell him that it can never happen again. He has a girlfriend and I'm too busy raising my son to get involved. I'm just not ready for anything regardless, right? *Ugh.* If I can't convince myself of this, how do I expect to convince him? Get it together, Skylar. Just get it together. I exit my car and head toward Neal.

CHAPTER 6

NEAL

Skylar pulls up and Drake jumps out of the car running over to me. I'm just changing the oil in my Charger. I slide out from under the car. "Hey, what's going on, Drake?"

"Where's Benny?" he asks. I should have known he didn't come over to see me.

"I had to take Benny to the vet today. He had his shots and he's not feeling too well right now," I explain to him. His little face crumples up as though he's in pain.

"Ouchy! He needs some soup and some crackers. That's what my mom gives me when I'm not feeling well," Drake tells me.

I laugh. Skylar walks up behind him. "Is he over here talking your ear off?" she asks.

"No, he's fine. I don't mind the company," I answer.

My eyes find hers and I immediately smirk devilishly. I don't care how much she wants to deny it, I know she is thinking about last night just as I am right now. My eyes drink her in as they go over every inch of her body. Her cheeks redden as she watches me. She asks Drake to go inside so she can speak with me. Uh oh. This doesn't sound good.

I get up and wait for her to speak. We stand here in an electrical silence. I want nothing more than to grab a hold of her waist and pull her into me, but I don't think that would be a very smart thing to do in the open where neighbors could be watching and Missy could happen to pull up at any time. Anyways, I can see by her tense stance it would scare her away from me.

"I just wanted to talk with you about last night," she begins, twirling her hair nervously.

I give her my most charming grin. She smirks just a little, then rolls her eyes. I wipe my hands on the rag attached to my pants. "What about last night bothers you?" I question.

"It can't happen again," she snaps.

I contemplate this answer for a moment. "Why's that?"

I don't think she was expecting this question. She looks stumped. "Well, one: because we barely know each other. Two: because you have a girlfriend. And three: because I can't be distracted while I'm raising and protecting my son."

"Who are you protecting Drake from?" I question. I want her to tell me the truth, because I still need to tell her what I've found out.

She pauses a moment before answering. "Listen, Neal. There are just some things in my life that I can't talk about. Do you remember what I told you about Drake's father?" she asks.

"Yes."

"He is a very dangerous man, and he has a lot of connections. I'm just trying my best to stay clear of him," she finishes.

Now it's my turn to be honest. She may not have told me everything, but she said enough. "I know who he is, Skylar. I looked up his file," I confess.

Her brows furrow. She looks confused almost. "Are you allowed to do that?"

I chuckle. "Yes. I can look at any file I please. He's still in jail, so you don't have to worry about him right now," I inform her.

She snorts. "Yes, I'm aware he's still in jail. Like I said, he has connections. He wants my son."

My brain shifts gears just a bit and homes in about him wanting Drake. This doesn't sound good. "Skylar, is someone chasing you?" I walk toward her. "I can help you if you would just let me," I say, getting ready to slide my hand down her cheek, but before that happens and before she can answer me, Missy pulls up. *Fuck!* Why? Why does she have to pull up now? I drop my arm to my side.

I take my phone out of my pocket and realize I have missed her calls and texts. I was so caught up in our conversation that I didn't even notice my phone vibrating in my pocket.

"I'm sorry. I didn't realize she was stopping by," I tell her.

She watches as Missy gets out of the car. Missy looks between the both of us leaving her eyes on me. I can feel the tension already and I pray to God, she behaves herself. She comes up to me and plants a lingering kiss on my lips. This is completely awkward.

She then turns to Skylar. "Hello, you must be Skylar. I'm Missy, Neal's girlfriend."

Skylar smiles politely, but I can see that she's a little uncomfortable. "Yes, it's nice to meet you finally. I was actually just heading inside. I need to start dinner. If you both would excuse me," Skylar says.

"Of course," Missy replies.

Then she turns to walk into the house without saying another word. I wait a moment just to see if Skylar turns around before going into her garage, but she doesn't. I wanted to at least mouth that I was sorry. Missy was a little rude to her if you ask me, but what did I expect. This is just how Missy gets when she feels threatened.

I head into the house. Missy is sitting in the living room with a glass of wine already poured. She doesn't even wait a moment to dig into me. "You two looked pretty cozy when I walked up."

I lean myself against the wall of the entryway. "We were just having a conversation."

She looks at me head on. "About what?"

"She's just having some issues with Drake's father. I was just letting her know that she had nothing to worry about while I'm next door. That was it," I try to explain without giving away Skylar's secrets.

"Well, aren't you so generous. I was calling you. Why didn't you answer?"

I run my hand over my head. Benny comes up next to me, and I reach down to pet him, maybe just stalling a bit to come up with a good enough answer. "My phone was on silent. I thought I had it on vibrate." This is the best reason that I can come up with.

Missy stands up and walks toward me. "Should I be

worried, Neal? You've been very distant this last week. Are you not interested in me any longer?" she asks, sticking her bottom lip out just a bit.

"Missy, I've been busy just like you. You've been going out with your friends after work. You leave before I get up in the morning, and our schedules are a bit opposite right now. What do you want from me?"

She wraps her arms around me, and for the first time, they feel as if they don't belong. "Okay, maybe you're right. Let's go upstairs," she suggests seductively.

This normally always got me no matter what type of argument we were having, but not this time. I'm not even a bit interested. Actually, I'm hoping to go see Skylar tonight so we can finish our conversation.

I unwrap her arms around me. "Not right now, Missy. I'm starving. I'm going to make something to eat. Are you hungry?"

She looks stunned, because I have never turned down sex before. "Neal, I've been seeing someone," she blurts out as I'm walking toward the kitchen. I stop mid walk and turn slowly. Did I just hear her correctly?

I have to admit, I wasn't expecting this. Especially, after she just wanted me to go upstairs to fuck her. The crazy part is, I'm not that upset. I mean, after last night, how can I ridicule her?

"How long have you been seeing him?" I question calmly. I stay right where I am. There's no need to get any closer or to turn fully around.

She stalls for a moment. "It's not a him. It's a her. I've been seeing a woman," she discloses. I'm taken back just a bit. I don't even know how to respond to this. I'm completely speechless. Is she serious? It takes me a moment to gather my thoughts. "I'm sorry. I should have told you, but I didn't know it was going to turn into a thing. I was hoping me fucking you might change my thoughts about her. I'm still not sure how I feel, I mean, I still love you. I just enjoy fucking her as well," she tries to clarify.

I turn completely around to face her. "Maybe you should give her a chance then."

She begins to stalk toward me with some intention on her mind. This can't be good. "What if we both fucked her?" she suggests.

My eyes pop out shocked, and I almost choke on the air I'm breathing in. Holy fuck! Did I really just hear that out of her mouth? Wow. Every guy dreams of this moment. These are the words that I've been waiting for my entire life. It's like the holy grail for men. Unfortunately, I no longer have any interest in it. Crazy to say considering it may have been a possibility just last week. I may have dabbled a bit, but now? All my desires and thoughts are of one woman and one woman only—*Skylar*.

"Wow, Missy. What an offer – " I tell her still trying to wrap my head around this. "But I'm not interested in doing that. It's just not my thing right now. Listen, you should give it a real chance. You never know where life can take you. Maybe this is just a sign that us being together isn't the right thing," I encourage her, letting her down easy as possible.

She looks a bit sad. I walk up to her and wrap my arms around her; give her a kiss on her forehead to send her off on her way. She looks up at me. "I still love you, though."

I remove my arms and back away to give us some distance. I can't lead her on, because once she walks out that door, I will never go back to her. I know that with every inch of my being.

"Missy, it's just not going to work for us anymore. You're going to have to let go. It's just time we moved on. We haven't been together for a long time now. I think we've been holding on to the idea of a relationship, not actually being in the relationship," I explain to her finally being able to tell my truth.

She looks surprised then realization hits her. "Is this because of Skylar?" she asks.

I knew this question was coming. "No, not solely, but yes, I feel a sort of connection with her. I don't know what it means exactly, but since you're being honest with me then I feel it's only fair for me to do the same," I admit. "Missy, I still care about you. That's not the issue. We've just changed. What we want in life has changed. We've held on long enough."

She has tears rolling down her cheeks. I wipe them away. "Maybe you're right, but that still doesn't make any of this any easier," she finally says. "If you ever change your mind or get lonely, you know how to reach me."

I nod. She turns and stops at the door. "Goodbye, Neal," and then shuts the door behind her walking out of my life for good. I blow out a deep breath. This is just crazy. I'm still trying to wrap my head around everything she has told me. Being cheated on stings just a bit. I'd be lying if I said it didn't, but losing to another woman feels just a bit better. I head upstairs to lay down. My head is completely spinning. After all this there's still the fact that Skylar wants me to stay away from her, and I just don't know if I can do that.

Something wet slides up my cheek; now over my mouth. I push it away and turn my head. I blink then open my eyes to darkness. What the hell? I hear Benny whining, furiously trying to wake me up. I look over at my alarm clock and it's almost 9pm. Damn! Did I really just sleep that long? I bounce up, wipe the crusties from my eyes, and tell Benny come on. He needs to go out before he pisses all over my carpet.

My brain is still swirling from my conversation with Missy. I can't believe we're really done. I'm not sad. I just don't know what to do with myself. It was a sort of safety knowing in the back of your mind that there's someone out in the world waiting for you, and now—nothing. It's kind of an eerie feeling. Maybe a little bit of an empty feeling, but then my mind drifts to Skylar.

Skylar is sort of an enigma. One moment she's ice cold and the other she is on fire. She's giving me whiplash while trying to figure out her feelings. I know she has no trust for men, and because of that I'm okay with backing off a bit and taking it slow. I want to gain her trust more than anything. I want her to let me in so I can help her— protect her.

I let Benny in, then decide that my conversation from this afternoon with Skylar needs to continue. There's much more that I need to discuss with her. I throw on some sweats and a T-shirt and head over there. Hopefully she's still up like last night.

I notice a car sitting diagonally from the house. One that I've never seen before. It's a dark grey older Cadillac which looks to have only one man sitting in it. Before I step out I backtrack, attempt to write the license plate down but there isn't one, and grab my gun from my holster. I unlock the safety and tell Benny to stay. I don't want him scaring him off. He whines not wanting me to leave without him. I head straight for the car; the whole way checking my surroundings. I just have a bad feeling that this guy is up to no good. The driver must have caught my reflection in the rearview mirror as I walk up because he speeds off screeching the tires as they turn the corner.

Shit! I kick the garbage can in front of me pissed. I should have scoped him out longer and took my time rather than walking straight up to the car. Who was he waiting for? Was he here for me or for Skylar. Me I can take, but the thought of her and Drake is something I cannot.

I shoot Johnny a text to see if he can get a hit on the car. I'm going to hunt this guy down and do whatever it takes to see who he is working for and what it is he was looking for.

I return my gun to my house first before I walk over to Skylar's, knock lightly on her door, and wait. She opens the door, but this time wide enough to allow me in.

"Neal? Is everything okay? Where's Missy?" she wonders, looking behind me toward my driveway.

I look at her before I head to the kitchen. "She left. We decided that it would be better if we were apart. She was seeing someone else, so I ended it."

Her brows lift in shock. "Oh," is the only thing she says.

She leads me into the living room instead of the

kitchen. Then waits for me to speak. "Skylar, I came over because I wanted to finish our conversation. I think there's some things that we still need to talk about."

She tilts her head to the side. "Like what?"

She sits down on the chair, and I take a seat on the ottoman next to her. "Like Drake's father."

"Okay, what is it that you want to know?" she questions.

"What is it that you know about him? How did you meet him?

She takes a deep breath and looks down at her hands. "I met him just before I was about to graduate. It was pouring outside, and I was walking home from school. He offered me a ride home. I told him no. It was freezing out, and he wouldn't take no for an answer. I know it was stupid of me to get into a stranger's car, but what more could he have done to me? I was at a low part in my life being shipped from foster home to foster home. At that point, I felt anything would have been better than where I was living."

"The family I was living with at the time was my last family. I had only lived there for about six months and already I had to fend off the man of the house, Fred. He had been coming into my room and touching me. Making me do things to him that I don't even want to remember. The next step was him forcing himself on me. That was coming any day, and I knew it. The only thing that was stopping him was his eldest son.

"He knew what kind of vial disgusting person his father was, and he hated him. We were both seniors in school. He was just biding his time, waiting to graduate, and then he was out. About a week before I met Antonio,

Fred came into my bedroom, and his son, had walked in on us. He threatened to go to the police if he ever came near me again. After that, his son slept on the floor of my room every night. I have him to thank for my virginity.

"Antonio was sweet to me. He picked me up and dropped me off every day until I graduated. When I turned eighteen and received my diploma I left with him. I trusted him. He was a life raft, and I held onto him tight. But things eventually changed. He became controlling and then violent. I was trapped again. After enduring him for almost two years, I found out I was pregnant with Drake. After Drake was born things took a turn for the worse, so I ran. Took whatever money of his I could find and ran."

This woman in front of me is my hero. I am in awe of her. The things she has endured and overcome are things no one should ever have to go through. I swear to God from this moment on I will do everything in my power to protect her. I will never let anyone hurt her again including me.

"And he followed you?" I wonder.

"Yes," she answers quietly.

"Is he still after you?"

"Yes, but he's hired people," she divulges.

This is worse than I thought. I can't tell her too much. I can't give her any information on the investigation, but I want her to feel safe with me. "Are you afraid they might find you here?" Shoot, I'm afraid they might have *already* found her here.

She looks torn. Like a part of her wants to trust me, but the part of her that's been depending on herself all this time doesn't trust me. *Can't* trust me. I think the one man she trusted broke her. I have to make her understand that that's not going to be me. "Skylar, you can trust me. I promise. I would never put you or Drake in harm's way," I tell her. "Please, just let me help you."

She looks up at me, staring into my eyes for a moment as though she's trying to read me. "Neal, they're cops," she says.

I take a deep breath, run my hand over my head, and stand. This isn't good. I've always known dirty cops are planted in the force. Hell, I have attempted to uncover who they are but haven't been successful in figuring it out, but to hear this from her solidifies that all precincts are tainted. I need my grounding for this. I knew Ray Castro had connections with law enforcement, but this just validates it. She would never know these things unless they were true.

I pace for a moment, then stop, and sit back down. "Do you know his family?"

She shakes her head. "He told me he didn't have too much family. That's why we connected so well because we only had each other to depend on. Now, I wonder if that was also a lie. He lied about being on parole, and he lied about living a dangerous life. So, now, I don't know what the truth is."

Now I have no choice but to tell her since she's been walking around blind. "He did lie to you. Skylar, his family is very powerful and very dangerous. His brother is connected to the cartel. Have you been watching the news?" I ask her.

"Yes."

"Have you heard the name Ray Castro?"

She begins breathing heavy. "Yes."

"That's his brother," I inform her.

Tears begin to slide down her face, and she begins to shake. I pull her into me holding her as tight as I can. I'll be her strength for tonight. I want to take all her fears away. The point of this wasn't to scare her, but I had to inform her. Information is power and I can't just leave her a sitting duck. I rub her hair as I hold her close. "Skylar, I want you and Drake to come live with me." I don't know what came over me just now, but I don't care. I want this. I want them both in my life.

She immediately pulls away from me. "Are you crazy? We barely know each other! The whole point of me running is to give Drake a normal life. Not to move in with the first man that gives me attention!" she says, raising her voice. She pushes off me and heads to the kitchen. I follow.

Way to go, Neal, I think to myself. "Okay, maybe you're right. I went a little overboard. I just feel like I can protect you better if you're both with me."

She turns around to me. "What are you not telling me, Neal?" she asks, crossing her arms over her chest. She has a fire in her eyes as though she's ready for a fight. I see the protective mother in her and maybe she's not the scared woman I just saw a minute ago. Maybe I've underestimated her.

I just need to say it. She deserves to know. I just pray she doesn't run. "Antonio gets released in a month."

She gasps and puts her hands over her mouth. Panic envelops her. Exactly what I was afraid of. I need to calm her down before she makes any sudden decisions. I walk up to her and grab her hand entwining it with mine. "I'm here. I'm not going to let anyone hurt you again. I already have surveillance around the house because of my job, and you need a new car. They're probably looking for that Buick as we speak. I can help you with that."

She nods her head, then looks up to me. "Thank you, Neal. But I don't want to drag you into this."

I place my palms on either side of her face, so she has no choice but to look at me. "I don't think you understand what I've been saying. I'm not going anywhere, and I am not letting you go through this alone," I tell her. "We'll figure this all out – *together.*" I give her a light kiss on the forehead, but when I look at her again, she now has desire in her eyes. I become unhinged just looking at her.

"You're so beautiful," I whisper to her.

I run my thumb along her bottom lip. She gently reaches her tongue out to taste my finger. My dick gets hard instantly. God, I want her. I want every part of her. I want her to be mine and only mine. I know this is soon, but she's been in my heart for years now. She left an invisible print on my life that can't be erased, and I don't want to lose her again.

She now nips at my finger, then brings it into her mouth, licking and sucking gently sensually while gazing at me with those big brown eyes. *Jesus.* I want to ravage her like the beast I am and take over every part of her body. I want her melting in my arms as she comes repeatedly over my cock.

"Do you even know what you're doing to me?" I ask her. She's making it hard for me to take things slow.

She shakes her head with a small smirk. Oh, she knows. She's purposely being a vixen. I lean down to kiss her like it's my last kiss on this earth, with passion and raw openness. Every feeling I have being laid out on the line with just this kiss. Her lips are soft and taste like absolute heaven. I wrap my hands through her hair pulling her closer to me. She moans as my hard cock presses against her pelvis through my sweatpants.

She smells of flowers on a beautiful sun shiny day as I trail light kisses down her neck, nibbling and tasting her deliciously sweet skin. I want to devour her like a succulent piece of candy bursting into my mouth. Each moan of hers is like a direct line going straight to my cock. She's driving me unbelievably crazy. I reach down to the hem of her sweatshirt and begin to lift it upward. Screw taking it slow. She raises her arms without hesitation, and with this I know she is on the same page as me. She wants this just as much as I do.

Her chest heaves up and down as the swell of her breasts overflow her white lace bra. I tuck my fingers under her bra straps pulling them down over her shoulders just enough to release her taut nipples. I lean down and take one into my mouth. She cries out as I suck and graze my teeth gently against her. It's such a turn on that she's so responsive to me. I move to the next and she bucks up against me, digging her nails into my arms. The pain is welcomed. I reach around her back with my left hand and unsnap her bra dropping it to the floor.

Her chest is now bare to me, and she is unbelievably perfect; *everything* about her is just perfection. We gaze at each other for a moment until I can't take it any longer. I reach down, grab her ass, and place her on top of the counter behind her. I smash my lips with hers in desperate need. I can't get enough.

"You're so fucking beautiful, Sky," I whisper to her.

She smirks shyly, then lifts the hem of my shirt and I

comply. I watch her hands roam over my chest and down through the peaks and valleys of my abs, exploring with her fingertips over each clenched muscle making me shiver. I want this so badly but I'm afraid she may regret this if we go any further. Do I stop? Or do I continue selfishly because I know it's what I want? Just as I'm about to pull away Drake walks in.

"Mom?" Drake calls out, rubbing his eyes as he looks around in a sleepy haze.

Skylar pushes me back, jumps off the counter, grabs her sweatshirt from the floor and quickly yanks it on. "Why are you up, baby?" she asks, kneeling to him.

"I couldn't sleep. I was looking for you and I couldn't find you," Drake says, the worry now vanishing. He looks over Skylar's shoulder to me. "Did you bring Benny?" he asks, in his munchkin voice, with a glimmer of hope in his eyes.

I chuckle. "No, bud. Benny's home sleeping," I tell him as I pull my shirt back over me. He looks toward his mother then back toward me again, confused. "Are you guys having a slumber party?" he asks excitedly. I smirk. I would love to have a sleepover with his mom.

This time Skylar answers. "No baby. Neal was just leaving. Come on, let's get you to bed." She turns him back toward the hallway, taking his hand to lead him up the stairs.

Disappointment swells my insides, and I take this as the night is over. Even though I was going to suggest taking things slow, I was also hoping for some more of the make out sesh to continue. The adrenaline that kicks in when catching a perp doesn't compare to the adrenaline that I feel when touching her lips to mine. She's addicting in every sort of way. "I'll let myself out. Make sure you lock the deadbolt after me," I tell her. "Good night, Drake."

"Night!" Drake yells out as he's walking up the stairs.

I make sure the bottom lock is locked and head out into the night on high alert.

CHAPTER 7

SKYLAR

"Well good morning, sunshine! You look like you could use a big cup of coffee," Jess comments as I walk toward my desk. Great, I must look like death. She gets up and heads to the break room without saying another word. I set my things down, exhausted. I didn't get much sleep last night after Neal left.

First, his words about Antonio kept repeating in my head. How did I not see the connection? I googled all night articles on his brother, Ray Castro. Their resemblance is uncanny. I also learned they have a sister whose son was just arrested a town over. Do they know about Drake? Most of Ray's business is run through Miami, so why choose to be in upstate New York?

I've had nightmares for years when it came to Antonio, but the stakes have now changed. I don't know how much longer I can run from him. When it comes to Antonio's brother, Ray Castro, no one can hide. He's a cold-blooded killer that always gets what he wants. If Drake is what Antonio wants, then Ray will have no qualms about taking me out to give his brother what he wants. My countdown has officially begun. I thought I had time to plan for the day of Antonio's release and now, a month is all I have.

I need to spend each day as if it's my last. If something happens to me, I want Drake to always remember these last days. I want him to know how much I sacrificed for him because he's my world and I'm okay with giving my life for him. But most of all I need him to know how much I love him and how happy he has made my life. I don't regret one moment of it.

A tear slides down my cheek. Jess drops a cup of coffee on my desk. I quickly wipe the tear away. "I thought you may need this ASAP," she tells me with a calming smile. "This morning's meeting is canceled by the way."

"Thank you, Jess. It's exactly what I'm in need of. I woke up late and didn't have time to brew any at the house," I explain. I'm just glad I didn't have to pack a lunch today either.

She sits back down at her desk; turns away from me to greet a mother and her daughter. After they leave, she turns back to me. "Ugh! That is the worst. Waking up late throws the whole day off," she adds. "How is Drake doing in class?"

I log into my computer. "Miss Turner says he is adjusting extremely well," I reply while clocking in.

"Oh, that's so good to hear! Some kids have such a hard time adjusting to new surroundings. Mrs. Turner is such an amazing teacher. She's been through so much but always comes to work with a smile on her face," Jess informs me.

My brows furrow. I must look a bit confused. "She recently went through a very messy divorce. Her husband was a nasty man. I don't know what she even saw in him but I'm glad she finally left him," Jess finishes explaining.

I wouldn't have considered this by just meeting her. Of course, you just never know what someone may be going through unless they choose to open up to you and I'm a walking cliché of this fact. I walk around with a smile on my face most days, but that doesn't mean my life is all roses, clearly. It just means I've gotten to be a professional at masking things.

"I couldn't even imagine having to go through something like that. Divorce most definitely brings out the worst in people," I add.

She huffs. "Who are you telling? My first husband was a joke! We got married right out of high school; eloped. I thought I was in love and knew it all. Everyone had warned me about what kind of guy he really was and *boy* they were right. He was a cheating son of a bitch. He ended up getting my best friend pregnant," she reveals. My eyebrows shoot up shocked, I gasp smacking my hand to my mouth. I can't even imagine. "To this day I thank god it was her rather than me!"

"So, what happened after that?" I ask.

"I left his sorry butt and got an annulment. Years later I finally met my Stan." She absolutely melts when saying his name. "We've been married thirty-two years now. So, you see, everything happens for a reason. I may have never been at the coffee shop down on Main Street that morning I met my Stan. My life could have turned out a lot differently if that dimwit never cheated. I thank God for that every single day," Jess admits.

Thoughts of Neal pop into my mind. Then the thought of last night comes front and center. I feel slightly flushed with the memories. I look down toward my computer to hide the embarrassment of possibly revealing myself and my naughty thoughts. Every time I'm around him, engulfed in his intoxicating haze, I can't get myself together. He just does something to me, and it scares the crap out of me, honestly.

I was so sure I could keep my distance and stay away from him. Hell, it was my idea! But the moment he looks at me with those drug overdosed eyes I'm a goner. I'm out of my element with all these crazed feelings.

With Antonio, it was about safety and comfort at first, but with Neal, it's about the burning desire that lights between my thighs every time I'm near him. It's hard to tame the fire once it spreads and by then, who the hell wants to? I knew I should have stopped myself last night but as soon as I felt his lips against mine, I was a goner. If Drake hadn't walked in on us, I may have experienced my first one-night stand. I'm not sure how I would have felt about that afterwards, but in the moment, I sure didn't care.

I've only been with one man, and he ruined me to the point of losing interest in being intimate with anyone else. My association with sex was the memories of being terrified and manipulated—that is until Neal came along. There's just something so different about him. Something that terrifies me, but in the most exciting way possible. He makes me want to explore my sexual side. He makes me feel in control and sexy, but most of all he makes me feel safe with him.

"I can't imagine being with the same man for more

than half my life. How did you know that he was the one you wanted to spend the rest of your life with?" I ask Jess.

"When you meet your soulmate, you just know dear. There's a familiarity with them, like you've known them forever. Being together and around each other comes naturally. Some relationships you have to work for, but I believe those are the ones that maybe were never meant to be or they're just a convenience or a warm placeholder until you do find your one," Jess answers so profoundly that it hits me hard because that's how I'm already feeling about Neal and I've barely gotten the chance to know him yet.

Before I'm able to ask another question Richie walks through the doors. After he greets Jess, he turns his attention to me. "Good morning, Skylar," he sings with the brightest smirk.

I smile politely internally wishing he would walk away. "Good morning, Richie."

"How's working with Jess?" he asks, winking her way.

Jess waves him off blushing. "Jess is great! She's truly such a blessing to work with."

"Will I see you in the break room for lunch?" Richie asks.

Thank God I already made plans. "No, I actually am going out to lunch with Emily today," I tell him, grateful I don't have to make up a lie.

He looks disappointed. "Ok, well maybe tomorrow then. Gotta go clock in. Bye, ladies!" he says, turning to head toward his office.

I guess tomorrow will be lunch with Drake for me. Jess looks over at me, and I know exactly what she's thinking. "I'm not interested," I tell her, rolling my eyes. She clearly loves to play matchmaker.

LUNCHTIME FINALLY ROLLS AROUND. My stomach is growling. Emily grabs me here in the front office. We take her car since she's familiar with the area.

"So, what's your thoughts on Richie?" she asks as she turns out of the school parking lot.

"Um, he seems nice," I reply. "I'm just not interested in dating though," I tell her semi honestly.

"I totally get that. Moving to a new area is stressful enough. Then add kids and a new job on top of it; a new man I'm sure is last on your mind," she says laughing.

I nod while my mind drifts to Neal.

"Well, I think he has a thing for you, but he also seems to get a thing for all the new girls. I was going to warn you of this but since you're not interested, there's no reason to," Emily explains.

Great, he's one of those. He's like a kid always wanting the shiny new toy. "Was he like that with you as well?"

We stop at a red light; she looks over at me. "I was going through a divorce when he began teaching at this school. So, I made the mistake of going on a date with him. I'll admit I liked the attention. I craved any sort of attention at the time, good or bad. My husband wasn't much on compliments and making me feel special. Richie came along and was the complete opposite—at least I thought. Once he realized that I wasn't too open to the idea of casual sex he moved on to the next," she informs me. "That seems to be his MO. He did me a favor by being a douche and I sure wasn't going to let him do the same to you."

I feel touched and grateful that she cares enough to want to warn me considering she barely knows me. It's sweet she's willing to stick her neck out for me. "Thanks, Emily. I really appreciate the warning. How long were you married for?" I ask, hoping I'm not prying considering I'm asking the questions I hate myself.

"Just a little over three years. I don't even know why I stayed as long as I did. He was controlling and possessive. He wouldn't allow me to have a social life because he was afraid people would see what kind of a man he really was and tell me to leave. At first, I thought he was just protective, and I always made excuses for him, but as the years went by it had gotten way worse. He tore me down so I would believe I didn't deserve anything better. He was simply a coward," she explains.

"So, what made you leave?" I question.

She takes a deep breath before answering. "He hit me."

I gasp. "I am *so* sorry, Emily. What a coward. I am glad you left. Who knows what could have happened if you stayed."

There were moments when I thought Antonio might hit me, but he never did, surprisingly. I'm sure if I stayed long enough it might have gotten to that point. Instead, he went straight to almost killing me in front of my son. So, I'm not sure which is worse. I just wish I could walk away like Emily and be through with it all. Death will be the only way out when it comes to Antonio, and that's not an option for me.

We pull into the parking lot of a small burger joint.

Emily parks then turns to me abruptly, "So, what's your story, Skylar?"

At this point she has been completely honest with me. Maybe I should do the same for once. I mean, the details may not be as important, but I can at least let her in a bit. I've never had a girlfriend. It would be nice to finally be able to talk girl talk with someone. I'm dying to get someone else's opinion on Neal, and I've never had anything to gossip about until now. I could use some woman advice since I am lacking experience.

We get out of the car and head into the burger joint to order. The place is packed. We place our orders and locate an empty booth in the back corner. "The night Drake's father went to jail there was a cop on scene. I don't remember much except for him being very attentive and kind. Everything was a haze that night, but he remembered me. He's my neighbor now. I moved in right next to him and didn't even realize it," I tell her.

Emily grins sitting up a little taller. "Oh my. You have a thing for him, don't you?" she asks excitedly.

My smile must give me away. "I've tried to stay away from him. I even told him that there would be nothing between us. But every time he comes near me my brain shuts down. I can't think. It's like my body is taken over. I have no control," I admit. It feels nice to finally get this off my chest.

Emily laughs. "I see. It's not that you're not into dating, you're just not into dating Richie. Well, it's sounds to me that you may have found your one."

I squint my eyes at her. "My one?"

The employee comes over to drop off our food. "Yes, your match. When you find chemistry like that then he's a definite keeper. And he's a man in uniform? Oh girl, you are in some trouble," Emily says giggling.

Boy, don't I already know this. I take a bite of my burger and put my straw into my cup. I ponder for a moment what Emily just said about finding *my one*, could this possibly be true? "He has or *had* a girlfriend; I'm not too clear on this. He was seeing this girl Missy but then he told me last night he broke it off. That's another reason I was trying to stay away. I have no interest in being the other woman. I would just rather remain alone," I divulge.

Emily takes a sip of her soda. "Do you think he could have broken it off for you?" she wonders.

I shrug. "I honestly have no idea."

"You need to find out if what he said is true. Then, see who really broke up with who. That can make a big difference. If she broke it off, then there still could remain feelings there and you don't want to be the rebound. But if it was the opposite, then I would say hang out. See where things go. There's no need to rush if you're not ready yet," she advises.

Emily has a point. Neal and I haven't really discussed his relationship. What if what we have is just strictly physical? I know I've already begun to develop feelings for him. I don't know if I can deal with heartbreak on top of everything else.

"You're right. Next time I see him I'm going to have this discussion. It's just, these feelings are new to me. The only person I ever had a relationship with was Drake's father and that was more like a dictatorship than a relationship," I tell her.

I finish up the last bite of my burger. I haven't had one

this good in a long time. I'm totally bringing Drake here soon. He would love it here.

"When does Drake's father get released?"

"In a month for good behavior. I don't know what we're going to do. He wants Drake and is willing to do anything to get him. I can't let that happen. His family is very dangerous, and I wasn't aware of this when we started dating. I'm afraid of what he'll do," I confess.

Emily reaches her hand over the table and grabs mine. "Skylar, that's horrible. I'm so sorry you have had to go through this alone. Please, if you need anything, anything at all, don't hesitate to ask."

I nod and smile slightly. "Thanks."

We head back to work. Our lunch break is only an hour, but I could sit and talk to her for days. I feel comfortable with Emily, which is unusual for me because I never let my guard down with anyone. I probably shouldn't take the risk, but I think the fact that she's also been through a traumatic experience bonds us somehow. I can relate to her in a way I haven't been able to relate to anyone.

The rest of the day goes by extremely slowly. I'm getting antsy thinking about heading home. Will Neal be outside? If not, will he show up at my doorstep tonight? Maybe I should wear something a little more revealing. *Oh gawd, Skylar!* What is wrong with me? What am I thinking? I don't own anything of that nature regardless. Of course, he didn't seem to mind my sweatshirt and shorts last night. Those are about the most provocative things I own.

I grab Drake from class, and we head home. "Mom, Desire tried to hold my hand at recess," Drake tells me. I do my best to hide my smile. I want to tell him that's adorable but I don't think that's the type of comment he's looking for.

"Oh yeah? And what did you do?" I ask him.

He crinkles his nose. "I told her that was gross and that I don't like girls!" he says so enthusiastically.

I try to conceal my laugh. If only he could stay this way forever. "That wasn't very nice, bud. Next time just tell her no thanks. It's okay to be direct but it's important to still be respectful."

He thinks about what I've just said for a moment then tells me, "But Mom, girls have cooties. You told me so, and I don't want no cooties," he tells me.

He's right, I did tell him that. My fault. "It's I do not want any cooties," I say, correcting his grammar. "And you're right, I did tell you that, and I shouldn't have. But that still doesn't mean you can go out and get a girlfriend," I tell him joking.

He makes a face of disgust. "No girlfriends for me! Yuck!" He sticks out his tongue and blows, spit going everywhere. My sweet boy. Little does he know he's going to have girls flocking to him for years to come. It's my job to make sure he becomes a gentleman, and that's hard to do as a single mom. These are the times when a boy needs his dad or a male role model in his life.

I turn the corner to head down my street. I notice a car parked on my right as I look through my rearview mirror. I haven't seen this car before. I couldn't make out the figure in the driver's side, so I have no idea if they are male or female. My heart picks up a bit. I've been so preoccupied with Drake and thoughts of Neal that I've forgotten to pay attention to my surroundings. This is bad. This is *very* bad. It just takes one moment of distraction for things to go south. This is why I never allowed anyone in my life. I can't afford to be careless.

I press the garage door opener as I pull into my driveway. Neal's house looks quiet and still. His car or truck is not in the driveway so he must be at work. Should I mention the car when I see him? Or am I just being paranoid?

"Mom, can I play with my ball outside?" Drake asks.

I look back outside, and the car is now gone. "Yeah, baby. Just let me change first then I'll come sit outside with you," I tell him. I can't leave him for even a moment alone out here after seeing that out of place car. Seconds is all it would take for someone to grab him. Then I would never see my son again. Just the thought of that scares the crap out of me. It makes me never want to leave the house again.

I change but before I head outside with Drake I need to speak with him. Give him a reminder. I kneel down so I am at eye level with him. "Drake, I need you to remember that you never talk to strangers. It's very important because we just don't know who the bad guys are, okay? I don't want anything to happen to you. You're my life. I love you," I tell him while holding his little hand. My intent is not to scare him but to inform him and make him aware so if that moment comes and I'm not there then he will know what to do—I hope.

"I know, Mom. I will protect you from the bad guys," he says so matter-of-factly.

My heart melts. "Awe, baby, thank you. But that's not your job. That's my job."

I put my pinkie out and he links his to mine. We both

kiss our thumbs, then I embrace him for a hug. How did I get so lucky? This little boy is just amazing. The light of my life. I couldn't imagine my world without him.

Drake grabs his basketball, and I take a seat on the front step. I see the old lady across the street letting out her cat. She stands in front of her door for a moment looking around. She notices me looking in her direction and waves. I wave back a little mortified for getting caught staring. I used to think nosey people were a nuisance but it was those very nosey people that scared the men away from my last house long enough for Drake and me to escape. I'm forever grateful for that. Now, I see them as a blessing.

Just as I begin to relax while watching Drake bounce his basketball, I see Neal pulling up. The beat of my heart picks up pitter-patting awfully fast now against my chest. I feel uneasy and a little queasy as I hold my breath. Maybe he will just go inside. Here I am sure he's going to come walking up, completely full of myself, and he doesn't. He pulls straight into his garage and shuts the door behind him.

I let out the breath I'm holding and chuckle to myself. I've never had this happen before. I hit pure panic mode the moment Neal is in my sight. It's like all sense of composure goes right out the window with my brain. I've heard of this feeling in the movies, but never real life. I never believed for a moment that feelings like this could exist with barely knowing a person.

It's not only my brain that goes haywire; it's the endless intense throb between my legs that's goes into overdrive. How the hell do I stop it? I was once a teenager, but never did I even come close to this corrupt insanity. I know that was because of my history; my upbringing wouldn't allow these types of things to happen to me when I was younger due to the abuse I endured; a curse that ripped my teenagerhood away from me.

I catch movement from my peripheral vision and when I turn to my right Neal is standing next to me. Benny has already found Drake from the shriek I heard. I look up and Neal is looking down at me smiling. "Hey," he says with his hands in his pockets.

"Hey."

My eyes drift down his body roaming and lingering over every contour; his biceps flex as if on demand. I store the memory as if I may never have the chance to lay my eyes on him again. I lick my lips unknowingly. My mouth has gone dry suddenly and I can barely form a cohesive sentence. So, I move over some on the step giving him room to sit instead.

As if ogling him wasn't enough, I get engulfed in his mouthwatering aroma. It's light and fresh like the crisp air on a beautiful morning day. I almost want to close my eyes and inhale, but I stop myself. That might get a little awkward. I'm not sure how I would explain that one.

"So, how was your day?" Neal asks, keeping things light.

"It was good. Not too busy. I had lunch with Drake's teacher, Emily. It was nice to have some girl time. I've never really had a girlfriend before," I tell him.

Neal glances sideways toward me. "No? Every girl needs some girl time. I've learned this over time. You girls tend to get a little crazy without it," he jokes chuckling.

Well, it's clear he really doesn't know me at all. "It's not that I haven't wanted to get close to anyone, I just never saw the point in it. I'm bound to leave at any time, and I just couldn't risk the questions I would have to answer while getting to know someone. How can I tell anyone about my past; about the men who are after Drake?" I try to explain. Then chuckle to myself while watching Drake chase after Benny. "Shit, anyone who knew the truth would run from me, and who could blame them? Crazed men hunting me down – not many people would want anything to do with that."

"Skylar, if they are any kind of friend they wouldn't run, they would just support you. Hell, maybe even help you!" he says, then turns to face me. He grabs my hand and entwines it with his. His hand is warm and soft. He has two calluses near his pinky and ring finger. But his touch is calming; something I'm not used to. There's a sort of strength that exudes out from him and makes me immediately feel calm.

"I'm not going anywhere. Whatever you need from me, all you have to do is ask. You need a friend – I'm here. You need someone to talk to – I'm here. And if maybe just maybe your feelings begin to grow as mine are – than I'm here for that too," he assures me.

I can't look away from him. I'm caught in his trance. My mouth opens to respond but nothing comes out. No one has ever said these words to me. I'm not sure whether to run or kiss him.

I shake my head and close my eyes. I need space. I can't breathe in his intoxicating words. If I do, then I might believe them, and it will crush me if he doesn't follow through. I can't risk depending on someone else to take care of Drake and I. Hell, I've only known him for less than a week now.

I open my eyes back up, but this time with my brick wall up and stable. "Thank you for the offer, Neal. Really. But I can take care of Drake and myself. I've been doing it for years now and I don't need anyone to help," I tell him cold and so-matter-of-factly even though I want desperately to say yes.

He looks a little hurt and angry as his brows furrow. He lifts our entwined hand up to his lips and kisses my fingers softly. When he looks back up at me, I see understanding and confidence. "I know you can take care of yourself. I'm not doubting that at all, Skylar. You've been in my thoughts every day for years now; always wishing I could have done something different that night to help you. You are an amazingly strong woman for what you have endured, but I *want* to be here for you. Not out of pity but because I care for you and Drake. If I have to prove my commitment to you both, then that's what I'll do. I'm here and I'm not leaving," he says.

I think he just poured his heart out to me, and here I am wondering if what he's saying is even real. I am one fucked up person. God, I want to believe him, I really do. "It's going to take time for me to trust again. Please, just be patient with me."

Neal smiles and nods his head. "I can do that," he replies clearly relieved that I'm offering him a chance.

It's time to change the subject. There's something that's been on my mind since my talk with Emily. "What happened with Missy? You mentioned you broke it off last night," I ask.

He blows out a breath, releases my hand, and rubs it over his head. "She was cheating on me," he reveals.

I remember him mentioning this briefly last night. "Oh gosh, I'm so sorry, Neal."

"It's fine. It's actually not what you think. She's been seeing another girl," he clarifies.

My hand goes over my mouth trying to stop my giggles. I can't tell if this was a good thing or bad for his ego. "Oh wow, that's not what I was expecting to hear."

He chuckles seeming to enjoy watching me laugh. "Yeah, you and me both. She had the nerve to tell me she wanted me to see both of them," he informs me, eyeing me. My mouth now hangs open in shock. I really don't know what to say to that. "Every man's fantasy," I reply with a smirk.

"Yeah, well, it's not mine any longer. This all unfolded at the perfect time because I wanted to break it off with her anyways. She was overly possessive and after a while our connection just burnt out. We haven't been seeing eye to eye for a while now. She just isn't for me," he explains.

Wow. A man that turned down the ultimate offer. I'm impressed. I never understood the hype, but I'm also not a man. "So, how did she take it?"

"Mom, mom, watch me!" Drake shouts. We both look over to him. He's attempting to spin the basketball on his tiny little finger.

"Wow! Good job, bud!" I tell him with a tiny clap.

"He sure does love basketball, huh?" Neal asks.

I smile. "He does."

We continue where we left off. "Missy wasn't thrilled, but I think she knew it was coming. Regardless of if she was with a man or woman, it's still cheating, and clearly, I had some of my own dilemmas happening as well. But I have no ill will feelings toward her. We ended cordially which was nice. No drama," he finishes.

I'm happy with his answer. Though, I don't think he broke it off for me, he did break it off for himself. That means no strings or feelings left on his part. That means he's truly a single man now. I wouldn't be a side chick or a homewrecker. The idea of being labeled this brought guilt upon me that I did not need.

"Good. If you're happy, I'm happy," I reply.

He nudges his shoulder with mine. "Sitting here with you makes me happy."

Before I can even think I ask him to have dinner with us, and he immediately agrees. I'm not going to rush anything but having someone around is new and comforting to me. Drake already adores Neal which can be a good thing and a bad thing all in one.

CHAPTER 8

NEAL

*D*inner was good as hell. Between the two of us we can really throw down. Skylar was relaxed for once and seems to be falling into a sort of comfort with me. She's funny and sexy as hell when she lets go and laughs. I love how she tucks her hair behind her ear shyly when she notices me staring; I just can't help but stare at her every second I get. Her smile is contagious and the glimmer in her eyes mesmerizes me. The more I'm around her, the more time I want to spend with her, getting to know her learning what makes her tick.

I want to taste every inch of her skin and embed every delectable piece of her body into my mind. She brings out a need in me that I never knew existed. I'm craving to touch her again. I finally had a chance to experience it and I'm already completely addicted. This is all so crazy to me. I feel as though I'm thinking like a girl, but I don't care. I'm not ashamed of what I'm feeling. I'm ready to embrace it.

She comes down after putting Drake to bed. I must

admit, I'm getting a little attached to him too. I'm enjoying spending time with him just as much as I'm enjoying my time with her. "Is he all settled?" I ask.

"He is," she answers, heading into the kitchen. She stops mid-step. "Oh, wow. You cleaned," she says amazed.

"Yes, I've cleaned a kitchen or two in my time," I reply jokingly with a wink.

She laughs. "Yes, I'm sure you have. Thank you. Would you like some coffee or maybe a glass of wine?"

I have the day off tomorrow, so indulging in a little wine is fine for me tonight. "I'll take some wine, but only if you will have some with me," I coerce her just a bit.

Skylar smiles and heads toward the cupboard that holds the wine glasses. She pours us two glasses of red and brings them over. She takes a seat next to me instead of across from me which makes me smile inside. To know she has shared with me things from her past that she hasn't shared with a single person, and to see her sitting beside me comfortably and relaxed makes me feel gratified. This is all I have wanted since the moment I realized who she was. A girl like her has no reason to trust anyone let alone me, and this is how I know I am doing things right by her—like I swore I was going to do.

Yes, *I* want to be her knight in shining armor. This dire need is all so new to me, but I like it. I just hope she understands that she doesn't have to run again. I'm here for her and Drake. I will do whatever it takes to make sure they are looked after, I mean *whatever* it takes.

I take a sip of my wine, then turn to her. "Skylar, I was thinking—I have off this weekend, and I would love to take Drake and you somewhere special. Somewhere my mother took me all the time as a boy. I think Drake would really enjoy it," I tell her. I'm unsure if this is all too soon for her and I'm praying this doesn't scare her away, but the truth is I need to get her out of town.

I'm unsure if the man in front of our homes the other night was for me or for her. I have Johnny and Cam staying at my house this weekend staking out the surroundings in case he comes back. I want to tell her about the man to see if she's seen anything or at least to warn her, but if I do this, will she up and leave in the middle of the night like she's always had to do in her past? I need to tread carefully so this doesn't happen.

She ponders my offer for a moment. "Where to?" she asks.

I smile. That isn't a no. "There's a cool little secluded campground out near Dansville. It's about an hour away from here. I rented out a friend's cabin already and there's a nice river to do a little fishing. I always felt free and so happy there growing up. My mom seemed at peace there and I liked seeing her that way. It was our little sanctuary. I thought I could teach Drake how to fish, and we could hang around a campfire at night making some s'mores. No pressure though," I assure her.

I take a sip of my wine as she plays with the stem of her glass. I can tell she's really thinking about her decision. I'm sure she's never gone away with someone before, and it may be difficult trying to weigh the pros and cons. So, I sit quietly while she deciphers them in her head.

She finally looks up at me with a shy meek grin. "Okay. We will go."

I can't help it. I immediately lean down to kiss her. My whole body was rigid like ice waiting for her answer and now the tension has melted off. I don't think I realized how much I was depending on her response. I never cared about little things before. I never held my breath or became disappointed when Missy declined my invitations. So, why now? How has Skylar changed me so much in such little time without even trying? This is all so foreign to me and the craziest thing is that I *like* it. I like these feelings that she's bringing out of me.

When I release her face, I stay close to her; nose to nose while staring into her beautiful brown eyes. "I don't think you realize just how happy you made me," I tell her honestly.

She giggles. "Well, I'm glad, because Drake and I really like being around you. To be honest, you scare me a bit. I'm not used to any of this. I'm not used to putting my life into someone else's hands, so to speak. Clearly, trust just doesn't come easily for me."

"Well, you are right. Camping can be *extremely* dangerous. But I can most definitely protect you from those bears with my gun," I tease her. "Skylar, you never have to worry when you're with me. I just want you to know that." I feel as though I need to keep saying this so there's no doubt left in her mind.

She looks as though she's recalling something. "There hasn't been a day that has gone by that I have not worried. It's a little hard to stop now. It has become almost as simple as breathing to me. My anxiety has been with me since I was a small child; worried about the next family I would have to endure to what would lurk in the shadows at night and now Drake. I never slept soundly or peacefully, and I've never really felt at home until now. But here I am, now scared of having to lose this feeling yet again because of my stupidity in choices I made years ago."

I take a deep breath and ponder her words for a moment before I speak again. They're deep and full of sadness. Filled with darkness that I hope one day to lighten. I want to be the cause of her smile every day, and to see the twinkle of life in her eyes emerge, but most of all I want to be her and Drake's security and stability in life. Someone she can depend on and hold on to when she has all these emotions. I just want to love them both and show them a life they both deserve. A life filled with comfort, unconditional love, and safety. And maybe, just maybe, a life filled with more children – a family.

Wow. These thoughts are so not me. Where the hell did this all come from? Who is this person I am becoming? I have never wanted any of this, and yet, here I am having thoughts of a family and a life beyond what I am. I've never wanted a family before because of my job. My job was my life. My job has been who I am for so long that anything else didn't seem possible for me – especially after my partner was murdered and his family was left behind.

These emotions have finally dawned on me. I've only technically known her for less than a week, but she's been etched in my soul from the moment I laid eyes on her. I have thought of her every day since then. She has consumed my dreams. Now here she is finally sitting in front of me as though my dreams have finally come true. I am in love with this woman, and I felt this the second our eyes connected years ago but never knew exactly what that feeling meant—*until now.* I have loved her all this time.

This is such a revelation but now what to do with it?

There's no way I can reveal this to her without causing her to push away from me.

I allow her words to sink in before I respond. "Skylar don't blame yourself for the choices you made years ago. You were merely surviving. I'm not going to lie, what lies ahead next isn't going to be easy, but I promise you, we're going to figure it out together. I'm going to help you get through this. You *will* survive this, and Drake will be safe. I won't let anyone hurt either of you," I tell her, trying to console her the best I can.

She looks at me with a meek smile and reaches her hand to my cheek slowly grazing her fingers down the side of my face. My skin scorches from the rake of her touch. My breathing hitches and begins to accelerate as I gaze into her dark beautiful eyes. "Neal—" she says softly.

I can't take my eyes off her. There's an intense shift in the air around us. "Skylar –" is all that seems to come out in a horse whisper.

She leans toward me and kisses me tenderly on my cheek over my already flaming skin. The fresh smell of lavender caresses my nose as she leans down to rest her head against my chest. I wrap my arm around her and hold her tight. Never wanting to let go. We sit in the serene silence for what seems like forever. Nothing spoken. Just us being and learning to be in each other's space.

Somehow this feels more intimate than any moment I have encountered thus far. Everything feels perfect. Just how it's supposed to be. But this doesn't stop my mind from drifting to what lies ahead. I have some work to do. I need to figure out how to take care of these Castro brothers once and for all.

SKYLAR STIRS RIPPING me into a groggy daze. We must have fallen asleep. "Shit. Neal, it's 3am. I'm so sorry. I didn't mean to fall asleep," Skylar says embarrassed.

I chuckle as I rub my eyes. "Well, I'm not sorry," I admit as I stand up and follow her to the door. If I didn't have Benny next door I may have just slept on her couch for the night. But he's probably wondering where I am and needs to be let out, poor guy.

I give her a kiss on her forehead telling her goodnight. I wait outside to listen to the locks clicking in place before I head over to my house. The air is crisp with a promise of winter coming soon. I can see the fog of my breath as I exhale.

I look around. Surveying my surroundings; checking to see if I see anything off or out of place, but nothing. It's kind of an unnerving stillness as though something is on the verge of changing. I can taste the assault of danger with every breath I take. A chill rides through my shoulders and down my spine as I take one last look around before I head inside.

I WAKE to the sound of a car engine pulling out of a garage, and realize I've slept in. Benny hasn't bothered me this morning since I let him out in the early hours when I came home from Skylar's, but as soon as he hears me stir, he's hovering over me with his tongue across my face.

"Alright, alright! I'm getting up," I tell him, pushing his

snout away from me trying to gain reprieve from his slobbers. I stretch, then drag myself to my feet. "Come on, boy. Time to go outside."

I take a quick peek out the front window after coming downstairs, everything seems calm, nothing out of the ordinary. I think back to my night with Skylar and smile. It feels amazing that she's finally opening up to me and trusting me enough to let her guard down some. I feel pride knowing that she's giving me the opportunity to get to know her and said yes to her and Drake coming away with me this weekend. I honestly wasn't so sure she was going to agree.

I grab my phone and shoot Johnny a quick text letting him know that the stakeout at my house is a go. He's coming today to set up more cameras and get everything else set up for the weekend. I'll be trading cars with one of the guys so my car will be here to look as if I'm home. I need to be sure they are coming for me and not for Skylar and Drake, then I'll know how to proceed accordingly.

After I let Benny out of the backyard, he goes right for his leash with his most pathetic whine and puppy dog eyes. How can I say no to this?

I chuckle. "You telling me it's time for a run?" I bend down asking him while giving him a scratch behind his ears. I down some OJ, grab my sneakers, and attach his leash to head out for our run.

The crispy morning air feels awakening, opening my senses as I breathe in the freshness. There's nothing like an early morning run to clear the mind and awaken the soul and with Benny by my side I can let loose a bit because I know he has my back.

Tomorrow night is the night of the drop from the tip

we got. My guys have been staking out the place, movement and security is on the rise, so I'm pretty sure this lead is right on point. We've been preparing for a big bust like this. It's time to get them where it hurts, with money and product, because this will cause an uproar and people tend to make mistakes when they're upset and looking for revenge. And that's the exact moment when we step in.

Johnny's waiting in his car in my driveway as Benny and I head back to the house. I knock on his window as I head toward the front doorstep. Benny waits for him to get out.

Johnny shuts his car door then kneels. "Hey, Benny. How's my handsome wingman doing?" he jokes while giving him scratches. Benny is in his glory, tongue out.

"Hey Neal, when you gonna let me take him for a ride with me so I can pick up some chicks?"

I shake my head unlocking the door with them right behind me.

"Dude, you'll be out of luck. They'll want to take him home, not you," I tell him laughing.

Johnny dumps his large black duffle bag on the table. "Yeah, but we'll be a package deal. Then they won't be able to say no," he says with a huge white toothed grin.

"What happened with Janice? I thought you were into her?" I ask, grabbing Benny's dog bowl and filling it.

"Nah, she was just something to fill the time. I don't know man; these chicks just can't keep my interest. Once we do the deed, it's like my brain shuts down and I'm done. I think I just need to stick with one night hook ups," he admits.

I grab the eggs and bacon from the fridge, the pans

from under the cupboard, and start whipping up some breakfast for us.

"Honestly, I just don't think you've met the right woman yet. When you do, you will know, and things will just feel different," I explain while thinking of Skylar. Shit, I knew without even understanding what I knew. All it took with her was one gaze into her eyes and I was haunted for years.

"You talk as though you know this from experience," Johnny hints as he begins taking the equipment from his duffle bag.

I shrug, not really wanting to reveal too much. If he knows that I'm involved with Antonio Castro's ex, then things might get too sticky. He won't approve of the connection or me getting close to someone so connected to this case. It's enough that he knows she's my neighbor, but being involved with her is crossing major boundaries, and I just don't care.

"I saw the love Simon had for his wife. He would talk about when they met, and how he just knew she was it for him. He said she consumed his thoughts until he finally had the courage to make a move, and after that it was history," I tell him.

Just bringing up my old partner's name crushes me. It's something I hate to do. It brings all the guilt and sadness rushing back to me like a tsunami almost knocking me off my feet. I grab a hold of the frying pan and squeeze, nails digging into my palm almost drawing blood, to let out my emotions through pain because I can't allow myself to break down. It took me way too much work to get to this point of being okay.

There's still not a day that goes by that I don't think of

him and his family wishing it was me they took out and not him. This kind of guilt can eat a man alive, it almost did. It consumed me for months until I finally forgave myself, because deep down inside I knew we both took the risks, it was the cost of our job, and we both accepted the possibility – *he* accepted that possibility knowing he had a family.

And now here I am, in love with Skylar knowing she has a son, and thinking of the possibility of a future with her knowing mine could follow Simons, so is this fair? Is this fair of me to want her to be a part of my life knowing that danger may always follow?

"Damn man, I miss that guy. I guess you're right, because the way he talked about his wife made us all want to settle down and find a good ass woman," Johnny admits.

I cover a plate with napkins for the bacon and pour the beaten eggs in the pan listening to it sizzle. I pour two cups of steaming hot coffee while waiting for everything to be done.

Johnny takes a sip before talking. "Thanks, man. I ran out of the chick's house this morning before she woke up and didn't have time to grab some coffee."

I shake my head. It's been a while since I've had a one-night stand. The thought no longer appeals to me. "Were you out with Cam last night?" I ask, scooping the scrambled eggs on our plates.

"Yeah, we went over to the pub last night after work. We needed to blow off some steam before tomorrow night. Cam was trying to convince her and her friend to come home with us both, but they weren't having it, so we went our separate ways. It was fun while it lasted, but when I woke up with her next to me, I couldn't get out of there fast enough," he divulges.

I'm not going to lie, thinking about tomorrow night gives me a bit of anxiety. This is always the calm before the storm. The anxiety kicks in before the pump of excitement runs through my veins. The adrenaline always kicks in, sizzling and coursing through me, right as the team is putting on our gear getting ready for action. There's nothing like it. It's what I've always lived for – *until now.*

Now, all I can think of is Skylar and Drake. The vision of them pops up front and center. This never happened with Missy. I always knew there was a possibility of not making it home, but now this possibility scares the shit out of me. Leaving them to fend on their own with men coming after them has me wanting to drop to my knees.

I place our plates on the counter. "Hey man, you okay?" Johnny stops what he's doing to ask.

"Yeah, man. I'm good. I'm just thinking about this raid. I can't help but wonder if we got something wrong?" I admit, normally always feeling great with our intel, never doubting our leads at this point.

Johnny comes to join me at the counter. "Listen Neal, we staked out the place, our guys are on point. If there was something off, they would have found it. You know this."

He's right, but something in my gut tells me otherwise. The informant was pretty adamant about the shipment being in connection with Ray, but Ray didn't make it this far by being sloppy. What if this is a setup? What if he's on to us and wants information on our team? Or what if the drop was leaked here to keep us away from the real drop? I rack my brain to go over the informant's background and criminal history. It feels as though I've missed something.

"Johnny, I think once we're done here, we need to get back to the office and go over everything again with a fine-tooth comb. I can't help but feel like we're missing something, and I need to be sure before tomorrow," I tell him.

He shovels some eggs into his mouth before agreeing. "Okay, so tell me where you want these cameras set up then we'll head back to the office."

WE GET EVERYTHING HOOKED UP. Johnny set up more hidden cameras surrounding the outside of my house giving me a view of Skylar's as well. I feel a little guilty not telling her I'm watching her house; she might think it's an invasion of privacy, but I need to make sure whoever is out there isn't there for her. This is the only way I can figure it out.

I called in the team so we could go over all the intel detail by detail. I had the informant's file pulled, and I found some discrepancies. He told me that he got involved with Ray's crew down in Miami when he was younger, but his file shows he grew up in his family's home with many foster children throughout the years. This last known home was here in New York. There's no background to him ever living in Miami, but when I questioned him on this, he said he left home as soon as he turned eighteen and moved around a lot after.

I head into my office and shut the door. I sit down at my desk opening the file backup that Johnny provided me the other day. I must have missed something. It runs through the night of Antionio's arrest, and the details of the domestic dispute with Skylar AKA Jennifer Bishop. I hate remembering that night and how wounded and broken she looked.

The next paperwork is Jennifer's background. It goes through all the foster homes she went through and my heart aches reading how many she was transferred through. You would never know the instability she went through as a kid by just meeting her. I know she holds secrets and scars from these places, but she carries them with such strength and courage that it makes me proud. I know she does this for Drake. He's her reason for not drowning in her past and it makes me smile. I can't help but admire her strength.

I get to her last foster home, and the address looks familiar. Where the hell did I just see this? Then it dawns on me. *Fuck!* I run out toward our locked room where all our information on the case is held and pull up my informant's file – it's the same address.

I remember Skylar telling me about the last house she was at when she met Antonio and how the older brother slept by her bedside to protect her, but she never mentioned his name. If it's James Connor, then we have a serious problem.

I look at the clock, it's noon and she's probably still at work. I can't wait. I need to go find out if this is the same man from her past. I run back into my office, grab my keys, and head out to the elementary school she works at.

Twenty minutes later I pull up to the school parking lot. Fuck, I wish I would have gotten her cell phone number. Why didn't I ask her for it? This would have made things so much easier if I could have just called her.

I walk up the sidewalk and hit the little red button at the door. A woman answers. "Good afternoon, how can I help you?"

"Hi ma'am, I'm looking to speak with Skylar," I reply.

"Sir, may I ask who's looking to see her?"

I look up at the camera. I know she's watching. This makes me happy knowing they are protected.

"Can you let her know that her neighbor Neal is here to speak with her?" I ask.

A moment later I am buzzed in. I go to the left where I see an older woman sitting behind the desk and far in the distance Skylar stands up walking over to me. I smile at the older woman.

"Oh, aren't you handsome." She smiles giving me a wink. "I'm Jess. It's nice to meet you, Neal."

I nod to her with a curt smile. "Nice to meet you too."

"Neal, is everything okay?" Skylar questions nervously. I can see the wheels turning in her head probably considering the worst.

I feel a little guilty worrying her. "Yeah, everything's okay. I just needed to talk to you a moment about something," I advise evasively because Jess is listening. "Is there somewhere we can go to talk privately?" I ask, looking around as some of her co-workers pass by the halls.

"Sure," she replies as she walks out the side door to meet me.

She looks unsure, and unsettled, but grabs my arm to lead me to a room off to the side. This looks like it may be a teacher conference room where meetings are held; a large oval table engulfs the room with chairs surrounding, and one small window facing out to the parking lot.

She leaves the door cracked. Before I can begin a man pops his head in looking between us both. "Everything okay in here?" he questions, looking oddly concerned.

I can see him eying me up and down. It's clear he may have a thing for Skylar that goes beyond a co-worker's concern. I squint my eyes giving him a warning look to back off as I fold my arms over my chest in a protective stance.

Skylar immediately jumps in. "Yes, Richie. This is my neighbor Neal. Everything's fine, I'll be out in a moment," she responds, waiting for him to get the hint and leave.

He nods disapprovingly and leaves. I blew out a breath, not even realizing I was holding one. The green-eyed monster has risen which is not my style at all normally.

"What did you need to talk about, Neal? Is this about Drake's father?" she asks with a crease now formed in between her brows.

"I'm not really sure what this is completely about to be honest. I'm trying to put some pieces together to understand some things I've come across," I tell her honestly. She waits to allow me to finish speaking. "The boy at the last home you were at before you left with Antonio, the one who slept beside your bed to protect you, what was his name?"

She looks completely baffled and thrown off guard now. "Why? Why do you ask?" she questions, brows furrowed.

"I know this sounds like a strange question, but something has come up in my investigation. I can't go into detail, but this person connects to you. Their last known home address is the same address of your last foster home," I try to explain as best as I'm able to.

She backs up a moment. "Wait, how do you know where my last home was? Have you been checking into my past, Neal?"

Fuck, it didn't even cross my mind of having to explain myself on invading her privacy, but she had to have known this would have happened with her relation to the Castro brothers. Though I haven't exactly told her that Ray Castro is on my team's target either. She needs to know I'm only trying to protect her.

"Skylar, you know what I do for a living, and there are things I can't openly say even though I wish I could, but when you told me about Drake's father and knowing who his family is, I had to do my research. I want to help protect you and Drake. So, in order for me to do that, I needed to know everything I can about yours and his past."

I see the wheels turning in her head while taking in my explanation. She finally takes a small breath, exhales, and nods. "His name is James Connor."

Shit. Shit. *Shit!* I can't help but internally swear to myself. I nod curtly and give her upper arm a squeeze before heading past her toward the door. "Thanks, I gotta go!" I call out behind me. I grab my cell out of my back pocket as I'm walking out the door and click on Johnny's number.

"Neal! I don't understand –" she shouts after me, her voice fading in the distance as I run past the red security doors and toward my car.

"Hey man, what's up?" Johnny answers.

"Get the team together. I have some new information. I'll be there in twenty," I tell him and hang up.

I rush to the precinct making it in record time. I climb up the stairs and head straight down the hall to our locked conference room. The guys are waiting and talking amongst themselves. I figure it's about time to come clean with everything – including my new neighbor. I thought I would be able to leave her out of this but that's no longer the case, things are becoming too entwined and too messy, and I can't risk missing something or leaving my team in the dark by holding information that can keep us all safe – including Skylar and Drake.

"Damn, Neal. So, why do you think your informant lied?" Cam asks, standing like a bull with his arms crossed with concern.

I shake my head. "That I'm unsure of but we need to find him before tomorrow night and find out. This connection between him and Skylar just seems odd. He cared for her as a kid. So, why get involved with Antonio's family if he's not up to something?"

Jacob stands up. "I'm on it. I'm going to get a trace on his phone to figure out his last whereabouts," he notifies us as he opens his laptop.

"Good. Cam, Johnny, you two start at North Street area, and I will head to his parents' house," I direct. Everyone nods heading out, and Jacob advises as soon as he gets a ding at his last known location he will call.

CHAPTER 9

SKYLAR

"Is everything okay?" Jess asks as I walk back toward my desk seeming worried.

I feel so unsure and confused right now. I'm not even sure what to think. What the hell was that? Why is he asking about James? And why didn't he tell me he's been looking into my past? I know about Ray and Antonio's connection because he's the one that told me, but does that mean he's also connected to this as well? When he says protect me, does this mean he's working the case to try to take Ray and his empire down? If that's the case, then I feel sick to my stomach.

What if there is retaliation? Antonio is a monster, but what I've read about his brother, he's the devil. How can Neal really protect us from evil like that? I'm caught up in this mess of my own doing from my young desperate choices, but this could just be insanity pushing myself further into the chaos.

I feel a soft hand on my shoulder bringing me back from my thoughts. I look up at Jess. "Hey, you look white as a ghost, Skylar. Is everything okay? Do you need to talk?" she asks concerned.

I clear my throat. "No, no. I'm okay. Really," I tell her. She looks as though she doesn't believe a word I'm saying right now. "Neal's the cop I was telling you about. He just had some questions about Drake's father. That's all," I lie only telling her half the truth hoping she will back off with the questions.

"Oh my! I know you've mentioned Drake's father not being in the picture. I'm glad to hear you have someone near you that can look out for you both. Just know I'm here to talk if you need; no judgments," she offers kindly.

"Thanks, Jess. I really appreciate it," I tell her gratefully. She really is so kind, not one malicious bone in her body. She's just a real genuine person and I haven't come across a lot of these types of people in my life.

I work through the morning like a zombie; my mind is just not here but instead replaying the conversation with Neal on repeat in my head dissecting every single word said. Then my mind drifts back to *that* house.

My heartbeat bangs through my rib cage as the door handle begins to turn. My palms are sweaty, my ears begin to ring, and my body begins to shake uncontrollably. I pull my covers higher over me trying to shield my body from what's to come. I knew it was only a matter of time before I felt his hands on me again and smelled his stale whiskey breath against my skin making me want to vomit.

I take a couple of deep breaths readying myself for a fight. I won't let him near me without fighting for my life. I refuse to allow him to touch me again. Last time I fought him off with my hard cover schoolbook I had been reading before bed. I whacked my foster father upside the head with the book as he tried to climb on top of me winning myself a hard backhand in return from him right before James came running into the room standing in between us.

If it wasn't for him, I don't know what would have happened to me that night. He was my knight in shining armor at only the age of seventeen. He stood up to his father for me with no questions asked or no favors in return.

I watch the light begin to spill through my dark room as the door slowly opens. I'm terrified, but I have to calm myself down so I can think clearly. The floor creaks as he takes a step forward and just as the door opens wider, I hear my name.

"Jenn?" he whispers before taking another step forward.

My body deflates immediately. I shake my head and take a deep breath trying to calm myself. Tonight, I'm going to be okay.

"Can I come in?" James asks now, standing in full view in front of the doorway.

I nod not knowing if he can see me. "Yes, come in."

He has a pillow and blanket under his arms. "My dad just got home from the bar, and he's been drinking. Is it okay if I sleep on your floor?" he questions.

I exhale. "Yes, please."

AFTER THAT NIGHT there was an unspoken word between us. He slept on my floor for months. He never mentioned anything further regarding his dad, and his dad stayed away from my room since then. James and I would talk the night away as we lay there waiting for sleep to take over. He was my best friend, my first friend, and I still feel guilty for leaving him so abruptly without a word.

I always wanted to find him and thank him, but with Antonio turning my life upside down, there was no way I wanted James to get involved in it. He was better off with me staying away from him. Destruction seems to follow me wherever I go swallowing up the innocent.

But now Neal came here saying there was a connection in an investigation to us? What in the hell could be going on? This whole thing has thrown me into a whirlwind.

"Earth to Skylar –" Hands wave in front of my face.

I shake my thoughts barely hearing what Emily is saying. I clear my throat. "Hey, I'm sorry. I must have just zoned out," I tell her, seeing her brows furrow with concern.

"You were in some serious deep thoughts there. I called your name a couple of times," she informs me with a light chuckle. "Everything okay?"

I smile faintly. "Yeah, I've just had a really weird day. I think exhaustion has kicked in. Maybe I stayed up too late last night with Neal."

She squeals. "Oh my! Okay, I came to see if you wanted to grab lunch tomorrow and now, I'm not taking no for an answer!" she insists.

I laugh. Her demanding bossy personality is beginning to match that fiery red hair of hers. I give in, "Yes, lunch sounds good."

She claps her hands. "I can't wait. If only we could have wine on break –" she says jokingly. "Maybe next time we should make it a dinner date instead."

"I wish I could, but I have no one to watch Drake for me."

She looks understanding. "I know, but who knows, maybe that will change for you one day with this hunky neighbor of yours around," she hints with a shoulder shrug. "Okay, gotta run! Kids are coming back from recess!" she yells from behind her as she scurries down the hallway.

THE REST of the day flies by quickly considering my thoughts have been pulling me elsewhere. I pick up Drake from his room, and we head off to the grocery store for some dinner supplies.

"I was thinking of making some stuffed shells, what do you think?" I ask Drake as he's busy looking out the window with his stuffed turtle tight in his arms.

He lifts his pointer finger tapping his bottom lip. "Mmmm, what about Dino nuggets and mac & cheese?" he replies with his most adorable squeaky voice.

I roll my eyes. I should have known. If I keep letting him choose these non-nutritional dinners, then I'm going to eventually have to be rolled out of my house.

"How about we leave that dinner as a weekend treat?" I counteroffer while watching him through the rearview mirror.

He takes a moment to think. "Can we make some brownies too?"

I chuckle. "We can make some brownies and get some vanilla ice cream too."

His eyes light up with glee. "Okay! Then I can wait until this weekend. But Mom?"

I park the car in the grocery store parking lot. "Yes?"

"Can Neal and Benny come for dinner this weekend too?" he asks.

I forgot I didn't tell him about our getaway weekend with them. "Actually, we're going to go on a little cool trip this weekend with them. Neal has a cabin and wants to teach you how to fish," I explain to him.

"Really?" he asks with excitement.

"Yep, just the four of us."

He bounces up and down in his car seat. "Can we buy a bone for Benny?"

I laugh as we both unbuckle ourselves and hop out of the car. I grab his hand in mine. "We can and I'll even let you pick it out."

"Mom?"

I look down toward Drake. He's looking at me like he has something important to ask. "Yes, baby?" I reply, giving his hand a little squeeze.

"Can Neal be my papa? I really like him."

Oh no. My heart just melted and broke in a million different ways. He doesn't mention his father very much anymore. I had to tell him he was far away and couldn't see him. How the hell do I explain to this precious innocent boy that his father is a monster? I can't. So, how the hell do I answer this question that I wasn't prepared to even answer – *ever*.

We make it out of the parking lot and into the entrance of the store. I squat down to Drake's level. "Hey buddy, even though Neal would be lucky to have you call him Papa, Neal is just a friend, and I know for a fact he likes us too," I explain to him, then pinch his little nose.

He giggles. "Okay, Mom. Neal and Benny are my *best* friends then!" he squeals.

"Yes, they can be our best friends. Now let's go get stuff for dinner," I tell him, standing up, grabbing his hand again to pull him along.

We head down the pasta aisle; I'm still holding onto Drake's hand while pushing the small cart. I notice a man with jet black hair and a black leather jacket in my peripheral view. This is the second aisle I've seen him in which doesn't say much since I've only been in two.

I grab the shells, a jar of sauce, and we head off to grab some ricotta and mozzarella cheese.

"Mom, can we get some ogarts?" Drake asks.

"It's *yogurt*, Drake. And yes, pick out what you want."

I look to my right and see the man in black standing a couple of feet away from us pretending to busy himself with the cheese blocks. The hairs on the back of my neck begin to stand up. I hold Drake's hand a little tighter now. This isn't just a coincidence; he's been following us throughout the store. I know how this works, I've been in this predicament multiple times now.

I take a deep breath, walk by him and grab the cheese I need. I turn toward him to get a better look at his face, and our eyes connect. He has a scar running down the left side of his cheek, dark brown soulless eyes with tired under bags, and a five o'clock shadow as though he hasn't slept or shaved in days.

He disconnects from me looking down toward Drake momentarily trying his hardest not to look obvious and continues with his nonchalant shopping. Little does he know; I'm seasoned with this behavior, and my sixth sense has kicked in overdrive.

I walk fast along the aisle until we reach the checkout lines. I see a manager at the front, but before I get his attention I look back and can see the man heading in our direction. My heartbeat pounds against my chest as the adrenaline swarms my body.

Drake notices the tension I'm radiating. "What's wrong, Mom?" he questions with concern.

My sweet little boy is always so in tune with me. He just melts my heart. I squeeze his hand. "Nothing for you to worrying about, baby. I'm just going to ask this nice manager over there if he can help us carry these groceries out to the car with us."

I wave down the manager getting his attention. I let out a breath of air as he begins to walk toward us. "Is there something you need, Miss?" he asks.

I look behind me, the man in black is almost on my tail. The manager follows my gaze looking toward him as well. His curiosity now turns to concern. "Do you need assistance?" he questions, looking back and forth between us.

I nod. "Yes, please. I was hoping you could help us with getting these groceries to our car?"

He nods understanding my request. "Of course, I'm just going to walk to the counter to make a quick phone call, and I will be right back," he says loudly, making sure the man in black hears him.

I mouth thank you to him before he walks away. I see out of the corner of my peripheral view the man walk past our lane and out the door. I take a couple of deep breaths trying to relax myself for Drake's sake.

The manager is waiting for us at the checkout; he helps put the bags in the cart. "Thank you so much. We really appreciate your help."

He has a sweet genuine smile. "Please, it's my pleasure.

I called the men in uniform," he hints after looking down toward Drake quickly not wanting to scare him. "They should be waiting outside to help escort you to where you need to go," he explains.

"Look, Mom!" Drake points to the car with lights on top excitedly. "It's a police car!"

I give him a small smile watching him wave to the police car. They flash their lights, and Drake jumps up and down. I'm happy that the past isn't haunting him like it does me. I'm proud of myself for sticking to my word of not letting my nightmare affect him by giving him flashbacks of that horrid night when they dragged his father off to jail like it does for me.

"Yes baby, it a policeman just like Neal," I tell him.

He snaps his head at me with wide eyes. "Neal and Benny are policemen too?"

I laugh as I buckle him in his seat and place the grocery bags on the floor in front of him. "Well, yes. Neal is a policeman, and Benny is his police dog. They both have a job in protecting people," I explain to him as I jump into the driver's seat and shut the car door.

I pull out of the parking lot and see the police car following behind me as we head home. I just pray that this man isn't on Ray's payroll. I need to remember to go back and thank that manager for what he just did for us. But now the question is – does the man know where we live? Will he be waiting in the shadows for us tonight forcing us to leave? How did he know to follow us at the store?

"Will they protect us from the bad men, Mom?"

My chest constricts immediately with that question as my eyes tear up. "Of course they will, baby."

He seems satisfied with that answer as he holds on to

his stuffed turtle looking out the window. I click the garage door opener, pull the car in, and as the door begins to shut, I see the officer pull away in the rearview mirror.

I let out a deep breath feeling a small bit of relief, but still not completely settled. I didn't notice any movement at Neal's when we pulled up. It's at this moment I wish Benny and him were outside being a nuisance so I could tell him what just happened. He's declared multiple times that he wants to protect Drake and I, so I need to really start letting him in. I need him to know so he can tell me everything will be okay. I need to feel his arms wrapped around me so I can feel safe again.

"Come on bud, help Mommy and grab a bag for me," I ask Drake trying to teach him early how to be a young gentleman.

"Okay, Mom!"

We drag the bags into the kitchen. I decide to walk around the house making sure to double-check the doors and window locks. Drake and I head upstairs, and I follow the same routine. Drake watches but doesn't question me since he's seen me do this a million times. He's become accustomed to this.

"Okay, why don't you play for a little while so I can get dinner together, or would you like to watch some cartoons?"

He starts walking past me to the stairs. "Cartoons, please."

I shake my head smiling and mess up his hair as I catch up to him. "Okay, cartoons it is."

Dinner takes about a half hour to make. I sit down next to Drake on the couch waiting for it to bake. I look at the clock and it's now past 5pm. Neal is usually home by now. I get up to look out the front window, but his car isn't in the driveway. I wish I had asked for his cell number earlier. I'm sure he's working late but I have this off feeling deep down inside scratching and gnawing at me that something isn't right. It's almost as if every time I pass a window the hair on the back of my neck stands up in warning. Last time I ignored it the men pretending to be police almost caught us.

I decide to call Emily. The phone rings a couple of times before she finally picks up.

"Hello?" she answers sounding all breathy.

I stall a moment before responding almost wondering if this is a bad idea. "Skylar is that you?" she asks.

"Hey, sorry yes, it's me. Did I call you at a bad time?"

She laughs. "No, was just finishing up my workout. You know, a girl's gotta keep in shape," she retorts. I smile. "Is everything okay? You sound a little off," she notices.

"I was actually wondering if you wanted to join Drake and I for some dinner tonight. I could use some company, and I've made more than enough," I offer, praying she will say yes.

"Of course I would! I'm starving, and I have nothing at home to cook. I was going to stop and grab something. Is there anything you need me to bring?"

I feel relieved. "I have everything here. Even a nice bottle of red," I tell her. "I'll text you the address. Drake's going to be so happy to see you!"

She laughs. "You know I love me some little Drake! I'll see you in a few."

Ten minutes later Emily pulls up. She looks adorable with her hair pulled up in a messy bun, pink cheeks, and a body to kill for in her red workout pants. I whistle as she walks up the sidewalk. "Wow, I'm surprised you don't have an entourage following you at all times," I say joking.

"Girl, I wish. The only ones that seem to follow me lately are the crazies," she replies, rolling her eyes.

Drake runs from the living room into Emily's arms. "Miss Turner! Miss Turner! Do you wanna come watch *Paw Patrol* with me?"

She gives him a big squeeze then releases him. "Actually, I'm going to have a little visit with your mom. How about after dinner if that's okay with your mom," she tells him looking to me.

I nod. "Of course, we'll have our brownies and ice cream on the couch after dinner for a treat before bed."

"*Yes!*" he says excitedly with a fist pump and runs back to the living room.

She follows me into the kitchen. "You look stressed. What's going on? Is it that neighbor of yours?" she asks, twitching her brow up.

She takes a seat at the kitchen table while I pour some wine for us. I take the stuffed shells out of the oven to let them sit for a moment.

I take a deep breath and begin to open up about my past with Drake's father up until the present. Her mouth hangs open in disbelief or maybe it's shock, regardless, she is speechless. Then I go into detail about what happened at the grocery store earlier.

"Skylar, this doesn't sound good. I think you really need to tell Neal about this ASAP," she suggests.

"I know, I'm planning on it once he gets home. I just

couldn't be alone, and I didn't know who else to call. I don't have any friends around here and because of the situation with Drake's father, I haven't been able to make any friends in the past," I reveal to her.

It feels good to finally confide in someone on a friendship level. I feel as though I can trust Emily, and she won't judge me. It's a weird sensation to feel after all these years. Between Neal and now her, I feel as though they are breaking down my barriers bit by bit. Or maybe I've just had enough of being closed off for so many years and finally need another adult human being in my life.

My life has been such a lonely road, and even though I've craved friendship along the way, it was pointless, but I feel as though something has changed. Maybe it's the safety I feel with Neal, even though a part of me is still not fully convinced he's ready to take this all on, but there's still comfort in knowing he wants to try.

She grabs my hand. "Well, I'm glad you called me, and you can call me any time. I don't care what time of day or night it is, if you need me, I'll be here even if you just need a listening ear or a friend," she offers so genuinely.

I'm not used to this sort of kindness and I'm almost unsure of how to respond. "Thanks, Emily. I really appreciate you, and I absolutely love how Drake adores you. He needs good people around him. People that can show him the world can be a good safe place. I feel as though I'm failing him at times. The guilt can be so overwhelming and debilitating some days, but I have no choice but to keep going for him."

"And you're doing a damn good job at it all, Skylar. You are one strong woman, and you should feel proud of yourself because even though you both have been through hell, Drake is doing great. He is one amazing boy, and *you* did that. No one else. You have been the one to protect him and he's lucky to have you as a mom," she states so profoundly.

A tear slides down my cheek, but before I can respond Drake runs into the kitchen.

"I'm starving, *Mom*. My tummy is growling. Is dinner ready yet?" he asks, holding his belly dramatically. Emily and I both laugh.

"Yes, my love. I was just waiting for it to cool down while Mrs. Turner and I talked," I explain to him.

I bring the shells over to the table along with the salad and garlic bread I made. We spend the next hour laughing and listening to Drake tell recess stories. I never knew recess could be so dramatic, but I guess when it comes to slides, swings, and taking turns there's a lot to maneuver.

After dinner we sit down in the living room while Drake eats his dessert watching cartoons and Emily and I quietly talk.

"So, tell me, what's the dating life like?" I asked her intrigued.

I've never had the chance to experience that part of life. I've heard stories, but going on an official date was something I thought I may only get to experience while watching it through a movie. Ever since I've met Neal, my curiosity has been piqued.

She sighs heavily. "It's honestly horrible. Every guy I come across seems to only want one thing from me and the ones that I think may be okay turn out to be creeps a couple of dates in. *And* let's not talk about the dating apps! Every man thinks the new language of hello is sending a dick pic. The whole thing is exhausting and I'm just ready to throw in the towel and be single with my vibrator forever," she divulges with a light chuckle.

I shake my head laughing along with her. I've never experienced this type of girl talk, and I think I'm going to grow addicted to it now. "Wow, I guess I was expecting to hear about car doors being opened, red roses, and romantic dinners. Clearly, I have been watching too many movies," I joke. "But seriously, I can't imagine going through all those toads just to find your prince, but I think it will happen when you least expect it. You deserve someone good by your side."

Before she can say another word, there's a light knock on the door. The look on my face must show my horror as I sink into myself then immediately look toward Drake.

"Skylar, you good? Do you want me to see who it is?" she asks.

I stand up heading toward the door slowly. Every hair on my body is standing up now after that run-in with that man at the grocery store. I'm just not sure who could be on the other side of the door. What if it's the man from earlier? Or what if those cops found us again? Who knows who it could be this time around. Between Antonio and Ray, they have every resource at their fingertips. I'm merely just a pawn on their chess board.

"Can you just stay with Drake?"

She nods.

My heart is palpitating a mile a minute. The palms of my hands are slick with sweat as I try to anticipate who might be behind the door. I stand in front of the entry, take a deep breath, and slowly peek out the side window. Relief immediately invades my body as I stare at Neal standing on my steps.

I unlock the door, swinging it open. He instantly steps toward me worried. "Skylar? Is everything okay? You don't look so good. You look like you have seen a ghost," he states while looking over my shoulder.

I nod not being able to form a sentence. Without warning, he wraps his arms around me in a safe embrace. My body immediately melts into him feeling cocooned in a safety blanket. I don't think I've ever been hugged like this. This hug feels like a home I've never had. Tears begin to run down my face as the weight of sorrow, loneliness, and the exhaustion of survival is being lifted momentarily.

I'm tired. I'm tired of doing this all alone. I'm tired of having to be strong every waking moment of my life. I'm tired of waiting for the world to cave in on me at any moment. I just want to live free from worry, be free from the constant looking behind me, but most of all I just want plain freedom.

Neal backs his head up so he's able to look at my face. "What happened, Skylar? Let me in so I can help you," he asks gently.

I slowly reprieve myself from his hold to stand on my own. I wrap my arms around my waist as a coping mechanism. "I think they have already found me again."

"Shit!" is the only thing he says before he starts pacing. "Did you see someone here?"

I shake my head. "No, Drake and I were followed at the store. There was a man following us and I had the store manager call the police. They followed me home and I'm not sure what happened to him after that," I explain.

The floor creaks behind us, startling us both.

"I'm so sorry. I didn't mean to interrupt," Emily says, walking toward Neal. "It's nice to meet you. I'm Emily, I work with Skylar."

Neal reciprocates her handshake. "It's great to meet you, Emily. I'm sorry, I didn't mean to interrupt," he says then turns to me. "I can come back later –"

Emily steps in. "No, please, stay. Skylar needs you. I need to get home, take a shower, and feed my cat. It was really nice to meet you, Neal," she tells him then turns to me giving me a hug goodbye before she leaves.

"Thanks for coming and being here for me. It really means a lot," I tell her.

She smiles. "Anytime, girl," she says before walking out the door.

CHAPTER 10

NEAL

Before Skylar and I can say another word, Drake comes barreling around the corner. "Neal! Did you bring Benny?" he asks excitedly.

I kneel to his level. "So, I was thinking maybe Benny and I will stay for a sleepover tonight if your mom says it's okay," I suggest, looking back toward her hoping she won't be too upset for not bringing this up to her first. I just didn't want to give her a chance to say no. I would rather take a little heat, than have something happen to them.

Drake jumps up and down. "Please, Mom? *Pleaseeeee –*" he begs, dragging it out with a little pout.

Skylar looks as though she wants to strangle me, then rolls her eyes sighing. "Sure. *But* Neal must sleep on the couch and Benny has to sleep on the floor," she agrees. "Now go upstairs and get ready for bed so I can talk to Neal for a moment."

"Yay!" Drake screeches while heading toward the stairs. "Okay!"

I laugh and stand so I can now face Sklyar knowing I'm in trouble. I wait for the wrath I know I'm about to receive. I may not know Skylar that well yet, but I know women, and I know what that face means.

"Neal, you can't just put me on the spot like that. That wasn't fair to use Benny against me. If you want to be in our lives like you say you do, then I need you to respect me and not step on my toes. I already feel guilty enough for having to say no to him for almost everything and always having to uproot him just when he's feeling at home. So, please don't make this any harder on me," she asks sternly.

Now the guilt kicks in. I didn't see it that way and she's right, I overstepped. I step closer to her, gently rubbing my hand down her arm. "You're right, Skylar. I wasn't thinking. I got too ahead of myself, and I should have asked you first. I was only thinking about wanting to be here to keep you guys safe and I didn't want to give you the chance to say no. I told you I want to protect you both, and being over at my house after what just happened at the store freaks me out," I explain.

"I think Benny and I are your best bet for security in case they come here to look for you both. I'm going to put a call in to see if the cop that followed you home saw anything; maybe the kind of car he was driving or if he was alone or not. That might give us a bit of an edge and tomorrow once you get out of work, I'm going to take you to my friend's used car place and we're going to get you a new one," I tell her, praying she will forgive me and won't tell me to go home for the night.

She exhales loudly. "I'm sorry for coming off too harshly. I'm just not used to letting anyone in and I'm definitely not used to someone wanting to look out for us without wanting anything in return. So, I appreciate you wanting to come and stay the night to make sure we're okay. Knowing you're going to be here has me already feeling better and maybe I'll get some sleep tonight," she says, opening up just a bit allowing me in.

I lean in to give her a soft kiss on the cheek. "You go tuck Drake in. I'm going to go over and grab Benny and throw some sweats on. Just lock the door behind me. I'll come back with a light knock."

She gives me a seductive smile before I leave that immediately stirs my southern region awake. I shake my head and close the door behind me. I need to get my thoughts at bay before I head back over. Now is not the time for them.

I look around scoping every inch of the street in detail. I know this street, I know every tree, bush, and all its shadows inside and out. So, if anything is off, I will know. It also helps that every movement is recorded and sent to my phone. This is something I'm eventually going to need to come clean about with Skylar. I'm not sure if she's going to feel comfortable in knowing this or feel that her privacy is invaded, but it's better to come clean before she finds out on her own and feels as though I am hiding something.

I let Benny out, change my clothes, and grab a bottle of wine hoping she's still in the mood to talk. There are some things I need to talk to her about still, like how I had to visit her last foster home, and had to speak with her former foster parents. It took everything I had in me not to beat the ever loving shit out of the bastard who touched her.

Just looking at him smoking his cigarette, wearing his dirty stained tank top smelling of booze and reeking of a child predator had my adrenaline pumping through my veins furiously and his wife was no better. I'm just thankful he was banned from fostering any more children years ago due to numerous reports of neglect and improper activity.

The house was dirty and in complete shambles, completely inhabitable and who knows the state it was in years ago. Imagining Skylar living in that place made me angry and wishing I could just burn it all down with him in it. Now I need to bring this up to Skylar because something about James isn't adding up and now that he's disappeared isn't helping the situation.

I lock up behind me with Benny in tow and head back over to Skylar's. I knock lightly so I don't scare her. She opens the door and my heart stops plastering a goofy smile on my face. Every time I see her, I feel like a teenage boy all over again. I take one last look around behind me before heading inside.

"Benny, upstairs," I direct him.

"I'll show him where to go. Come, Benny!" Skylar calls for him heading back upstairs after him.

AFTER A COUPLE of moments Skylar comes back down. I poured us both a glass of wine and hand her hers as she enters the kitchen.

"Thanks. I set a blanket and pillow out on the couch for you," she tells me.

"Did you want to sit for a moment? I have some things

I want to talk to you about and I still need you to tell me in detail what this guy looks like that followed you in the grocery store."

She nods heading toward the couch taking a seat, leaving enough room for me to sit next to her. This makes me internally smile again. We sit in a comfortable silence for a moment. I allow her to gather her thoughts before we start talking about what happened earlier.

"Neal, I'm so sick of running. I just want to settle down and live a peaceful normal life. Always having to look over my shoulders is exhausting. I don't know how he does it, but Antonio finds us faster each time. I barely have time to breathe," she admits. "I've never seen this guy before. It's always someone new to throw me off. Thank God for my gut intuition because if it didn't alert me, I'd probably be dead by now."

She tells me in detail of what went down. I already have Johnny looking into which street cop followed her home. Once I talk to him, I'm hoping he will have a little more information for me. I'm also going down to the grocery store tomorrow morning to see if I can look at their CTV so I can get a good look at him.

If I can get an ID somehow then maybe I can pull him in for questioning or get an idea of his location so I can keep an eye on him. I already know who he's working for but maybe he can lead me right to Ray Castro as well. This isn't going to be easy but it's worth a try.

I grab her hand rubbing my thumb back and forth for comfort. "You are so fucking brave, Skylar. I know it's hard for you to give up control and I know it's hard for you to trust someone. I get that, but I'm going to spend as long as you need showing you that you can trust me and that I'm here for you and Drake.

"My boy Johnny that I work with came by yesterday and helped me set up some cameras around the perimeter of the house. Any movement is recorded and sent directly to my phone. There's one pointing toward your house as well. I'll understand if this upsets you, and if you want me to, I'll remove it, just say the word. I just felt better knowing while I'm at work I'll be able to keep an eye on things around here," I explain, hoping she won't find me stalkerish.

To my surprise she jumps up and wraps her arms around me tightly. "Thank you, Neal," she says in a low whisper.

I smile and bury my nose into the nape of her neck inhaling her mouthwatering scent while enjoying the feel of her body against me. She fits like a glove in my arms, and I have no intention of letting her go. She leans back just enough to give me a sultry look making my dick twitch. I reach my arm over the couch placing my glass of wine on the table next to us, then grab hers placing it on the table next to mine.

She bites down on her bottom lip driving me crazy. I take my thumb rubbing it along her lip releasing her hold so I can claim it for myself. I lean in just slow enough for her to be able to pull back and when she doesn't, I close my mouth on her mouth coaxing her to open for me.

Our tongues collide in a slow sexy dance. I trail my fingers under her tank top and up her spine reaching the back of her neck grabbing a tight hold of her hair pulling her in closer to me. She lightly moans sending a jolt straight down to my cock. I pull her onto my lap fully so she's now straddling me. Every bit of this feels so damn right.

I have to control myself. I want nothing more than to flip her around and dive deep into her until she screams my name, but I need to take things slow with her. She already means too much to me to scare her away. She moves her hips ever so slightly grinding against my now prominent bulge. I groan loving the feeling while digging my fingers into her hip. There's no hiding the magnitude of my desire standing stiff in my sweatpants between my legs, but she seems to be enjoying the feeling as she continues to grind against me.

"Neal –" she whispers raspy between kisses.

I slow myself down praying she doesn't ask me to stop. "Skylar –" I respond while still devouring her lips.

"Don't stop," she begs, giving me the green light to push forward. I internally high five myself as I make the move and flip her over, so I am now on top of her in between her legs.

I continue to devour her mouth as I feel her nails digging into my back. I trail small kisses over her jawline, down the side of her neck, nipping and biting my way down. I lean up on my knees reaching between us to the bottom of her tank top, but before I lift it off her, I look to her for permission.

She bites her bottom lip and nods giving me the go-ahead. Fuck this woman is so damn sexy and the fact that she's trusting me with herself after not being able to trust a single man is even more of a fucking turn on. I'm going to make her mine. I'm going to make her fall in love with me as I've already done with her. I've loved this woman since the moment I laid eyes on her, haunting my dreams and invading my thoughts for years. There's no doubt in my mind that it was love all along.

I lift her tank top over her head, then she reaches behind her back with eyes intensely boring into mine as she unclips her bra and slowly glides it down her arms throwing it on the floor. My little vixen is making my dick even harder if that's remotely possible. I'm looking at pure perfection as she lays back down.

The hunger radiating off me feels wild and restless. The need to consume her is undeniable, like I've been starved craving what I've been denied for so long is now a mouthwatering sight in front of me and I plan to enjoy every delectable bite.

"You're so fucking beautiful," I whisper as I lean down taking a taut nipple into my mouth.

I roll it around with my tongue then graze her with my teeth as I move to the next. Her back bucks up as her breathing increases. She smells of lavender and tastes of sweet nectar. The perfect aphrodisiac for my libido. I can't get enough. I'll never be able to get enough. She is now my kryptonite.

I slowly drag my hand over her rib cage, down the side of her stomach landing just above the top of her stretch pants while gliding my fingers slowly underneath. She grabs my face bringing me back up to her and smashes her lips against mine in a desperate need to be close. The way she just took the initiative makes me growl with hunger. She's clearly beginning to let her guard down with me and I'm going to soak in every movement of it.

I slide underneath her panties slowly gliding over her clit and she immediately bucks up with a moan while kissing me harder. I run my finger in slow circles over her tiny bud, working her up lathering her in her own juices before I finally descent in between her drenched folds teasing her and getting her ready for my invasion.

I slip one finger inside while still rubbing her clit with my thumb, and the moan that rips out of her as she rocks her hips while riding my finger almost undoes me. I feel like a teenager about to come in my pants. I continue to kiss her, swallowing up her pleasure as I slide my finger in and out of her tight little pussy.

She feels like heaven, making me want nothing more than to be buried deep inside of her being completely engulfed in every inch of her. I can feel she's on the verge of coming as her breathing becomes more sporadic and her walls begin to clench my finger in a tight grip as she growls out, she's about to come into my ear.

I pick up the pace pushing her over the edge as she comes hard and fast over my hand. The way her face morphs with pleasure is now etched into my mind forever locked away in my spank bank. I've never seen anything so fucking sexy in my life. I continue small light strokes over her clit until her orgasm finally subsides and her eyes glaze over contentedly.

I bring my soaked finger to my lips as she watches me suck my finger, tasting and lapping up every bit of her. She tastes like fucking perfection, an addiction that I never want to overcome. Her eyes grow wide in shock as she watches.

I smirk mischievously. "You taste so fucking good. I can't wait to have my tongue deep in your pussy eating you like a dessert."

She giggles, smacking my chest. "Neal, just shut up and fuck me already," she demands.

I feel like a kid on Christmas hearing these words. Just as I'm about to remove my shirt, we hear footsteps heading down the hallway from the stairs.

"Shit! Help me find my shirt," she asks stressed, panicking and moving from beneath me looking for her shirt. I quickly grab it from the floor handing it to her so she can yank it over her head before Drake walks in.

"Mom?" Drake calls out looking around rubbing his eyes with Benny following close behind.

Benny comes over to sit beside me on the floor next to the couch while Skylar kneels in front of Drake.

"Hey bud, what are you doing up still?"

"I had a bad dream. I went into your room, but you weren't in there. I thought the bad guys came and got you," he tells her so calmly.

Jesus fucking Christ. My heart breaks hearing this and the fact that this seems to be a topic he is used to instead of being a normal kid screaming and crying when scared makes the whole thing worse, he's acting like this is an everyday thing.

Skylar sighs wrapping her arms around him for a big hug. Drake looks to me over her shoulder. "Neal, can you tuck me and Benny in?"

Skylar looks between Drake and I a little caught off guard. "How about we all come up and tuck you in?" she suggests.

"Okay," he replies, then walks over to me and grabs my hand. I smile loving the way he feels so comfortable with me. I can picture myself holding these little hands for years to come.

I get up passing Skylar and she mouths thank you to me. I give her a kiss on the cheek and pat my hand on the side of my leg for Benny to follow. Drake leads us all upstairs to his room climbing in his bed waiting for me to tuck him in.

"Benny, down," I direct him to the floor next to Drake's bed, then bring the covers up over his body tucking him in tight as a burrito. I have no experience doing these sorts of things, but somehow being with them just seems to come naturally and feels so right.

Skylar comes to the opposite side of the bed and sits down. "I'm going to be right across the hall, so if you need me or have another bad dream, then come get me. Okay?" Skylar tells him.

"Will Neal be there too?" he asks, looking to me with big blue eyes.

I have no idea how to even answer this question, and I have most definitely learned my lesson regarding stepping on her toes, so I look toward her and wait for her to respond.

She looks at me unsure as she's debating which answer she will choose but then takes a breath and nods. "If Neal wants to come stay upstairs so you will feel better, than I will leave that up to him," she says, leaving the decision up to me.

I'm a little caught off guard to be honest, I mean sleeping in bed next to her is a no-brainer but I sure as hell didn't expect her to even consider the idea. The thought of falling asleep enveloped in her smell and the possibility of her body wrapped around me is like the heavens just opened and blessed me.

"Of course I'll stay up here. Nothing is going to happen while I'm here. Benny and I will protect you and your mom if the bad guys come. I have muscles," I say, making a muscle with my arm. "And Benny has big teeth that will scare the bad guys away," I tell Drake trying to comfort him.

Drake giggles leaning over the bed to pet Benny's head. "See, there's nothing to worry about my sweet boy," Skylar tells him kissing the top of his forehead.

Drake reaches his arms out to me almost making me choke up as I lean down to give him a tight squeeze before getting up to head to the door. Skylar says goodnight one last time turning off the light, and I follow her out to her room.

She immediately turns to me before I can take a step across the threshold.

"What I asked for downstairs – I think we should cool it for tonight in case Drake wakes back up," she suggests.

I nod. "I agree. I can grab the blanket downstairs and sleep on top of the covers," I suggest.

She shakes her head. "I think we're grown enough to control ourselves in the same bed under the same covers."

I chuckle. "Speak for yourself," I joke with a wink.

She bites her lips with a mischievous twinkle in her eyes. "Can I be honest?" she asks as she walks over toward the bathroom.

"Of course."

"The last time I slept with a man in bed was when I was with Drake's father. I really don't know how to do this. I don't know how to be normal or even know what a normal relationship looks like. I know you have experience, but I don't even know if we're going to be here tomorrow. How is that fair to any of us? How am I supposed to get Drake used to you when we may have to pick up and leave at any moment?"

Fuck my life. Hearing these words scares me and pisses me off all at once. There's no way I'm going to let her walk out of my life again. No fucking way. I rush up to her grabbing her face with my hands gently rubbing my nose against hers.

"I swear to God Skylar, I will protect you both with all I have. There won't be a need to run anymore. This is your home now. *I* am your home now and I won't let anything happen to you or Drake. I shouldn't have walked away from you years ago. You have haunted my dreams ever since and I'll be damned if I let you walk away from me now," I tell her while staring deep into her eyes willing her to believe in me.

I feel as though I've known her forever. As though we're two separate pieces of one soul. I'm not sure how this is possible, but I now understand the saying soulmate. She's it for me. She's my twin flame, my everything, and the thought of losing her makes me more determined than anything.

"I will figure this out. *We* will figure this out together. And as far as relationships are concerned, I have no expectations with us other than I enjoy spending time with you both. You and Drake are growing on me," I say with a small side smirk. She smiles. "And just seeing this smile on your face and knowing I'm the one that put it there makes me happy."

I can't rush all my feelings on to her just yet. I know she's still fragile and figuring life out, and I can see there's a thin line from her wanting me here to her also wanting to push me away, so I need to walk the line very carefully until she finally lets her guard down completely with me.

Once that happens then I can reveal to her the magnitude of my feelings toward her.

"But can you do me one little favor?" I ask, praying she doesn't turn me down.

She looks skeptical but nods.

"Instead of running away, can you run toward me if anything happens?" I request, running my thumb over her bottom lip.

She closes her eyes momentarily so she can inwardly think, almost as though she is letting go of one tether so tightly bound, then puts her hands over my wrists and opens her eyes. "I can try my best."

I exhale with relief that she agrees to try. I'll take whatever I can get. This is a small win in my eyes. I lean in for a small intimate kiss of gratitude before letting go. Even though I want to ravage the shit out of her, I am respecting her wishes of toning things down tonight. I need to show her that she can trust me, and that she's safe in my arms.

ONCE SHE FINISHES up in the bathroom, she heads over to her side of the bed wearing her tank top and some small shorts. I do my best not to undress her with my eyes but fuck it's so hard to do when she comes out of the bathroom looking like my young teenage self's wet dream.

It takes everything in me to calm the beast. What I wouldn't give for a taste of her right now. To lay her down on her back, remove those tiny shorts, spread her legs, and make her come all over my tongue. Thank God I'm already propped up in bed with the covers over my now rock hard cock.

She looks a bit nervous and unsure as she slides under the covers. I lean over pushing a strand of hair from her face. "Hey, don't be nervous around me," I tell her trying to ease her mind. I open my arm for her. "Come. I don't bite – *yet*," I joke.

She laughs with me and scooches over, allowing me to wrap my arm around her bringing her closer to me. I kiss the top of her head and silently sniff her hair loving the aroma of lavender mixed with a hint of coconut. I feel her body begin to relax and conform to me as she exhales deeply.

"This feels nice," she admits quietly.

"This feels perfect. To be honest, Missy and I never laid here like this. Everything always had to be about sex with her. I had realized for a while that I wasn't happy, but I kept trying anyways hoping that things would grow deeper with us," I explain.

"Did you ever try to talk to her about it?"

I think back a moment. "I thought I did but maybe I didn't say enough because I didn't care enough. There was always something missing with us. I couldn't put my finger on it until you came along. I'm not sure how to explain it so I don't sound insane, but I feel as though the world keeps putting us together for a reason. It's like two stars colliding in a galaxy twice, which has rarely been heard of. I feel like we are those two stars," I tell her.

I feel her vibrating beneath me trying to hold back a laugh. I lean my head to the side to get a better look at her while she tries to hide her face. "Oh, you think that's funny do you?" I crack a smile letting go of the seriousness.

"I'm sorry, I didn't mean to laugh but I think you just surprised me with how in tune you are with your feelings for such a big bad cop. I guess I'm just not used to a man having emotions or even sharing them with me. Antonio was rough and rigid, and he told me love wasn't real. Women were meant for a man's needs only. And after my experiences in my foster homes, I believed it. So, hearing you talk like this is almost too good to be true like when is the other shoe going to drop? I'm sorry, I know you're just trying to be honest, but I told you I'm broken. I don't know if I'm ever going to be good at something normal," she confesses.

All laughing aside again, hearing this just kills me. My heart aches for her. I am now going to make it my mission to put her shattered pieces back together again. I wrap my arm tightly around her bringing her up closer to me, so her face is now tilted up toward mine. "I don't care how broken you are, none of this scares me. I'm going to move heaven and earth to show you how a real man is supposed to treat a woman. You deserved to be loved and cherished, Skylar. I want to be the man to help heal you and prove to you that we're all not like that."

Before I can say another word, her lips are on mine. I feel a tear slide down her cheek falling into our kiss with a salty quench. She runs her tongue along my bottom lip then bites down sucking it into her mouth driving me insane. I groan pulling her over me the rest of the way, so she is now straddling me. I know I told myself I would behave but fuck it. I can't seem to control myself around this woman.

There's no doubt in my mind that she feels my hard rod in between her legs as she grinds slowly over me. She's going to be the death of me. I may end up with blue balls every time I look at her.

"I know I said we should hold back tonight but I want you. I want you in our lives and I want you inside of me *now*," she says in between our kisses.

God, she knows just the right words to get me riled up and as much as I want this too, I promised her I would keep things PG for Drake's sake, and I want to keep that promise to show her this isn't all about sex. This is about way more than that. This is about trust, respect, friendship, and eventually partnership.

She begins to reach down between us and before I can grab her hand, her fingers are wrapped around my cock over my sweats gliding her hand up and down. "*Fuck, Skylar!*" I growl. "You're going to be the death of me."

Dammit, I don't want her to stop. I wrap my fingers through her hair and smash her lips against mine with a fierce desperate need. The thrust of our tongues and the friction of her hand against my dick makes me want to combust. The image of me sliding inside of her is all I can think about. Just before she attempts to reach inside my pants, I stop her.

"Hey, hey," I say, trying to softly get her attention. "Even though it's killing me to stop right now, and the thought of being buried deep inside of you is all I can think about, Drake could walk in at any moment," I remind her.

She lays her forehead on my chest as we both lay in silence breathing hard. "Shit, you're right. I got too carried away. It's been so long since I've had the touch of a man, let alone someone that I feel this connection with."

I can't help but grin ear to ear. Hearing that she's starting to feel the same feelings as I have for her, lands me on cloud nine. She slides over so she's now against my side again with one leg propped over me and her head lying against my chest. "Thank you for not taking advantage of the situation," she whispers.

I kiss the top of her head. "We have all the time in the world for that. Having you wrapped safely in my arms means everything to me."

CHAPTER 11

SKYLAR

I wake up to the bed tilting and a shadow of a small body climbing up onto the end. I sit up looking over toward Neal who is still sound asleep. "Hey bud, did you have another bad dream?"

"No, but I woke up and couldn't fall back to sleep," Drake tells me.

I open the covers next to me. "Come on, climb in."

"Can I sleep in the middle?" he asks.

"We don't want to wake Neal," I whisper to him.

I feel a shift on the bed. I can see Neal's eyes open just slightly from the moon lighting a small glow inside the room. He pats the space between us. "Come on, bud," Neal says in a raspy sexy unawake voice.

Drake scurries between us under the covers laying his head down against my pillow. I wrap my arms around him enjoying the snuggles because I know one day he's going to be too old for this. "Better?" I ask him.

"Much better!" he says loudly with a smile. Then he turns to Neal. "Where's Benny?"

Neal looks over the side of the bed. "He's lying right here next to the bed."

Drake nods his head and yawns. Neal is now lying on his side looking at me intensely. Butterflies begin to wildly flutter throughout my stomach. "What are you thinking about?" I ask him.

I can already hear Drake's quiet snoring between us.

"You. Me. This. How perfect this all feels in this moment," he confesses.

I continue to gaze at him feeling the heavy intenseness of his words. "I'm afraid if I let myself fall, I won't recover," I admit to him being as completely honest as I can.

He reaches out grazing his fingers over the side of my face. I close my eyes and nuzzle gently into them. "I promise, I will catch you always."

When I open my eyes back up, I see an openness and sincerity within him as though he's allowing me to see a side of him no one has ever gotten to see. He's breathtaking and sexy as hell, and the fact that he seems to want to take on the male role model for my son is such a turn on. Now if I can just get out of this hell, maybe Drake and I can have a shot at a normal life.

I CRACK open my eyes and realize my bed is completely empty. I haven't slept this well in, well, I can't remember how long, but now I begin to panic wondering where Drake is. Did something happen while I was sleeping? How did I not hear them get up? I'm always so in tune with every tiny little noise around me. How did I miss this?

I throw back the covers heading immediately down the stairs but before I reach the last step I hear giggling, the smell of bacon, and the aroma of coffee coming from the kitchen. I stand here for a moment trying to slow my breathing and heartrate, so I don't run into the kitchen looking like a psycho.

After a moment to myself, I head in. Drake is at the kitchen table talking Neal's ear off looking relaxed and content as ever holding his stuffed turtle, and Neal is divvying out the eggs on three plates with bacon in only sweats. *Jesus fucking Christ!* It's like I'm watching a weird fetish porno about sexy men in the kitchen. I need to wipe the drool off the corner of my mouth before he witnesses my ogling. His toned back, and bubble ass, are more than I can handle at this time in the morning, but God help me when he finally turns around with his bare chest and abs I felt last night on full display – I'm not sure how I'm going to contain myself.

I give Drake a kiss on the top of the head, and he immediately looks up at me with a huge smile. "Hey, Mom! Did you sleep well?" he asks.

"I did," I reply as I walk past him to grab the coffee cup Neal is holding out for me with a smile. It takes every ounce of power I have not to drink in his whole body right now, so I concentrate hard on keeping my eyes on his.

"Neal told me and Benny to let you sleep in, so we came down to make you breakfast," Drake says proudly.

I give Neal a half thank you smile. "Well, thank you both for this. I didn't even hear you two get up. Very, very *sneaky*," I joke as Benny nudges my hand for a pet. This hairy guy is growing on me just like his owner is.

I take a seat putting my coffee down and give Benny my full attention. "Sorry about the hair, he's shedding like crazy. He has a groomer appointment tomorrow before we leave for the cabin."

I think I'm surprised with how calm I am reacting to Neal taking control of this situation as though we've been in each other's lives for a long time. Even though panic did strike me for a brief moment, something in my gut is telling me I can trust him. This is all still going to take some time, but this is a good stepping stone for us all.

"It's fine. Really, I don't mind. He's the closest thing to Drake ever having a dog, so it helps not having to say no constantly from him asking," I clarify.

Drake jumps in. "Yeah, Mom *always* says no because we never know when the bad guys will come and we have to leave," he explains.

I close my eyes taking a deep breath to calm my shame. The guilt of Drake talking about this like it's a normal everyday thing, and the fact that he can't have a dog because we might have to run on the drop of a dime consumes me. I feel like such a shitty mother.

Fingers gently wrap into mine. Neal's thumb rubs back and forth in a comforting touch. "Hey, Sky, don't shut down. I'm not judging. I can see this is hard to hear," Neal tells me in a soft voice. I crack a tiny grin at the nickname he just gave me. I like it. It feels right.

I open my eyes then clear my throat, so I don't get stuck in his gaze as I know Drake is watching us. "I like that," I confess shyly.

He copies my smile. "Like what?"

"What you just called me," I explain.

He nods giving me a wink. "Good, because you will be hearing it a lot."

"I want a nickname!" Drake yells out.

I can't help but laugh. "Okay, hmmm –" I say, tapping on my lip pretending to think hard. Then I turn to Neal. "What are you thinking?"

"What about Scooby-Doo?" he suggests, waiting for Drake to respond.

Drake giggles. "No!"

"Okay, how about Little Dee?" he adds.

Drake's eyes light up, and I can't help but laugh as I sip my coffee. "How about *Big* Dee?" he retorts.

I jump in. "How about just plain Dee?"

They both think about it for a moment. "I like it," Neal agrees.

Then Drake jumps in happy. "Me too!"

"Okay, now that we got that settled, you need to finish your breakfast and then head upstairs to get dressed for school," I tell him.

He begins scarfing down his food, making a mess as Benny sits under him collecting his droppings from the floor. I've barely finished my coffee before he's putting his plate in the sink and heading off upstairs.

"Come on, Benny!" Drake yells from halfway up the stairs.

"I wish I had the energy he has in the mornings, and it looks like he may be taking over your dog," I inform him.

He waves me off. "Benny needs a little squirt like him to wear his energy off. He gets bored with me unless we're working or training." He looks away in thought for a moment like he has something to say. "Skylar, about yesterday when I came to the school –"

"Regarding James Connor?"

"Yes, I can't go into too much detail since it's regarding an open case, but I had to go to his parents' house to see if I could get any information on locating him –" he explains but waits for my reaction before going any further.

I stare past him as I'm immediately brought back in time.

SKYLAR, *I think you're going to like this family. They have a son your age and a couple other teenagers living with them as well. It's walking distance from your new school, and the parents seem to be interested in the well-being of your future.*

The father has a good job, and the mom stays home, so you will have some support. Just keep your head down and stay out of trouble, Skylar. You only have one school year to get through, and then you will be eighteen and graduated. This is your last hope before you end up in a facility, so don't mess it up.

"SKY? SKYLAR?" I hear from a distance. I feel light shaking on my arm, and when I look up finally back into the present Neal looks worried. "Hey, there you are. Where did you go?" he asks.

I shake my head willing myself from the past. "I'm sorry, just hearing about that place rehashes all those old memories I've tried so hard to push down. The memories sometimes just suck me back in," I admit, trying to shake off the thoughts.

"Shit. I didn't mean to bring up those memories for you. I just wanted you to know so you didn't hear it from anyone else."

He grabs my hand for comfort. "Did you find James?" I ask.

He shakes his head. "No, his parents haven't seen him in years. They said he left one day shortly after his eighteenth birthday and haven't heard from him since which I guess confirms he wasn't lying about that part like I thought."

"I don't understand. How did you even come across him?"

He sighs. "He's an informant. He was arrested during one of our raids a year ago. He works for Ray."

I nod slowing taking this information in. "I just don't understand why he would go and work for someone like that. He couldn't stand Antonio. He tried so hard to convince me to stay away from him. I felt so bad for up and leaving without a word or a goodbye. This just doesn't make any sense."

He's in deep thought for a moment looking as though his mind's going a mile a minute. "You're right, that doesn't make sense. I wonder if he realized the connection between Ray and Antonio, and maybe somehow hoped the connection may lead to you?"

It seems like a far stretch but I'm not ruling it out either. James really tried hard to get me away from him. I just thought maybe he was just trying to be the protective big brother, so I blew off the warnings. But what if he has been trying to find me after realizing the connections between them. Ray is even more of a monster than Antonio, so why work for the brother of the person he despised the most?

"I'm glad he got out of that hellhole, but going through all this trouble and working for Ray just to locate me seems a bit overboard. Maybe he just got sick of being the good guy or ended up getting into the wrong crowd and has no idea about the connection," I tell him.

He shrugs. "Maybe. But I need to find him to figure it all out. Do you remember any places that he liked to go as a kid?"

I try to think back to the days I blocked off and pushed down. Shifting through the murky memories I try to recall some of the places he talked about. "I do remember one place he seemed to mention a lot. It was a small fishing cabin that his uncle owned. I think it's about twenty minutes from the house near a small river but I'm just not too sure exactly how to get there. He took me there once, but it was so long ago," I inform him.

Neal nods. "Okay, I'll see if I can pull up any property records on his uncle to see if I can locate the place. I have to go into work late tonight, so I won't be around this evening, but I want you to have my number in case of any emergencies," he says, taking my phone and inputting his number then calling himself, so he has mine as well. He gives it back to me with a smile.

"Neal?"

He gives me his full attention.

"What were they like?" I ask almost wishing I hadn't asked.

He shakes his head. "Let's just say even though your situation isn't the best now, it would have been way worse if you stayed."

There's nothing more I need to know. That one statement says it all. Even though I left with a monster, I got away from an evil demon. I feel better knowing that I made the right decision regardless of it turning out to be a disaster.

We both finish our breakfast. Neal gets up and puts both our dishes in the sink. "What time do you get out of work?"

"3pm."

"Okay, I'm going to text you the place to meet me for the car. My boy will figure out something for you," he says.

He grabs his shirt and keys from the counter, and I follow him to the front door. He whistles for Benny and Benny comes charging down the stairs with Drake following. "Neal, Neal! Can Benny sleepover again tonight?" Drake yells as he's stomping down the stairs.

"Benny and I have to work tonight, but you will see him this whole weekend at the cabin. How's that sound, Dee?" Neal tells him with a smirk using his nickname we all agreed on.

Drake grins from ear to ear. "Sounds awesome!" he says ecstatic as he climbs back up the stairs.

We're both chuckling shaking our heads. "You raised one cool little kid."

I love that he enjoys being around Drake. And the more I spend time with Neal, the more I feel like he may just be the perfect man for Drake to look up to. I'm glad he has the training and the means to protect us, but what if his career becomes a hinderance instead of a good thing? Can I continue to be around the constant worry and danger that his job will put him in – *put us in?*

I shake these thoughts from my head for now. It's too soon to be thinking this way. We've just barely scraped the surface on getting to know one another. But fuck, as I graze my eyes over this sexified man staring back at me with that all knowing look, I almost melt in my panties. He just ignites something in me that no man has ever been able to do with just one look.

He slowly stalks toward me until my back hits the hallway wall keeping me in place. He sets his arm above my head and leans in so he's now only mere inches away from my face. "I think you're pretty cool too," he tells me with a sly sexy grin.

My heart begins to stammer as I gaze deep into his smoldering blue eyes. They twinkle with a hint of mischief as he looks to my lips like he's dying to taste them. I hold my breath with the anticipation of what's next. Every fiber in my being is screaming out needing to be touched by him.

"And you're fucking beautiful and sexy as hell too," he finishes before landing his lips against mine and thrusting his tongue into my mouth with pure domination. I run my fingers over the back of his head pulling him in closer to me as I dig my nails into his neck. An animalistic guttural growl comes from deep within him as he pulls my leg up and grinds his hard length into me.

"What are you doing to me, Sky?" he says, whispering between kisses.

Whatever I'm doing to him, I don't want to stop. I haven't known or experienced this side of me yet. It's thrilling and scary all at once, but I will take this over going back to being utterly alone again. He's beginning to show me trusting someone is possible, and just maybe there is a possibility that love is real and not just in the movies.

"Eww!" a little voice of disgust interrupts us, and we jump apart like two teenagers being caught. Drake starts giggling. "You guys are going to get cooties."

"Someday you might like cooties when you're older," Neal says with a chuckle.

"Nah, girls are gross!" Drake tells him with a scrunched up face.

I gasp. "What about your mom, Mister? I'm a girl –" I taunt him.

He rolls his eyes as he finishes his way down the stairs looking cute in his sweatsuit he picked out all by himself. "Yes, but you're my *mom!* That doesn't count," he states so matter-of-factly.

Neal bursts out with a loud laugh. "He's got you there!"

I smack him on the shoulder. "Shush it!"

He gives me a kiss on the cheek. "Okay, I'm heading out. I'll text you where to meet later. Bye, Dee!"

"Bye, Neal! Bye, Benny!" Drake yells after them.

I swear I have a huge goofy grin plastered on my face. I don't remember the last time I've smiled this much ever.

THANK God it's lunchtime because my stomach is roaring like a lion for the whole world to hear. I meet Emily out in the parking lot for our lunch date. I'm glad we had this planned because I completely forgot to pack lunch this morning.

"Hey girl, I'm freaking starving!" Emily says dramatically.

"Me too. Neal cooked breakfast this morning, but I feel like I didn't even eat. My stomach's been growling like crazy. Even Jess heard it," I tell her laughing as I fasten my seat belt in her passenger seat.

She freezes and turns to me. "Oh *girl*, you have got to spill it!" she squeals.

I shake my head realizing I walked right into this one. "Okay, I talk, you drive."

"Deal," she agrees as she pulls out of the parking lot.

I go into the whole night and some light detail of us together. I still like to keep some things just between Neal and I, but I tell her enough to get the gist of it all.

"I told you he's got it bad for you! So, tell me, how are you feeling about him?"

We pull up to the burger place we went to last time, order our food, and sit down waiting for it to be delivered to the table.

"I really, *really* like him, Em. He's given me every reason to want to trust him, and he's dead set on showing me that he's really interested in being a part of both Drake and my life. He asked us to go to a cabin with him this weekend. I guess it's a place that means a lot to him since he and his mom used to go there when he was younger."

Her smile grows wider. "And did you say yes?"

"I did. We leave tomorrow when I get out of work. Drake was thrilled when I told him since we never get to do things like this. Maybe I'll actually get a chance to relax like a normal person and stop looking over my shoulder for a moment," I tell her.

She grabs my hand. "Skylar, you deserve a moment of peace, and I'm glad that you will be with Neal, so I don't have to worry about you guys. I know he's going to keep you both safe."

I nod and exhale knowing she's right. Our food finally gets delivered and we spend a moment in silence eating like savages.

"So, I know I said I was done with dating for a while, but I got a message on my Facebook page from an old high school friend. He asked me to go for drinks with him tomorrow night to catch up," she discloses before shoving a fry in her mouth.

I clap excitedly. "Did you guys date in high school or were you really just friends?"

She smirks. "We were more like friends with benefits," she admits. "Our parents were close back then, so we kinda grew up together, then one night after a party we ended up hooking up and continued to do so for a while. But then he ended up getting a girlfriend, my family moved away, and I never heard from him again," she explains with a shrug.

My eyebrows raise in shock. "Wow. So, you guys really have some history then. Did you have feelings for him?"

She looks a bit sad. "I did, but I never had the balls to tell him. Then he caught interest in one of the cheerleaders, and I told him to go for it. I knew he was just using me to fill the time until someone better came along, so I let him off the hook."

"Well, show him what he missed out on all these years!"

She laughs. "Oh, don't worry about that. I plan on it, and I have the ultimate killer outfit too."

"Good! I can't wait to hear about it all when I get back."

CHAPTER 12

NEAL

I smile as I see Skylar pull up to the dealership I'm waiting at. I'll feel a tiny bit better once she gets rid of this gold Buick that stands out like a sore thumb. They park next to me, and the smile on her face when she sees me just brightens my whole day.

I spent all afternoon trying to locate that cabin, and when Johnny finally found it, it looked as though James might have been there at one point but he was nowhere in sight. So, back to square one with the search. Now I'm starting to wonder if something happened to him. Maybe Ray found out he was working for us and got rid of him, or maybe he's laying low or on the run from someone.

Based on my gut and the fact that the informant of the whole mission is missing, I made the executive decision to call off the raid. I had to plead my case to the chief but in the end, he agreed, and we decided to just observe to see if we could gather any intel based on that.

"Hey, Neal!" Drake runs up to greet me with a hug.

"Hey, bud." I rub his head messing up his hair.

"Are you going to get us a new car?" he asks not being able to stand still.

I chuckle. "I hope so." Skylar is watching us intently. "Hey, how was work?" I ask her.

"Good. Me and Emily went to lunch and there was a staff meeting at the end of the day, but nothing out of the ordinary."

Cal comes up to greet us. "Hey Neal, how's it going? What can I do for you?" he asks, shaking my hand, then turns to Skylar and shakes hers. "Cal. Nice to meet you."

"Skylar," she replies with a weak smile. I can tell she's already feeling uncomfortable and out of her element.

"Skylar here needs an equal trade in for her car. Do you have anything available on the lot today?"

He takes a walk around her car and pulls up his notepad to write down the make, model, and VIN number. "Why don't you guys look at that row of used cars over there. I'll go run some numbers and meet you both back over there," Cal advises, pointing behind us.

"Sounds good, man."

We head over toward the cars. "Anything you see that you like? I think you should concentrate on something that has a low profile," I suggest.

She nods while her eyes drift over each car as she walks slowly down the row. Drake runs in front of her toward the bright red Honda. "Mom! Look at this one! It's so cool," he yells with wide eyes as he looks through each of the windows.

"It is bud, but we need something not as bright. Maybe our next car can be red, but for now maybe this grey one will work. The price doesn't seem that bad," she says as she looks toward me.

I take a look at the price sticker, and it seems to be a good price range for a trade. I just need to know what Cal comes back with first. Regardless of knowing him for a while, I know he has a job to do, so I decided I'm going to catch him in the office to negotiate this trade without Skylar witnessing.

"Hey, I'm going to go inside and talk with Cal. This is the car you're interested in then. Anything else you see that catches your eye?" I ask before trying to close a deal.

She looks around one last time. "I think this one is perfect. It blends in just enough and seems to be in good shape."

I nod and head inside the building.

AFTER ABOUT TWO hours between negotiating, test driving, and completing all the necessary paperwork Skylar is handed her new keys. I watch her face light up, then she jumps into my arms enveloping me in a huge embrace almost knocking me back.

"Thank you, Neal. You don't know how much this means to me," she says lowly in my ear sending tingling vibrations all the way down to my cock. Just the feel of her breath against my neck does things to me.

I kiss the side of her cheek realizing Drake is intently watching us. "Of course. Anything for the both of you," I tell her, then lean back to look at her. "Ready to go home? I have a couple hours to kill before work. I can cook us up something at my house," I offer.

"Sounds perfect."

DRAKE IS busy playing with Benny in the backyard while Skylar sits at the kitchen counter watching me cook. I take in the view of them all for a moment and realize how perfectly content I feel. This picture perfect moment in front of me is something I can envision in my future for years to come. It's crazy that these ideas and thoughts aren't scaring the shit out of me, but more like doing the opposite, making me crave this life.

"That smells amazing, what is it?" Skylar asks while closing her eyes inhaling the aroma.

"Some cutlets and garlic mashed potatoes. My favorite comfort food," I inform her. "My mother always made this on celebrations days – when I got good grades at school, birthdays, holidays. It was her go-to meal that I literally could eat every day of my life. So, here I am carrying on that tradition I guess with you getting a new car."

Her eyes twinkle as she gives me half a sexy smile. "I like your mother already, and I like the tradition idea."

"I think I told you before, but you remind me a lot of my mother. She was such a strong woman and made sure at every turn that I was taken care of and even though we struggled, she always found small ways to make me feel special just as you do with Drake."

She looks down at her fingers, picking at her nail in thought, then looks back up to me. "Are you even real?"

I turn flipping the chicken quickly while turning it down low, then walk around the counter to her. "Oh, I'm real," I tell her with a wink sliding in between her legs. "And I'm all yours, *if* you want me."

She wraps her arms around my neck looking up at me with fuck me eyes. "Oh, I want you. If Drake wasn't outside right now, I'd make you take me right here on this counter," she states, making my dick hard as fuck.

I lean down slowly, grazing my nose against her while we lock eyes drowning in each other's need to be closer, and to invade the space in between us until there's not a morsal of air left, every piece of me wants to ravage her like a caveman, swoop her over my shoulder and take her to my room locking her up with me until I've tasted every inch of her but I know right now I have to behave because little eyes are always watching us. If I'm going to be in Drake's life then he needs someone to look up to and show him how to respect and treat women, and that starts with his mom.

"Do you know how sexy you are, and how much you turn me on?" I say to her in a low raspy voice.

I see her cheeks color with a light pink glow as she looks away from me with shyness. I gently grab her chin to bring her eyes back to mine. "You don't have to feel uncomfortable with me, Skylar. You're so fucking gorgeous. You never have to shy away from me," I tell her.

She bites down on her bottom lip driving me absolutely insane as I zone in wanting to bite it myself. Just as I begin to lean toward her, she stops me. "Neal! The chicken's burning!"

"Shit!" I yell, maneuvering around the counter quickly. Luckily, I caught it right before it burned. It's still a nice dark golden brown. I place the cutlets onto the napkinned plate to cool off. "That was a close one."

"You need my help with anything?" she offers.

I grab the bottle of cabernet pouring us both a glass of

wine. "No, I want you to just sit and relax," I direct her, handing over her glass. I just have to mash the potatoes and we're ready to eat.

"I'll go grab Drake. He needs to wash up before we eat."

I drain the potatoes, grab the milk, butter, and garlic. "Can you call Benny in too? I need to feed him."

"Sure thing!"

I watch her walk out the sliding door with a happy smile plastered back on my face. It's like we ebb and flow as though we are exactly where we are supposed to be. It feels great having them here in my house. This place feels alive. The stale stark white walls now feel bright and airy, and the giggles coming from the backyard ricochet through the house like music to my ears.

I catch myself whistling as I mash the potatoes and take a sip from my wine glass. I almost feel like I'm having an out of body experience. Jesus, I go from guns and chasing the bad guys to a bowl full of mush. I wish I could spend the whole night with her again. I would have done my best to convince her that it was in her best interest to have me sleeping by her side again but tonight I have a duty to my guys. I'm not going to lie, it's going to be hard to push her from my mind, but I am glad that I'll have my phone with me in case of any odd movement. The only issue I'm concerned about is being too far away and taking too long to get to them if they needed me.

I think it's time I introduced her to my mom. That way if I'm not available right away, she can call her or go to her house for safety. She needs more options to run to and more people surrounding her that she can trust. Emily seems trustworthy so far. I'm happy she's finally found someone she can confide in and call when she needs a friend around.

I look up as I'm setting the table and grin as Drake runs past me with Benny in tow toward the kitchen to wash his hands.

"Drake, stop running! You're going to hurt yourself," Skylar scolds as she shakes her head following him. "I'm sorry, he got into the flower bed chasing Benny. He's extra dirty," she advises me feeling a bit guilty.

I grab the dishes of food from the counter, chuckling. "I love it. Reminds me of me when I was his age. He's going to sleep good tonight."

"I hope you're right, then maybe I can get a good night's sleep too."

Drake climbs up on the chair. "Mom, can Benny and Neal sleepover again tonight when they're done working?" Drake asks, looking between us both.

I hand her the plate of cutlets. "I wish we could bud, but Benny and I may have a really late night tonight. But tomorrow we head to the cabin for the weekend. Are you excited?"

He bounces up and down in his seat. "Yeah!"

We all fill our plates. I jump up quickly and fill Benny's bowl, then come back to the table. "I grabbed some hot dogs, s'mores, and a bunch of snacks already. I figured we can cook them over the fire, so let me know if there's anything else you want me to grab while you're at work before we head out."

"Does the cabin have amenities? Like beds and a bathroom?" she questions before taking a bite of her food. "*Wow*, Neal, this tastes *amazing!*" she says with a small moan.

I do my best to keep my thoughts PG, but it seems to be getting harder with the more time I spend in her presence. "Thanks. I'm glad you approve," I say with a wink. "So, yes. It's small but it has one bedroom, a pull-out couch in the living area, a kitchen, and bathroom with a shower. I figured you and Drake can sleep in the room, and I'll sleep on the couch," I inform her, so she doesn't feel pressured.

"Can Benny sleep with us, Mom?"

She rolls her eyes with a small head shake. "We will see, okay? Don't forget, Benny is Neal's dog and he's also a working dog so he can't play all the time, right Neal?" She turns her attention to me and I'm getting the hint that she wants me to have her back.

I nod understanding. "Your mom's right, bud. But he has off this weekend, so I'll leave it up to your mom where Benny is allowed to sleep."

We spend the rest of the dinner talking about plans for this weekend. Benny and Drake head back outside to play while Skylar and I clean up. She rinses off the dishes while I load the dishwasher.

"So, what time do you have to leave for work tonight?" she asks, handing me two glasses.

"Around nine. Can you do me a favor?" I ask, turning toward her.

She hands me a plate. "Well, that depends on the favor," she responds with a teasing smirk.

I can't help but match her energy. "God, why do you have to be so cute?" I shake my head grabbing the plate from her. "Sky, if anything feels off, I want you to text me and call your friend Emily to come here until I can get back."

She grins. "I can do that."

"Good. Now give me that last dish so we can go cuddle on the couch before I have to leave," I instruct her.

She does as she's told. "Wow aren't we getting bossy," she teases.

I put the last dish in the dishwasher and close the door. Then grab her hand leading her over to the couch in the living room. I sit first, then pull her onto my lap wrapping my arms tightly around her waist while nuzzling into her neck as she leans into me. I hear her exhale as if she's letting the weight of the world go from her chest. My emotions are running wild through me. Everything about this moment is just perfect.

"Sky –" I begin to say.

"Mhmm?" she hums in response.

"Tell me you feel this too? Tell me I'm not going crazy," I beg needing confirmation from her.

She gazes into my eyes – I mean I feel like she's *really* looking into the deepest depths of my soul as she's trying to decide whether I'm a safe space for her to reveal her feelings. "I do, Neal. I feel it all too. I just don't know what to do with it all. To be honest it scares me. I've never felt this way for anyone before, let alone this fast. And then there's your job – I've been in fear my whole life, and your job comes with danger and so many unknowns. Where would that leave me and Drake?"

I knew my job would come up eventually. How could it not since I've also thought of this as well. Maybe I should have stayed away from her, maybe I should have just kept an eye on them from a distance but I'm a selfish fuck. I just couldn't, and now that I've had a small taste of her, I can't walk away and give her up now.

I bring her down to me for a slow soft kiss. It feels so good to hear those words from out of her mouth. She's finally admitting out loud her feelings toward me, and it feels amazing.

"Listen, I know there's a lot to deal with first before we talk about my job, but when that time comes and things have settled down, we will discuss my options. But for now, can I just gloat and savor the words you just spilled? I know in reality we have only physically known each other for a small amount of time, but Sky, I feel like I've known you forever. You feel like home to me. I feel settled and complete when I'm with you."

She sucks in a breath stunned. "Neal, this is all so insane, but the crazy thing is I feel the exact same way. This all feels so surreal. I never believed I deserved a man like you. And on top of it there is no way I can ask you to stop doing what you love. You told me you wanted this career since you were little, I can't ask you to give it up for us."

I see Drake running past the sliding door with Benny's ball in his hand and I chuckle to myself before I give my full attention back to her. "You deserve the world, Sky. And believe me, whatever I decide to do won't be because you are asking me, it will be because I want to do it, okay?"

She nods biting that damn lip again, but before I can lean in and take over, Drake comes barging in with Benny. I can't help but laugh at the interruption as Benny jumps up on the couch pushing his snout in between us trying to give Sky slobbery cheek licks.

"Eww, gross Benny!" she screeches pushing him away. Drake is rolling on the floor laughing.

My stomach hurts from laughing so hard. I snap my fingers and immediately Benny jumps off sitting next to the couch. "Sorry, he gets a little excited when he likes someone."

She leans over rubbing his head. "Awe Benny, I like you too."

I HEAD into the back locker room with the team already getting geared up and ready for tonight. The atmosphere is buzzing with electric excitement. Every time we suit up the energy crackles around us. These nights are what we've trained for, planned for, studied for. There's a brotherhood that evolved between us from these moments, and we live for this work like adrenaline junkies ready for our next fix.

I'm not going to lie, if I need to give this up in order to make a future with Sky, I'm going to miss it but not as much as I would miss her if I lost her because of this job. I've been walking through a life of dull grays with sprinkles of light, but now I feel as though every moment is filled with bright colorful light. I have a purpose, something to look forward to when leaving work, and now I'm on a mission to figure out how to free her from her hellhole so she can finally live in some form of peace.

"Caruso!" Johnny calls from across the room.

I nod my head walking in his direction. "What's up, man?"

"We got some intel on some sightings of James. Which means he's still alive and must be laying low for some reason," he advises.

This is good news. *Really* good news. This means I still have a chance to get some answers regarding Sky. He's the only connection I have between them all and he may be the only one that knows their next move regarding her and Drake.

"Good work, man. Let's give the guys a run-through on tonight," I instruct him.

He whistles getting the attention of our guys. We go over the expectations of the night and make sure they know whatever goes down, we're hands off, only observing for some intel. We need to see the players involved in these shipments, the trucks they are using, and work on getting some trails on the players so we can locate some other potential locations.

I have this gut feeling Ray is close by since his brother is only weeks away from being released. If we can locate him, then maybe we can cut the head off the snake. Unfortunately, with this line of work, we get rid of one leader, and another grows back in its place. It's the way of the world. The fight on drugs and money will never stop. But at least this way, Ray won't be able to fund Antonio as easily being behind bars – *hopefully*.

With gear on, guns in hand, and a plan in place, we all head out to scatter into our set places before the drop is supposed to take place. I can already feel this is going to be a long night as my thoughts drift to Sky.

CHAPTER 13

SKYLAR

"*M*orning, Jess."

"Good morning, Skylar. Can I say you look absolutely radiant today. Could it have to do with that neighbor of yours?" she questions with a wink.

I can't get anything past her. I put my lunch and purse on my desk before clocking in. "*Maybe –*" I answer knowing I can't lie to her. She sees right through everything.

"I saw the way he looked at you. That's the way my Stan looked at me when we first started dating, and he still looks at me that way. That's how I know you have a keeper," she informs me.

I love the way her eyes gloss over when she speaks about him. That's the kind of love I want – deep and pure. The love in books and movies seemed so far away for someone like me, but when I'm with Neal, it feels attainable like I can reach out and touch it.

"The whole thing is crazy. We've only just met, but when I'm with him it's like the rest of the world doesn't exist. He wraps me in a safety blanket, and I can let go for once. And he's so good with Drake. I'm just so terrified to let go completely though. Drake's father was kind at first too, and then he turned into a monster. I don't think I can handle that disappointment again."

She looks at me with kind motherly eyes. "Oh, Skylar! I can see you went through a lot with Drake's father but let me ask you one question – the way you have been feeling with Mr. Hottie, did you also feel this way with Drake's father?" she questions.

"No, never."

She gives me an all knowing smirk. "Then there's your answer. This isn't the same. What you have going on with this one is different. So, allow yourself to experience it. A life of love is better than a life with no love at all. You deserve this, and so does Drake."

God, I love her. She is so wise and just the sweetest soul. Maybe all my bad luck in life is finally turning around. With allowing myself to open up and be vulnerable, good people are finally entering my life.

"Thanks, Jess. I hope one day I'm as wise as you."

"Oh, my dear, you will be. Just remember one of my favorite quotes, 'there's no such thing as failure, failure is just life trying to move us in another direction'. If you can live by this, then you can see the positive in all life's lessons," she finishes.

Before I can say another word Richie comes through the front door. I internally cringe. After what Emily told me about him, I try to stay far away, but he's persistent so I never seem to get too far.

"Well, good morning, ladies. You both look beautiful

today," Richie greets us with his white toothed smile that now irks the shit out of me.

"Well, good morning to you, Richie. Aren't you chipper this morning!" Jess replies. I know she adores him, so I keep my thoughts to myself for her sake.

I silently sigh. "Morning, Richie."

He walks past the front counter and comes into the office. "Skylar, any chance I'll catch you for lunch?"

"Actually, I promised Drake I would have lunch with him in the cafeteria today," I lie, but looks like I'll be joining making it a truth.

He looks disappointed but covers it with a smile. "Maybe next week then." I nod, not giving him confirmation. "Okay, ladies, enjoy your day!" he tells us, then turns to leave.

Jess immediately gives me a look. I shrug not knowing what else to say. "Maybe it's time to tell him you aren't available so he can move on to the next," she advises. Little does she know, he's a fast mover.

"Maybe you're right. Next time I see him, I'll mention Neal," I agree, and she looks pleased.

IT'S NOW lunchtime and Drake is talking my ear off about recess. My phone dings from a text. I see the name come across the screen and smile. Neal placed himself under "Hot Neighbor." Fitting.

He sends me a picture of a packed up car.

"Can you tell I'm excited and ready?"

he texts.

I can't help but laugh.

"What's so funny, Mom?" Drake asks.

"Just Neal being funny," I tell him.

I text Neal back.

> "I can. Lol. I'm over here looking at the time non-stop."

He sends a smiley face.

> "Are you sure there's nothing you need me to grab before we leave?"

he texts.

> "Maybe some wine?"

I reply.

> "Already packed,"

he immediately texts back with a wink face.

> "Just be ready to hit the road as soon as you get here."

> "Okay, Mr. Bossy Pants."

> "Oh, you haven't seen bossy yet, Miss Kramer."

This sends a chill down my spine. I look around almost forgetting I'm sitting in a room full of kids and have to simmer myself down.

"Can't wait. See you soon."

THE DRIVE here wasn't too bad. Neal told some funny stories about his childhood and talked about some of his embarrassing moments in school when growing up. It was a nice distraction as I took in the view of all the colorful trees beginning to change colors.

The cabin is cute, tucked away deep down a winding dirt driveway enveloped by trees. Drake is already jumping up and down in his seat with excitement as we pull up while Benny is whining ready to burst through the car door.

"Neal, this place is perfect."

His grin is from ear to ear. "I'm glad you like it. I spend a lot of time here throughout the year. I'm actually thinking about purchasing it. My mom's friend owns it and is ready to sell," he tells me. "You should see it in the summer. There's a perfect little spot down at the river to swim. I know Drake would love it there."

The fact that he always thinks of Drake and his happiness makes my heart want to combust. I can't help but wonder how I got so damn lucky. This man is kind, protective, and most of all sexy as hell. This seems to be the theme of my thoughts lately.

"Drake loves just about anything that has to do with a dog and being outside," I tell him laughing.

As soon as we open the doors to the car Drake and Benny come barreling out. Neal and I grab some bags, and as soon as he opens the cabin door I gasp. It's the cutest thing I've ever seen. To the right is a small kitchen with a little table against the side under the window. To the left is a stone fireplace, cream furry rug, and two leather sofas with fluffy cream pillows strown about. The place isn't what I was expecting for a cabin. Whoever owns it has put some love and care into making it feel homey.

Neal grabs mine and Drake's bag setting it in the bedroom. We stop and look at each other with such a powerful desire that my body immediately engulfs in a tundral of flames. I have no choice but to shake this sexual tension off because Drake is outside.

Neal clears his throat. "I'm going to start dinner."

"Okay," I tell him, relieved that he's the first to break our connection.

THE SUN IS SETTING as we are all sitting around the campfire. Drake has ketchup all over his face from the hot dog he is chowing down, Benny is waiting patiently for any droppings that fall from Drake, and Neal and I are now sitting back with a glass of wine and full bellies just enjoying the fire in a serene silence.

"Can we go fishing now?" Drake asks with a mouth full of food.

We both chuckle. "The fish are sleeping, bud. I figured tomorrow morning we can go bright and early," Neal tells him.

"Do we have to eat them?" Drake questions with a scrunched up face.

Neal looks at him amused. "Nope, we can put them back."

Drake looks relieved. "Good, cause I don't like eating Nemo's," he says with conviction.

I shake my head. "Drake, Nemo's are in the ocean, not a river."

He thinks about it for a moment then nods.

After another hour I take Drake inside, getting him ready for bed. By the time I get Drake fast asleep and come back into the living room, Neal has everything cleaned up and a nice fire crackling in the fireplace. He taps the cushion next to him for me to sit and hands me my glass of wine.

He wraps his arms around me as I curl up next to him laying my head on his shoulder.

"Thank you for bringing us here."

"I plan on bringing you guys here a lot," he says then kisses the top of my head.

We sit again in comforting silence as we watch the fire crackle and sip our wine for what feels like forever. I think this is the most relaxed I have felt in my whole life. My mind drifts to Missy wondering if they sat here doing this as well.

"Did you bring Missy here?" I wonder, trying to hold my jealousy at bay.

He squeezes me slightly. "Just once. She hated it here."

I nod feeling a bit better knowing this wasn't *their* place together but could possibly become *our* place together.

I lean back so I can look at his face. "Neal –"

He looks down at me, eyes full of promise.

"Kiss me," I demand.

Not another word is said as he takes our glasses placing them on the side table, then pulls me over so I'm now straddled over his lap and kisses me with such conviction and force it takes my breath away.

Everything we've said to each other and mean to each other is thrown into this kiss. I moan ever so slightly as he kisses his way across my jawline to the nape of my neck while his hands slide down to the hem of my shirt pulling it up over my head.

My bare braless chest now on display between us, he leans down taking my taut nipple into his mouth lapping and sucking gently. Fuck this feels so damn good. Every piece of my body is singing as it comes to life. The twirl of his warm wet tongue over my sensitive skin sends tingles shooting straight down to my core. I can't help but grind myself against his hard cock that lies underneath his sweatpants.

I haven't had a man inside of me for years, but I am so fucking ready. I'm dying to be close to him in every way possible. I already feel my soul entwining and locking tightly with his, and my heart is ready to combust from the undeniable connection I'm feeling but now I want nothing more than to feel my body erupt like a shooting star lighting up the sky.

I grab the bottom of his T-shirt yanking it over his head in a desperate need to be closer. I'm in dire need to feel every part of him against every part of me and as soon as my eyes roam to his chest, then down to his chiseled abs, I almost melt in my panties. His body is beautiful like a Roman God ready to conquer and own my womanhood.

"Neal – I *need* you. *Please,*" I beg in between kisses.

He immediately flips me over onto my back kneeling between my legs as he reaches for the hem of my pants pulling them down slowly until I am lying completely nude in front of him.

He discards my clothing on the floor while his eyes roam over every inch of my skin. I try to close my legs feeling a bit self-conscious from being completely exposed to him, but he stops me. "Don't hide. You're fucking perfection, Sky. Every part of you is insanely gorgeous and I need to taste you," he tells me as he drops down on his knees to the floor, places my leg over his shoulder so his face is now inches from my core.

Before I can object, he swipes his tongue slowly up the center of my folds causing my ass to jolt up from the sensation. "Holy fucking *shit!*" I moan out.

He chuckles, enjoying my reaction, then laps his tongue around my clit in precise movements. This all feels euphorically foreign but most of all my whole body is now tingling with speckles of intense heat swarming through every inch of me.

I bring the back of my hand over my mouth and bite down, so I don't scream out. His tongue is magical as he twirls and sucks my tight bud into his mouth. I've never felt this before. I've heard about this but never in my wildest dreams did I think I would get a chance to experience it. Every lick and every suckle brings me closer to the edge until he laps his finger around my entrance then slowly enters me knocking me over the edge.

"*Fuck,* Neal. I'm gonna come –"

He continues to slide his finger in and out of me bending to hit the perfect spot. "Yes, baby. Come for me. Let me taste your sweet release," he says between licks.

And with one more stroke I am now catapulting off the edge straight into a catastrophic orgasm. Sweat beads my body as tremors flood through me. I hear him groan as he continues his motions bringing me down into a euphoric haze as he slurps up every drop of my juices.

"Jesus Sky, you taste like fucking heaven," he says as he climbs up onto the couch, chin glistening from my come as he wipes it off with the back of his hand before leaning in to kiss me.

I grab the band of his pants sliding them down his tight ass, hinting to him that I need more. I need him inside of me. "Fuck me, Neal," I beg.

He leans up removing his sweatpants and boxers discarding them on the floor with mine. I gulp as I look down eyes wide at his massive sized dick standing in full attention in front of me. It's been so long, he's going to rip me apart.

He must sense my apprehension as he leans down nuzzling the tip of his cock between my legs. "I promise I will go slow," he tells me while he runs his thumb over my cheek waiting for my permission.

"I know. I trust you. It's just been so long for me, I got nervous for a minute," I admit.

He leans his forehead against mine. "Sky, there's no rush. We don't have to do this tonight."

I shake my head. "No, Neal. I want this. There's nothing more that I want in this moment but to feel you inside of me, to be one with you."

He kisses me lazily and deliberately as he inches himself slowly inside of me. Each push forward stretches me and conforms me to him like a glove. My nails dig into his back as I adjust to the intrusion. Even though there are moments of uncomfortableness, he eases me with his kisses and once he is fully seated to the hilt, he stills himself allowing me to catch up.

"Fuck you feel so damn good, Sky," he growls, trying so hard to remain in control. "You okay? Do you need me to stop?" he asks, checking on me even though I know stopping is hard for him.

I shake my head to assure him. "Fuck me *now*," I demand.

This is all I have to say for him to move his hips sliding in and out of me feeling fucking amazing. I begin to move with him, meeting him with the same ferocity he's placing on me. The way he moves and grinds feels like we're dirty dancing in the most provocative way, gyrating to our own music. His hands and lips are everywhere and nowhere all at once as his pumps become harder and faster.

"*Jesus*, Sky. You feel like heaven. I'm going to come –" he growls, but before he lets go, he reaches down in between us to circle my clit.

The combination of this and him inside of me detonates another toe curling orgasm crashing over me in waves making me tremble and contract around his dick. He groans as he drives into me one last time before pulling out and pumping his seed all over my stomach.

Shit, I didn't even think about protection until just now. I got so caught up in the moment that the thought of condoms or birth control never crossed my mind. What a stupid girl I am. I slam my arm over my head trying to hide the mortification on my face.

Neal pulls my arm from my face looking confused. "Hey, what just happened?"

"I'm not on any birth control, Neal. Thank God you remembered to pull out, but I just feel irresponsible for being too caught up in the moment not to think about it," I explain.

His face softens with understanding. "Don't blame yourself. This is my fault. I should have been more prepared. I left the condoms in my glove box because I didn't want Drake to find them. Next time, I'll be ready," he says with a flirty grin.

He gets up heading to the bathroom and comes back with a warm cloth to clean me up with. This part somehow feels even more intimate than having him inside of me. I giggle as I watch him walk around unphased with his nakedness. He has such a confidence and sexy gracefulness about him in all his naked glory.

"Are you enjoying the view?" he jokes as he slides on his boxers. I nod, cracking a smile while biting my bottom lip.

"Well, my view is even better," he admits as his eyes drift down every inch of my body sending chills over my skin. "I'm the luckiest man alive."

I sit up quickly grabbing for my underwear and clothes now feeling a bit self-conscious. Neal walks over taking my clothes from me and kneels in front of me sliding my underwear over my feet, up my legs, and setting them in place followed by my leggings, then stands helping me with my shirt.

"Stop hiding from me, Skylar. You're a fucking goddess in my eyes. If I could, I would make you walk around naked for me for the rest of our lives."

I roll my eyes dramatically but then take a moment to think about his last words and my heart drops. *The rest of our lives.*

"Neal?"

He looks over his shoulder and immediately drops the blankets after seeing my face drop to come sit next to me. "Hey, what just happened? Why the face, Sky?" he asks gently while tucking a strand of hair behind my ear and holding onto my hand.

"What if I have to spend the rest of my life running, Neal? What if Antonio never stops? How is that a life for any of us? I've never allowed myself to think of the future because I've always only been able to think of today but being with you makes me want things I never thought I could have let alone want.

"Sharing a life with someone, *loving* someone, and having it reciprocated always felt out of my grasp. Not a reality or at least not my reality that is – until you came along. Now what am I supposed to do with this all?" I look up to him with tears in my eyes.

He immediately wraps his arms around me engulfing me in a tight embrace. "Shit, Sky," Neal whispers while just holding me in silence. I melt into him, allowing all my worries to begin to dissipate. After a long moment, he leans back so he's able to look at me.

"It's not what are *you* supposed to do with it, it's what are *we* supposed to do with it. You're not in this alone anymore. I know it's hard for you to believe but I'm going to figure out a way to end this all and I don't care how long it takes, I'm not walking away from *this*, from *us*. I love you, Sky," he confesses.

I suck in a breath.

"I think I've loved you since the moment I laid eyes on you years ago. I just didn't understand it until now. And I know you may think I'm crazy or this is way too fast, but I've never felt this way about another person before. No one compares to you. I can't picture my life without you and Drake in it. *Fuck*, the thought of losing you rips me up inside. You're my moon and I'm the stars. Ever since you walked into my life you have brightened my dark world," he tells me as he cups my cheek.

"Let me in, Sky. *Please*. Let me take the burden from you and be your protector. I know you're struggling with all this but just let go and lean on me. Trust in me to help you," he begs.

I can't help but start to cry. I've never in my life had someone who I could depend on, trust, and would cherish me with all their being. He's breaking down my walls piece by piece and even though it scares the shit out of me, and I've internally been fighting it every step of the way, I feel so blessed that it's him that's doing it.

He *loves* me.

And here I am still afraid to give him my heart fully after he's just confessed his undying love to me. How fucked up does this make me? I'm broken and have trust issues, and he still wants to be here and love me.

"Hey, don't cry," Neal says gently. "I know this is a lot for you. I get that and like I told you before I can be patient. You are worth the wait, and you're not alone anymore, Sky."

God, how did I get so lucky after all these years? My whole life I've felt as though I was being punished for something I never did. I've been beaten down, abused, and stalked like prey and somehow, I am still here standing. I just barely survived my younger years and almost gave up many times but after Drake was born, I had no choice but to push through no matter what. He's been my reason to keep going and to keep fighting, and now God is giving me another reason. He's giving me love and a great protector and maybe just maybe after all these years of suffering, I've finally earned some reprieve.

I've never known what true love was until this very moment. And even though I'm scared shitless, I know what I'm feeling is true and right. Every bone in my body is screaming to say the words back, to just let go and finally free myself from the walls that have caged me in for so long. But I'm afraid if I say the words out loud, he may just disappear like a mirage on a hot summer's day.

"God, I'm so fucked up, Neal. I want so badly to give you all of me but I'm a coward. I have overcome many things in my life but if I lose you, I'm not sure I will ever recover. Please forgive me, but I need to hold onto my guarded heart for just a bit longer," I beg of him hoping he will understand.

He gives me a small, charming smile. One that instantly calms me making me feel as though everything's going to be okay. "We have a lifetime ahead of us. You, me, and Drake. So, you take all the time you need," he tells me with a light kiss to the forehead.

"Now, how about we get some sleep. I have plans to take you both fishing early tomorrow morning."

I release a tense breath and nod cracking a tiny smile.

"Now help me get this pull-out couch set up so I can fall asleep with you in my arms tonight," he demands.

CHAPTER 14

NEAL

"*N*eal, we have a problem. You need to come home," Johnny texts.

Fuck. Johnny would never request this unless it's serious. I head outside onto the front porch, so Sky doesn't hear the conversation and dial Johnny's number.

"What's up, man? What happened?"

Johnny huffs into the phone. "We found James, and we found him in the back of Skylar's house looking through the windows."

I run my hand over my head pacing the porch. "*Shit*. He found her. Where is he now?"

He's down at the station being held for trespassing. I suggest you get your ass back here so you can get some information out of him. He said he will only talk to you," Johnny lets me know.

"Okay, okay. I'm going to pack up and head back asap. Keep me updated if anything new comes up."

"Will do," he agrees and hangs up.

THANKFULLY SKYLAR UNDERSTOOD and was okay with us leaving early due to work. We made it back in record time with the help of her packing everything up quickly. I already dropped her off at the house and I'm now walking into the interrogation room to speak with our informant.

"James, James, James. What happened to you? Why did you disappear on me, man?" I ask him as I take a seat in front of him with Johnny standing in the corner behind me.

"Yeah, James. You've been a hard man to find," Johnny adds in his two cents.

James looks run-down – bloodshot eyes, skin pale, and jittery as fuck. Something is definitely not adding up because he's usually so calm, cool, and collected.

"Ray's onto me, man. Somehow, he knows there's a snitch in the mix, and he's pointing his finger at me. I've been on the run. Moving around from place to place, trying to stay under the radar. He's been watching my parents' house, and they've been hunting me down at all my regular stomping grounds hoping to catch me. If they do, I'm a dead man," he explains.

"Do you know where he's getting his information from?" I ask, wondering if we may have a leak in our department.

He looks up at me, confirming my question with just one look. "Where the fuck do you think? You think this place is squeaky clean? Fuck no. Ray has uniforms on his payroll in every precinct. And the longer I'm held up in this place, the faster you're putting a bullet in my head," he confirms.

This I know to be true. We're going to have to be real careful with our next move when releasing him, but I'm not too sure how much of an asset he is now that Ray wants him dead.

"Do you have any idea what the officers may look like?" Johnny steps in.

"I mean, maybe if I saw a picture I could point them out, but off the top of my head, no."

I nod. "And what were you doing trespassing? What were you looking for?"

He blows out a breath. "I was looking for a girl I once knew."

He's clearly trying to be evasive but I'm not letting up until he tells me everything. I'm pissed. I'm fucking fuming that this piece of trash knows something, and I'll be damned if he's not going to tell me.

"And who's this girl to you?" I question.

"She was one of my foster sisters. She stayed with my parents when we were younger. Ray's been looking for her, and I finally tracked her down again to warn her," he clarifies, but is he telling the truth. Was he there to warn her or bring her back to Ray hoping he would give him a free pass?

"What does Ray want with this girl?"

"Jennifer is his brother, Anotonio's, son's mother. Antonio met her when we were teens. I tried to warn her off him, but she didn't listen. One day she just disappeared without a trace. No goodbyes, no letters, no calls. She just vanished. I went in search of her to try to find out where Antonio was. That's when I found out who his brother was. I knew just asking around was going to get me nowhere but trouble, so I decided to join forces with him. Get him to take me in, trust me so I could try to find Jenn and take her away. Unfortunately, that only got me further away from her and a ticket to Miami, but the longer I worked for him, I knew eventually I would find her.

"It wasn't until about a year ago he sent me up this way. At first, I didn't understand why but then he slowly started sending parts of his family up this way too. Then one night, a couple months ago, he had me as the driver waiting outside a house while two paid cops went in. I heard them talking about Antonio's son, and I knew it was Jennifer they were after. I alerted the neighbors who then made a scene allowing her and her son to get away that night and I've been looking for her ever since," he informs us.

Fuck. Even though I didn't want to believe him, I feel he's telling the truth. He just knows too much, and his story lines up with hers about that night and how she managed to get away.

"So, how did you find her this time around?" I ask, trying to sound curious but not overly zealous.

"I didn't, Ray did."

Shit.

"He's been looking for her car, and he got a hit at a grocery store. I overheard him giving orders to Devon to follow up, so I followed him there and waited. I saw the cops were called, and Devon hauled ass. I was worried, since I wasn't sure if this was a cop on his payroll or not, so I followed them to make sure she made it home okay. Honestly, I wouldn't be surprised if his men have already pressed that cop for information, and if that's the case, he's closer than she thinks. That's why I was there to warn her," he finishes.

I try my best to remain neutral and calm in front of him even though I'm losing my shit internally. I have to keep it together. I'm unsure if he knows the connection between us. I still don't trust him, and there's a small part of me that thinks Ray may have put him up to this all, but only time will tell.

"It sounds like you should be staying away from her as well. If Ray's looking for you and finds you at her house, then you're just giving both of you up. You're not giving her a fighting chance with you following her with an invisible noose around your neck," I remind him, hoping he will stay far away from her if he really gives a damn.

"Fuck. I didn't really think of that," he says almost to himself while looking down at the table. Then he looks back up at me with determination in his eyes. "I need to get a message to her. She needs to know that her and her son are still in danger!" he explains in panic.

I can see the desperation on his face. "I'll get the message to her. You just stay away," I demand. "Now tell me more about Ray," I direct him off the topic of Sky and onto something I can work with to help us take them down when the time comes.

I DIDN'T GET out of the station until late. Much later than I expected. Thank God Skylar took Benny over to her house or I'd probably be walking into a mess at home. I look at my front door, then toward hers, knowing she doesn't have to work tomorrow and decide to take the chance that maybe she will still be up.

I text her first telling her I'm outside before I scare her with knocking. She immediately comes to open the door with Benny in tow. After everything I heard tonight, I give her a slow leisurely kiss before letting go to give Benny some attention.

"How was work?" she asks as I follow her into the kitchen.

I've been debating on what to tell her. I'm afraid if I tell her everything she may run in the middle of the night, but I'm afraid if I don't, then I may be putting her in more danger. She has just been getting her life back on track, and I don't know what the right move is.

Do I ask her to leave and stay at the cabin? Or do I convince her to go into hiding? How is this even possible with Drake in school and she now has her new job. I need to be real careful on how I go about this all, so I don't lose her. We have changed her car, but now that I know Ray will most likely go after that cop for information, she's a sitting duck.

I was finally able to find out who he is so I can confront him tomorrow, but if Ray got to him first, there's no telling what lengths he will go to lie with a threat held over his head.

"Sky – "

She's in the midst of pouring some wine, while looking back with a smile from me calling her name, but as soon as she sees my face, her face drops. She brings the glasses over to the table and sits down cautiously next to me.

"Neal? What is it? Your face is pale as a ghost," she points out.

I guess there's no hiding my stress from her tonight. I just don't have it in me. I have no choice but to tell her everything and let the cards fall as they may and just hope she won't disappear out of my life.

"Sky, what I'm about to tell you is going to be a lot and before you react, I need you to just take it in so we can figure out a plan together," I tell her, hoping she will heed my advice.

She nods wide-eyed and silent waiting for me to continue. I start from the beginning. I come clean about some of why I asked her to the cabin this weekend, I tell her about Ray now being our main target since he's now in the area, and finally I tell her about James.

She's making me nervous as she's sitting like stone the whole time. No emotion, no movement, barely a breath taken. I reach out to touch her hand, but she immediately pulls away from me and my heart sinks.

She stands up and turns her back to me to look out the kitchen window. I'm at a loss for words right now and the only thing I can think to do is hold her, so I slowly get up and walk behind her wrapping my arms around her waist putting my chin over her shoulder holding her tight.

She leans into me taking a much needed long breath. We both stand here looking out the window into the night with the moon lighting up the sky highlighting her in the most perfect way. I'm afraid to speak but I'm dying to know what she is thinking.

"Sky, talk to me, *please?*" I beg.

She instantly tenses up as though she's now awakening from a trance and moves my arms off her turning around to push my chest, so I step back from her. I feel a bit rejected and unsure of what to do next. Usually, I'm good with an angry female. I was able to calm Missy and simmer down her outbursts, but with Skylar, I don't want to make the wrong move.

"Am I just a pawn, Neal?" she asks, crossing her arms over her chest.

My brows furrow confused.

"You lied about taking me to the cabin and running a stakeout. You didn't tell me the fact that you saw a car in front of our houses, I mean don't you think that's pertinent information to share with me?" she begins to raise her voice flaring her arms. "And now the fact that your whole job pertains around taking down Ray! What am I supposed to think about all of this?" She starts pacing in the kitchen.

I stand here knowing she's right. The way it sounds after coming out of her mouth is different than when it was all in my head. I need to rectify this. I need to make this right.

"Sky, you're right. The way this all seems, I can understand why you may think that but please know that is not the case at all. I couldn't tell you about Ray – I'm technically crossing an oath in my job for even telling you tonight but everything I have done was to protect you. I know that sounds insane and maybe a little selfish at times, but I didn't want you to up and leave," I tell her.

"Every time you leave, they find you faster but at least being here with me you have a fighting chance. And I set up that stakeout because I needed to know if the person in the car was there for you or for me, and now we know. I never once thought of you as a pawn, just a woman I'm in love with that I'm afraid of losing and causing me to do everything in my power to make sure you are both safe somehow, so if that makes me a liar or an asshole, then I'm sorry. Maybe I didn't handle it all perfectly, but I've also never been in this situation before with someone I love. Can you forgive me, Sky?" I beg.

She's now inclined against the counter with her hands leaning on the edge behind her while searching my face trying to decipher if what I am saying is the truth. It feels like an eternity as I hold my breath waiting for her to respond to me.

She finally releases a breath then in the next moment she pounces on me. She jumps into my arms and smashes her lips on mine. I momentarily freeze but then gain composure kissing her back hard. I lift her legs, so they are now wrapped around my waist and place her on top of the kitchen counter.

Everything in this moment feels intensely raw and open. I feel her love pouring into me as she kisses me with such a potent ferocity I almost forget to breathe. She feels the same as I do. I know this now deep in the depths of my soul. And I know she's just been too scared to say it out loud. So here she is saying it in the way she's kissing me, in the way her hands are grabbing onto me like she never wants to let go, and the way her body melts into me as we're two halves finally coming together as one.

She's forgiven me.

I reach the hem of her shirt, slowly pulling it up over her chest. She raises her arms for me allowing me to do so as we stare into each other's eyes. Nothing else needs to be said in this moment because we're saying it all with the connection of our gaze.

I throw her shirt to the floor, then reach for the hem of her shorts pulling them over her lifted hips and discarding them as well. She now sits in front of me in all her naked beauty and I feel like I'm winning at life.

"God, how did I get so lucky?" I say out loud, voice raspy.

She bites her bottom lip, driving me absolutely insane. I place my hands on her knees spreading her legs apart as I slowly drop down dying to have a taste of her. I lick my lips as her beautiful glistening pussy is waiting for me. She's watching my every move, her chest heaving up and down with anticipation as I lean in and swipe my tongue through her folds. She tastes like the best flavored ice cream on a hot summer's day. I groan with pleasure as her flavor of arousal bursts over my tongue making me hard as a rock as a moan of pleasure rips from her mouth.

I smile, loving how her body responds to me as I suck her clit into my mouth building her up into a frenzy. I take my time tasting her, licking every inch of her as her juices now drip down my chin, and the moment I enter two fingers deep inside of her she begins to let go.

"Yes, baby, come all over my tongue – " I tell her as I continue to run my tongue over her swollen clit, and massage her sweet spot deep inside of her.

It takes everything in her to hold back her screams as she bites down on the back of her hand while spasms of pleasure tear through her body. I've never seen something more beautiful than this sight in front of me right now.

I wipe her juices from my mouth with my shirt, then stand up and kiss her with everything I have. I've just witnessed one of the best moments of my life; her moans, her smell, her taste will forever be engrained into my memories for the rest of my life.

"Do you know what you do to me?" I say in between kisses. She giggles, shaking her head. "You fucking recked me, Skylar. I can no longer face a world without you in it. You're now etched into my heart and bound to my soul. Your moans will now echo throughout my dreams for the rest of my life. I'm now a complete addict, addicted to the very essence of you. You've single-handedly embodied every part of me," I confess to her.

Tears escape her eyes running down her cheeks. I swipe them away with my thumbs. "You have become the person I didn't think I needed or even deserved in this life, Neal. You have shown me what it means to be loved and even though we haven't physically known each other for that long, I feel as though a part of me has known you forever. I finally have visions of a future for the first time in my life, and you've made that possible for me," she tells me then pauses and takes a deep breath before speaking again.

"I love you, Neal. I was too afraid to say it out loud before, but tonight I'm deciding to look fear in the eyes and take a chance on my future – *our* future," she finally admits.

I slide my hands on the sides of her face breaking into a huge smile. "You literally just made me the happiest man in the world with those words," I tell her, planting kisses over every inch of her face as she giggles and squirms beneath me.

"Good. Now fuck me," she demands.

I immediately lift her off the counter, carrying her over to the couch and lay her down beneath me. I slowly strip off my clothes, never taking my gaze from her. The air is crackling with static energy as the anticipation surges.

She licks her lips as her eyes drift over my body, and I smirk knowing her thoughts are dirty and full of lust. I lay myself down in between her thighs with my cock now at her entrance, but before I move, I lean my forehead against hers.

"I love you too, Sky," I tell her then slowly push myself into her as I gulp down our moans with a kiss.

CHAPTER 15

SKYLAR

The last couple of weeks have gone by in a blur. Work has been great. I took Jess's advice and broke it to Richie that I was seeing someone, he has barely spoken with me since which works in my favor. Emily and I have gotten much closer. She comes over at least once a week for some wine and girl-talk while Neal works the night shift. It's been great finally having a friend and someone I can confide in that knows about my life. I don't have to lie or keep secrets from her or worry about her judging me, and let's face it, I could use all the guy advice I can get since I don't have much experience in the dating world or love department.

Neal and I have been almost inseparable. He's been staying over almost every night and some weekends when he doesn't have to work, Drake and I stay over his house. We have had a couple debates on Drake and I moving in with him, but I'm just not ready to give up my independence yet even though I understand his reasoning behind it.

Ray is still out there, and Antonio is set to be released in just five days. Things have been tense the past couple of days, and Neal has been overly stressed about having to work longer hours and leaving me and Drake unprotected.

He finally introduced us to his mother. He wanted me to have another person I was able to depend on in case of emergencies, and she's been such a great addition to my life. We talk a couple times a week now, and we've been spending time at her house for Sunday dinners.

We added a security system in my house and more cameras. I've been extra cautious by taking different routes to school and home each time I leave to help eliminate being followed, but ultimately, I know if Ray wanted to find us, he has the means. Which makes me wonder, why hasn't he?

What has he been waiting for? What's he planning?

I JUST FINISHED PUTTING Drake to bed. Now that Neal's been more involved in our lives, Drake's nightmares have subsided, and he's been sleeping through the night. I just wish I could now get a good night's sleep but with my stress level being at one thousand about Antonio being released soon, sleep evades me at every turn.

I smile as I walk into my bedroom and see Neal comfortable in my bed shirtless with all his muscles on view. Instant tingles shoot straight down between my thighs drooling over this perfect specimen in front of me. I crawl up the bed into his open arms cracking a small seductive smile and lay my head onto his chest.

"Hey you," he says kissing the top of my head. "Drake already asleep?"

I nod, leaning into him, taking a long inhale. God, I love the way he smells. He chuckles. "Ya, he had a busy day at school today. He was exhausted and he's now out like a light. Now if only I could sleep as good as him then maybe I can wean myself off the four cups of coffee I've been inhaling every day."

Neal chuckles. "Maybe it's time we invest in an espresso machine. And maybe it's time we talk about you and Drake moving in with me," he says, bringing up the topic again.

I begin to tense up.

He shifts his body so he's now able to look at me. "Before you tell me no, can you just hear me out a moment?" he asks, looking mighty serious.

I can see this means a lot to him, so I put my pride aside and agree with a nod.

He takes a relieved breath. "Johnny has a rental property now available. His tenants just moved out. He said it can be ready by next weekend officially. It's a whole house, on the other side of the town but still close to the school. It's located in a cul-de-sac and has a great fenced in backyard for Benny also."

"I know your set on being independent and I get that, but living with me doesn't mean your freedom and independence disappears. It just means we're partners. My shit is your shit and your shit is mine. We support each other, build each other up, and figure out life together. Plus, with Antonio getting out, it will give us the upper hand being somewhere new while we work on figuring things out," he explains.

"I want to start a life with you, Sky. I want to come home to you and Drake and do this with you every single night," he tells me, waving his hands around. "Can you just let go for a moment and stop thinking so much. Can you just follow your heart?"

"What will you do with your house?"

"Sell it. Keep it and rent it out," he says with a shrug. "I'll figure that out later."

I nod, looking away to think for a moment.

Wow. This is a lot to take in. I have to admit a couple weeks ago, I was totally against the idea, and I would have shot no out of my mouth immediately, but now, after the time we have spent together, and watching him and Drake together, I've been thinking about the idea frequently. I love being around him and falling asleep with him at night. Even though my sleep has been evasive, just knowing he's next to me eases my worries.

Neal not only told me but has also proved to me that he is here for us no matter what. He has been nothing but patient, supportive, and loving at every turn. But the fierce protectiveness he has over us isn't suffocating, it's beautiful and pure and something I've been longing for my entire life.

My heart is now forever imprinted with the love that I have for him. Every day I fall more in love if that's even possible, and every day he proves to me just a bit more that he's the man he promised me he'd be. So now it's my turn. It's my turn to show him that I'm willing to take a chance on him, on us, on our love. It's time for me to let go of all my fears and the past that's holding me back and trust him enough to take the leap.

I sit up so I am now fully looking at him. I see the

worrying of rejection in his eyes, and it breaks me just a little. I grab his hand and take a breath of strength before I speak. This moment is big for me – *huge* with me letting someone else in fully.

"Yes, we will move in with you," I finally answer him.

Instantly, his eyes dance with excitement as his white brilliant smile consumes his face while grabbing me into his arms and kissing me with such joy and elation. This kiss is pouring out with promises of our future and I can't help but melt into him with a contented sigh.

"Fuck Sky, you don't understand how happy you have just made me," he tells me in between kisses. "I can't wait to build this life with you. Thank you for having trust in me."

"Just promise me you will never change, and this is who you will always be – "

He caresses my cheek with his thumb. "I promise."

THIS WEEK HAS FLOWN BY. Neal has been extremely busy at work, and I have been over his house all week helping him pack while he's gone. I barely have enough for five big boxes to pack at my house, so whatever I need to move can just be put into my car. Neal on the other hand has years of things to pack. I'm grateful to my landlord for being understanding and allowing me to break the lease without any recourse.

We went over to the new house this morning and it's way bigger than I pictured. It was almost like living in someone else's dream. This can't possibly be my reality now, right? After all these years of accepting my life as is, I looked around the house feeling as though I'm beginning to live in an alternate reality. A reality filled with a possibility of normalcy and a simple life.

The cul-de-sac felt much safer being there was only one way in and one way out. Johnny is there this weekend setting up cameras and a new state of the art security system and making sure the locks on all the doors and windows are secure. He's become one of my favorites of Neal's co-workers and friends. He seems to have respect and admiration for me for all that I've have gone through and the fact that I'm still here standing strong which has helped me open up to him just a bit allowing him to get to know me some.

Neal has been doing everything in his power to make sure everything feels perfect and safe before moving in and I know the stress and worry over Antonio being released is taking a toll on him too. He tries to hide it, but I can see right through him. It's been impacting us both but we're trying hard to learn how to maneuver around each other graciously during this trying time.

I've finally finished packing up the last of Neal's kitchen as he walks through the door carrying a bottle of wine, a bouquet of flowers and a huge smile on his face.

"Hey, you," he greets me with a long kiss after putting down the flowers and wine, then wraps his arms around me burying his head in the nape of my neck and inhaling the scent of my hair. "God, I love your smell."

I smack his arm giggling. "I take it you missed me?"

He kisses my cheek before grabbing the flowers and handing them to me. "I always miss you when I'm away from you. Have you missed me?"

"Always. Flowers huh? What's the occasion?" I ask as I

head to the kitchen to look for something that's not packed up to put them in.

"You saying yes to us living together is most definitely something worth celebrating, don't you think?" he questions with a wink.

"Neal, Neal! Mom said I can paint my new room any color I want!" Drake yells, running in from the backyard with Benny following.

Neal lifts him up by catching him mid run. "And what color were you thinking?"

"Green! Green is my favorite color and Mom already told me I can get a tent for my birthday next weekend!" he says excitedly.

"Ah yes, your mom told me about your birthday. What do you want to do for your special day?"

He sets him down on the counter stool. Drake taps his pointer finger on his bottom lip pretending to think really hard. I can't help but laugh when he does this, he's such a goof. "I think I wanna go to a jump house!"

I roll my eyes laughing. "I think we can make that happen, bud," I tell him.

He immediately celebrates in his seat. "Yay! Can Benny come?"

Neal shakes his head chuckling while heading to grab Benny's food bowl. "Benny has to stay home, bud. Dogs aren't allowed there, but Benny can be with you when we cut your birthday cake and how about we invite Mrs. Turner too?"

His little face lights up. "Okay!"

"How about a break from packing? Maybe we could order a pizza and watch an afternoon movie?" Neal suggests.

"I love that idea. I could use a break."

MY EYES FLUTTER OPEN. I look around confused for a moment until I realize I must have fallen asleep during the movie and it's now dark outside. I start to push myself up to see where Drake is when I hear Neal's voice in the kitchen behind me. I'm not sure I'll ever get away from the need to know exactly where he is at all times. This obsession has now become a part of me.

"How was that nap?" Neal asks as he dishes out some ice cream for Drake.

"Yeah Mom, you slept through the whole movie!" Drake tells me, shaking his head at me in disappointment.

I stretch my arms over my head with an exaggerated yawn. "I must have been more tired than I thought." I stopped taking naps once Drake got out of his nap phase.

"Neal said if I was really quiet while you slept then I could have some ice cream," Drake informs me, a twinkle in his eyes.

I laugh. "That's a pretty good bribe."

"I'm learning from the best," he jokes.

"What time is it?" I ask, looking around for my phone.

"A little after eight."

"*Shit.* I need to run over to the house and grab our night clothes. Drake, you want to run over with me to change and grab your sleeping bag after you finish your ice cream?"

"Okay!"

Neal leans over the back of the couch giving me a kiss on the top of my head. "You need me to come with you?"

I turn my head giving him a kiss in return. I automatically melt into his soft lips with a sigh. "I think we can handle it. Will only take a minute."

Drake finishes his ice cream, and we head over to our house. Benny tries to follow but I tell him to stay. He whines, puts his head down, and waits at the front door. He's become extremely attached to Drake, almost like his personal protector.

I instantly shiver from the chill in the air now that fall has officially settled in. The night is quiet, almost an eerie silence that looms over the neighborhood. I look around feeling odd as the hairs on the back of my neck stand up. I grab Drake's hand protectively as I unlock my front door. Just for a split moment, going back to Neal's and not entering this house, crosses my mind but I quickly shake it away since we have cameras placed all over. He would have seen if something was amiss.

"Mom, you're squeezing my hand too tight," Drake whines.

"Shoot, sorry bud," I say quickly, letting go of his hand as I shut the door behind us and lock it immediately.

The house is completely pitch dark since I haven't been home since this morning and didn't have a chance to keep on a light like I normally would do. I never leave my house like this, and I'm pissed at myself for now having to feel my way to the light switch while my eyes become adjusted.

"Drake, go upstairs and change into your pajamas," I tell him as I walk into the living room to turn on the lamp. I try clicking it multiple times, but nothing happens. Is the power off? Now that I think of it, my alarm didn't go off as I entered the house either. The power has to be off. I sniff the air as I take a couple of steps. Something smells familiar but I can't seem to place it. I walk around after attempting to turn on the light and give everything a once-over to see if anything's out of place as I rack my brain trying to figure out that fragrance. My house has smelled the same over the last couple of weeks other than maybe adding a bit of dog smell, so this has me a little confused and on edge.

God, it's so familiar it terrifies me for some reason, but for the love of me I can't place it. My body shivers as though it knows something I don't. My brain feels mucky, almost like it's denying me access to a memory that's been buried for centuries locked away in a long forgotten tomb.

I spend a couple of minutes trying to pry the memory open in the pitch dark, then it hits me like a meteorite hitting the earth and everything begins to play in slow motion as I start to run upstairs after hearing a muffled screech. It feels like I'm stuck in a nightmare, I'm running and feel like I'm barely moving no matter how hard I move my legs. I push harder, skipping the steps of the stairs and missing one as I go falling flat on my face as I scream Drake's name.

I reach the top of the stairs running into Drake's room at full force and instantly stop dead in my tracks, my heart is banging against my chest ready to explode at the sight in front of me. My worst nightmare has finally come true. I'm officially in hell. Every sleepless night, every worried thought that has consumed me all these years, is now standing in front of me holding my son captive.

I hold my hands up trying to play offense looking harmless as I look between my son and Antonio. Drake has tears cascading down his cheeks as he tries to squirm out of Antonio's hold between muffled cries. His hand is covering Drake's mouth to silence him as a gun is in his other pointed at his little head. Drake looks so helplessly scared and confused. He's never seen a picture of his father, so for all he knows he is just another bad guy.

I do my best to hold in a sob as I try to remain calm while tears explode from my eyes blurring my vision. I need to try and stay one step ahead of whatever he may be planning. "Antonio, *please*, please don't hurt him," I beg. "He's your son and you're scaring him."

"Well, hello, *Jennifer*. It's nice to see you again after all these years," he says in a deep husky voice and a wicked smirk.

He looks much older than I remembered and worn down. Prison has aged him far past his actual age. His voice alone sends a shiver down my spine making me want to vomit. I begin to shake involuntarily trying my hardest to hold myself together for Drake's sake. I can't show him fear or he will eat me alive.

"*Please* Antonio, let him go. Can't you see you're scaring him?"

The look in Drake's eyes is shattering me. Every inch of my soul is hurting seeing my baby filled with absolute terror. He's been scared before, but not like this. He's terrified as he sobs in Antonio's arms.

"Antonio, take me. Let him go and take me," I beg again offering a tradeoff knowing I'm not what he wants, but I have to try.

He leans down and whispers something in Drake's ear then slowly releases his hand from his mouth. Drake attempts to stop crying while sucking in breath after breath hard. I reach my arms out and he allows Drake to run to me. I scoop him up in my arms and squeeze him tight, rocking him as I try to comfort us both. The feel of his little arms wrapped around me is the best feeling ever after a million horrible thoughts just flashed through my head.

"Pack a bag for him. You're both coming with me," he states as he walks toward me and now has the gun against the back of my ribs.

I flinch from the probe of the hard metal against my back and the feel of his hand wrapped around my arm. He moves my hair to the side grazing my neck with his fingers; I recoil and almost vomit in my mouth from the touch. All I want to do is yank my body away from him, but I have no choice but to try and remain calm; appease him in any way possible.

"Antonio, he's scared. Please, just leave him here and just take me. I'll do whatever you ask. *Anything*," I plead again still holding Drake tight.

Antonio laughs. "You think after all these years I'm just going to leave my son behind?" he begins to raise his voice then gets close to my ear. "You took my son from me, Jennifer. You put me in jail and ran off. Do you think that's something I'm going to forget? You're going to pay for that. I'm going to make sure of it. You're going to be begging for my forgiveness."

Before I can respond, I hear frantic pounding coming from the front door and Neal screaming my name. I let out a breath relieved he has realized something's wrong. It won't be long until he calls for reinforcements, and we will be saved from this monster.

"Antonio, you need to let us go before the cops get here," I warn him. "Neal's not going to stop."

He scoffs, grabs my arm hard and begins to drag me toward the stairs, shoving the gun harder into my back. "You fucking make a wrong move, and I shoot him," he threatens. I'm unsure if he's talking about Drake or Neal.

I know he's not bluffing either way. He would rather kill us both than let us go again. I know him and how possessive he is, and there is no way he is letting us go without a fight. I stumble down the stairs with Drake quietly holding onto me with all his might. I see Neal looking through the side window of the door and when he sees me, I lock eyes with him and shake my head to keep him back.

The last thing I need is him bursting through the door, and us in the middle of a gun fight. I can't risk it, and I know Antonio won't hesitate putting us right in the middle of it all to protect himself.

"Fucking move it!" Antonio yells, heading us to the garage door as I trip over my feet.

He makes sure to hold me tight against him as he forces us into the garage opening the car door pushing us in. "I swear to God Jennifer, you make one wrong move and it's over. Just do as your told and Drake will be okay," he says as he slams the car door shut.

"Mom, I'm scared," Drake whispers in my ear as his arms squeeze around my neck a little tighter. So much guilt is coursing through my body. I did this. Drake didn't choose to be born. I made that choice and now he's paying the price.

"I know, baby. I'm so sorry. Everything's going to be okay. I won't let anything happen to you. I promise," I tell him, trying my hardest to calm him down. I kiss the side of his head watching Antonio as he walks to the driver's side of the car and gets in.

"The cops are probably almost here. Neal probably called them already." I try to inform him.

He turns to me and screams. "Shut the *fuck* up!" We both flinch. "You don't think I know all about your little *boyfriend?* You could run, Jenn, but you couldn't hide from me for long. I *own* you. You're mine, and there won't be a place in this world you can run to that I won't find you," he threatens as he puts the car in reverse, slamming his foot on the gas, and storms backwards bursting through the garage door at high speed.

All I can think of is this is it. Neal is going to be outside the house waiting, and then it's going to be the end of us caught in a high speed gun chase, and Drake and I are going to be the casualty of war. I close my eyes and hang onto Drake tight as I prepare myself for the aftermath.

Antonio screeches backwards out of the driveway then shifts into drive and slams his foot down on the gas surging us forward. I open my eyes to look for Neal, but I don't see him. In fact, the whole street looks empty. His garage door is open, and his car is gone. Where the fuck is he? Did he just leave us? There's not one cop car in front or any lights or sirens in the distance. That can't be possible. It just doesn't make any sense.

How could he just disappear and leave us? He promised me constantly that he would protect us.

We drive at high speed for what seems like forever until we finally pull up to a barn behind an old, abandoned house in the middle of nowhere. I look around seeing only one large grass field surrounded by woods. Where the fuck are we? And why weren't we followed?

"Don't fucking move," Antonio demands as he gets out of the car looking around before he walks over to our door opening it up. "Get out."

I decide remaining quiet is probably the best thing for me to do. He could easily just get rid of me and take Drake if I become a nuisance for him. I need to play this smart. It's clear that some part of him wants me here since he could have easily left me behind but instead, he forced me along.

He takes me by the upper arm with Drake still wrapped around me dragging me along with him. I refuse to let him go even though he's becoming heavy. Thank God Drake is remaining quiet making it easier on the both of us. Antonio drags us into a large open barn filled with bales of hay, an old tractor, and other large farm equipment. There's a metal chair sitting in the middle of the floor with heavy rusted chains attached to two wooden poles.

I gulp hard immediately knowing I'm going to be chained down without the ability to protect my son. Antonio shoves me forward as he rips Drake from my arms. Drake begins screaming and kicking as I try to reach back out to him trying to snatch him back.

"Go sit the fuck down Jenn!" he yells, pointing the gun behind Drake's head.

I instantly give in backing up into the chair and sitting down. Antonio puts the gun down on a wooden box next to him and turns to grab a rope tying Drake's hands together to a piece of large equipment. He pulls out a bandana from his back pocket, tying it around Drake's head covering his eyes. My eyes dart to the gun as I calculate in my head how quickly I can run before he stops me, but before I can even make a move, he looks at me with a knowing smirk and places it down the front of his pants.

"Tsk, tsk, tsk, you think I'd fall for that again. Now strip!" he screams.

"Antonio, you don't have to do this. Tell me what you want, and we can talk it out. We used to talk all the time." I try my best to place us back to the old days when we first got to know each other. Maybe some small piece of him will remember those early days and soften just a bit.

"What I want is my fucking son who you have kept me from all these years and what I want is for you to pay for these years you have stolen from me!" he screams. I flinch. "He's mine! He belongs to me, and you took him. I saved you from a life of misery and this is how you thanked me? You put me in prison and took off with my boy!" he shouts as he stomps over to me pointing the gun to my head. "Now fucking take your damn clothes off!"

I slowly begin pulling my sweatshirt over my head leaving my tank top in place. Then remove my shoes with my toes, unbutton my jeans, and pull them off leaving me standing in only the tank top and underwear. Antonio watches every move licking his lips making me want to scrub every inch of my skin.

He grabs each of my legs one by one locking the chains in place. As he does, he puts his head in between my legs and inhales. Tears flood down my cheeks knowing this isn't going to end well for me. I try to close my legs as best as I can. He trails his hand up my thighs, over the waistband of my underwear, then under my tank top lifting it up on the way until my breasts are fully exposed.

"Antonio stop. You don't have to do this."

Before I can say another word, he leans down taking my breast into his mouth and clamps his teeth down over my skin biting so hard I cry out from the searing pain seeing white stars almost passing out.

Drake starts crying. Every inch of my being aches to wrap my arms around him and comfort him even though I'm submerged in my own pain.

"Now shut the fuck up. I don't want to hear another word from you. This is just the beginning for you. I'm going to break you in for the rest."

Antonio handcuffs my hands behind me to the back of the chair. I am officially imprisoned with no way out. I have no way to protect my son. I'm utterly helpless and now all I can think about is where is Neal. The bitemark has bled through my white tank, throbbing as a reminder of what may come next. This Antonio is different than what I knew before. He wasn't a kind man, but he was tolerable for the most part. This is no longer the case, and I have no idea who this man is standing in front of me.

My heart aches for Neal. All I want is for him to burst through the door and save us. Where the fuck is he? That asshole fucking left me – left *us*. My heart slices in two with the pang of betrayal. I believed in him and his words only to be lied to and deceived in the worst possible way. He's a fucking coward and now I'm going to be raped and tortured in front of my son.

I look to Drake as he's sniffling, looking over every inch of him from the distance to make sure he's not hurt thanking God he is blindfolded and wasn't able to watch what just happened and then it hits me – I forgot we placed a tracker in his shoe. Neal and I placed an air tag in his shoe in case something like this happened!

Holy fucking shit! Could Neal be tracking us? Could I be wrong about him leaving us and being a coward? Guilt now consumes me with the possibility I may have jumped the gun and he's been here for us all along. Maybe he hasn't left us. Maybe this was his plan all along – to track us and wait until he can get to us safely.

All my thoughts are interrupted with Antonio now standing in front of me with such hatred radiating off him as he begins to unbuckle his pants while kicking my knees apart. I start shaking my head unable to form any words.

A crackle from the stones echoes through the air as I hear a car pulling around the back, then multiple doors slam. I exhale with relief as he buckles his pants back up looking pissed from the interruption. There's no way Neal would just announce himself so blatantly by driving right up, so who the fuck is here now? Just mere moments ago I was relieved by the interruption, but now my breathing accelerates as panic begins to set in on who may be on the other side of those doors.

My chest heaves up and down frantically. I slam my eyes shut repeating the mantra, "You're strong, you can handle anything. You're strong, you can handle anything," to myself repeatedly until my breathing finally slows and I'm able to open my eyes again with a conviction of determination. I'm not going down without a fight.

I look over my left shoulder seeing three men walk in and two of them are dragging a half-beaten man along. They walk over dropping him in front of me. The man's face is so swollen and bloodied beyond recognition that he can barely open his eyes. Who is this man and why is he now lying in front of me?

I rip my attention away from the man lying in front of me to Antonio talking to one of the men who looks almost identical to him, I recognize him – *Ray Castro*. Neal has been working hard to locate him and now here he stands as he embraces his brother. They exchange commentaries before Ray looks over me then changes his attention to Drake.

He walks over to Drake squatting down in front of him with a misguided smile. I immediately jump in. "Please leave him be!" I shout.

They all snap their heads in my direction. Antonio begins to stalk angrily in my direction, but Ray stops him. "Leave her," he says loudly. Then he turns back to Drake removing his blindfold. "Hello, Drake. I'm your uncle Ray. If I remove the rope, will you be a good boy and listen?" he asks him gently.

Drake just nods quietly staying still. "Good boy," Ray praises him as he unravels the rope from his hands, rubs his wrists gently, then lifts him up to stand in front of him so they are now eye level. "Now, you are going to go spend some time with your father and your mom's going to come spend some time with me for a little while," he tells him.

Drake's lip begins to quiver. "But why?" he asks him.

"Your mom needs to make some money so she can help take care of you. And you're going to spend some time with your dad while she does this," Ray finishes. "I promise we will take good care of her."

Shit. Now I know why they brought me here. Ray is known for trafficking women and that's what his intent is with me. This is why he has come. I look up toward Antonio. "Antonio, don't let him do this. We can work on being a family again! I'll do whatever you want, be however you want, just don't do this!" I beg with everything I have panicking.

Ray takes Drake to the other side of the barn where we can no longer see each other. All my convictions from a moment ago have depleted as I watch him take my son away. Then Antonio backhands me hard across the cheek, enough that my head snaps to the side and I see tiny specks of light as my vision fades in and out. I immediately feel the searing pain burning across my cheek as he hits me again. He never laid a hand on me before, but I've always known this is what my future would have been like if I stayed.

I whimper as the pounding in my head begins to increase. He grabs a fistful of my hair yanking my head back hard, my skull burning from the tight hold as he tells me, "You're no good to me. You're a whore and you're going to be treated as such. I'm going to make sure you're used repeatedly until you're begging for me to end your life. You will never see Drake again and I'll make sure every day that passes he forgets you ever existed," he spits out.

Tears run down my cheeks shattering my confidence and strength. I am filled with despair and utter hopelessness right now. Who am I fooling? I have no way out of this. Here I am chained to this chair surrounded by men who only see me and my body as a means for money and there is nothing I can do about it. My only means of protecting Drake and I before was running; I never stayed around long enough to fight.

"Okay, I get it. You hate me, but just know if you do this, if you separate Drake from me, he will end up despising you. You won't win in the end. I can promise you this. I'm engrained in him and I'm a part of him and no matter what you do, he will never forget me," I snarl, not caring anymore what he does to me.

He snickers evilly. "You should be thanking me for the time you had with him. I already had you sold when you had me arrested. We were never going to be a family, and you were never going to raise my son. You were just a means to an end all along, and your whole purpose in life was to sell that pussy to make me money, I was just breaking you in," he says spitefully.

I laugh in his face. "And you were also a means to an end. Now look at you, pathetic and far from a real man. You're not even man enough to lead like your brother does. You're just a little puppet to him and my son will never be like you. So, do what you want with me, hit me, sell me, kill me, but just know that you will never break me. My soul will haunt you for the rest of eternity."

"Leave her alone, Antonio," the man on the ground says barely audible.

Antonio turns and kicks him. He grunts, barely being able to hold onto his stomach from the impact. "Shut the fuck up! How you going to save her now, James?" he taunts, reaching for the hair on the top of his head pulling it back so he can face him. "She was never yours. She was always *mine!* Now look at you, thinking all these years you were going to somehow protect her. What a joke, and now you're going to die for it."

I stare at the man on the ground studying him, noticing the similarities of the boy I used to know. James.

My sweet James, who saved me from the nightmare of his father, the boy who looked out for me, stayed up most nights making me feel safe and protecting me from his own flesh and blood. Now, here he is still attempting to do the same while risking his life. Why would he after I just up and left him in the dust all those years ago?

"James –" I whisper.

He looks over at me. "Jenn, I tried to come and warn you. I knew they were coming for you, but I was too late," he says right before Antonio kicks him one last time knocking him out.

I flinch hearing the crack from the collision.

"Jesus, why would you try to save me?" I yell at James' limp body as if he can hear me. I look back up at Antonio. "You and your brother are fucking monsters! My son will never be like you. I pray you're sent back into the depths of hell where you belong!"

In the next moment I'm knocked into a black silence.

CHAPTER 16

NEAL

"Caruso, we have confirmation of Ray entering the barn with two of his men. Tell us what you want us to do," Johnny says. "Everyone's on standby waiting to move in."

I look through the scope of my AR-15 hoping to get a visual on Drake and Skylar, but the barn windows are too high. So, we're going to have to make our way toward the barn slowly and carefully to get a better idea of what's going on inside. My team surrounds this location and beyond us the rest of the force is waiting on our signal. There's no way they are getting out of this. Antonio will be the demise of his own brother's takedown because of his obsession and sick need of control.

"We need to make sure Skylar and Drake are out of the way before we make a move. I'm going to get closer and get eyes on the inside," I announce through the mic.

I scope out the barn and see a ladder against the side leading to a ledge. I signal my direction of movement as I slowly creep my way toward the ladder. Johnny slides into my position to watch my back as I move inch by inch making sure not to make a sound. The grass quietly succumbs beneath me as I clear my way like a panther through the darkness like I've done so many times before. Only this time my life and my future lie beyond these walls, making this the most important thing I'll ever do.

There's so much riding on these next couple of moments for us all and I'll be damned if I make a promise to her that I can't keep. I told her I would keep her safe and I intend to keep every word I made. She is my world now, my everything. There's no me without her.

I reach the ladder, slide my gun over my shoulder to my back so I can begin to carefully climb the ladder testing each step before placing my whole weight against each bar. I get to the top of the ledge which holds a small window overlooking the place, the glow of dim yellow light beams from the inside. I have to be careful not to cast a shadow when looking inside so I gradually inch my head just enough to be able to see in.

Anger rapidly surges through my body as I see Skylar sitting limp chained to a chair barely clothed with a blood covered shirt. Her head's laying to the side and her face is covered by her hair. I can't tell if she's breathing from way up here. It's killing me that I can't burst in and save her, but I must play this safe and the fact that I can't see where Drake is is making me anxious. I study the inside reporting back to my unit through my microphone giving them intricate details on every inch of the barn. There's a man lying in front of Skylar not moving. I take a closer look through my scope and realize it's fucking James. God damn it, he went and got himself caught. I can't tell if he's still alive, but it definitely looks as though he was beaten and tortured. From a distance I hear voices of multiple men from what looks to be a small side room, then Ray comes out holding Drake's hand.

He allows Drake to run to Skylar hugging her limp body as he whimpers while trying to wake her up. That fucking piece of shit! This is the last thing a child needs to see. They purposely want this vision to be the last thing he carries of his mother. It's sick and inhumane just showing what type of men these are – *monsters.*

Ray rubs the top of Drake's head as though he's offering comfort, making me want to take every revengeful thought out on them right in this moment. My stomach coils with repulsion at the sight. My fingers squeeze around my black metal of death even tighter trying to control myself. Antonio squats beside Skylar uncuffing each of her legs then double checks her hand-cuffs are secure. Ray calls over one of the men to lift her and he begins carrying her off as Drake starts screaming attempting to run after her. Antonio grabs Drake mid-run holding him back.

I notify the guys to get ready to move. There's no way I'm allowing them to leave with her. I push open the window trying my best not to make any noise as I care-fully climb through it. I land on the barn's overhang where old equipment and some hay bales are stored. It's dusty and the air is thick up here. I lay down on my stomach as close to the edge as I can manage and get myself in place ready to take a shot if need be.

"I have eyes on them," I advise the team.

"We're almost to the target, sir," Cam says as I listen to them creeping in the direction of Skylar.

"Bring him to Helen's and drop him off then meet us at

the warehouse over on 5th Street. Jorge is coming to pick the girls up; you can say your last goodbyes there and take care of him. We have no need for him any longer. He was just a means to get to her," Ray tells him, pointing toward James before turning to head out.

They must have known the connection between her and James all along. They played him this whole time as he led them straight to her and now those fuckers are planning to sell her. My adrenaline picks up tenfold, banging my heart against my chest. My blood is coursing through my body putting me on extremely high alert. I listen carefully as I hear them quietly directing the men to get on the ground. My guys are quick and precise with very little commotion.

"We have her," Johnny announces.

I immediately let out a breath relieved. My whole life of being without her flashed by my eyes for a moment. I crack a tiny smile of victory to myself. She's going to be okay. Now I need to get Drake.

Little does Ray know my guys already have her in custody and his plans on trafficking her end tonight. All the torment, sleepless nights, and fear end tonight for Skylar as well. The triumph is real, but the job isn't done yet. Now we're just waiting for Ray to walk out to his own demise. It was only a matter of time before his karma caught up to him. I watch as he takes his last step over the threshold, then in the very next moment I hear yelling and then shots fired.

Fuck! This is not good.

I knew Ray would be harder to take down, but I was praying it would happen without someone getting hurt. We need him alive. He's the key player to take the whole organization down. Without him we're driving blind again. Antonio's been out of the direct game for too long to know all the players and without us getting inside intel from the direct source, someone else can just simply step into place.

Antonio quickly lifts Drake off the ground like a rag doll, telling him to shut up as he begins running toward the side door. Without a thought I jump off the ledge, roll, grab my gun, and sink into position.

"Don't move another fucking step, Antonio!" I yell behind him just as he's about to push the latch on the door to try and escape.

He slowly turns around, but he now has a gun pointed at the back of Drake's head. He makes sure not to allow his son to see what a shitty fucked up father he is by using him as a pawn. I remain calm as I've been trained to do for so many years.

"Put him down, Antonio. It's over for you," I inform him.

There're still shots being fired and I'm now hearing that one of my men has been hit. Ray's not giving up without a fight, and we now have backup on its way.

"Ah you're the infamous *cop boyfriend* –" Antonio begins to say.

"Neal, I want to go home!" Drake cries, trying his hardest to get out of Antonio's hold.

Antonio grip gets tighter. "Fucking stay still you little shit!" he yells shaking him. "Jenn will soon be a used up piece of ass. I'm going to personally make sure she's begging for you to save her as they rip her apart one after another. Better you move on to someone else and forget about her because you're never going to find her and if you do, she'll be in pieces by then," he growls.

I scoff with a grin. "Jenn is safe you sick fuck. We have her. Your little plan didn't work. Let go of Drake and get on the ground. It's over for you, Antonio," I tell him knowing I just ultimately pissed him off.

His face contorts with fury. I hear the news over the microphone that Ray is down, and they are working on reviving him. It sounds like chaos out there as they are all trying to keep him alive. We want him to pay for his crimes through justice not go out the easy way. He needs to atone for his sins in front of a judge and jury, but after another moment they call it. He's gone. Shit. Maybe this little news will convince his brother to give in and surrender himself.

"Your brother was just shot. He's gone now. You're better off surrendering so you don't end up like him. My guys have this place surrounded, there's no way of getting out of here," I try my best to convince him even though a small part of me knows if he ends up back in jail, he can still get to Drake and Skylar, but I made an oath to do the right thing.

"Listen, *cop boy*, if you think I'm turning myself into you, then think again. I'm going to walk out of this door with my son and you're not going to stop me. You're going to have to kill me first."

As soon as this leaves his mouth, all hell breaks loose outside again. There must have been some sort of backup plan set in motion if we got involved and now it's like World War II outside. I internally swear but refuse to show any falter in my armor. I hold my ground waiting for his next move. If he tries running, then I'm going to aim for his legs.

"What do you think you're going to get out of this? You think Drake's going to grow up just like you after what you just did to his mother in front of him? You're fucking traumatizing him, man. You're a weak man for doing this to your own flesh and blood. Just let him go and I'll let you walk out that door without a fight," I offer him hoping he will take it.

He snickers. "He'll soon forget his whore of a mother, I'll make sure of it. I'll be back for her too. Don't you worry about that. They both belong to me, so enjoy her while you can because it won't be for long," he states as he starts to back up heading toward the door to escape.

"Take one more step and I'll shoot," I threaten him.

He doesn't listen and makes the move.

I do exactly what I said and aim for his leg. He falters at the first hit, but it doesn't drop him, so I aim for the other taking the shot as he tries to take another step pulling open the door then he finally drops to his knees releasing Drake while trying to catch himself.

"Drake, run!" I scream, but right before I rush toward him in attempt to pull him behind me Antonio aims his weapon and pulls the trigger. Everything flashes before my eyes in slow motion. Drake is running, Antonio releases the shot, and before I can place my body in front of him as a shield, James beats me to it taking the bullet for Drake.

I quickly grab Drake, pulling him behind me waiting for retaliation. It would be so easy for me to just take Antonio out and end this all, but I can't be a part of that evilness. I need to show Drake that there are good people in this world that honor laws and carry integrity within themselves. A life of crime is not what anyone should strive for and there are consequences when you choose the wrong path.

"Antonio, give up man. You shoot again and I'm going to take you out myself," I try to warn him again.

There's still a war going on outside but it's beginning to quiet down as I'm sure his people were outnumbered.

Antonio climbs to his feet attempting to limp away. This time I allow him to leave. Drake's seen enough for a lifetime, I can't traumatize him even more. I need to protect what's left of Drake's innocence and hurting his father more in front of him will only damage him further. I know Antonio won't get too far in his attempt to run. He's hurt, and he's surrounded by some of the best. He only has two ways out – in cuffs or ending up like his brother.

I close my eyes already knowing how this is going to end as he walks over the threshold. I kneel hugging Drake burying his head into my chest as I listen to the blows happening outside. He's shaking holding onto me for dear life. I lift him up, tucking him into my body so he knows he's safe and protected.

"I got you, bud. You're safe now. No one is going to hurt you again," I whisper to him as I take him to the far end of the barn waiting for all fire to finally cease. "Stay right here. I'll be right back. I need to go check on James," I tell him.

I carefully run back over to James checking his vitals. Luckily, he was only hit in the arm. I take my belt off wrapping it around his upper arm creating a tourniquet, then help him over to where Drake is for cover.

"You did good, James. Thank you," I praise him for being brave enough to give his life for Drake. Things could have turned out to be way worse if James hadn't been here and I didn't make it in front of Drake in time. Hell has a special place for fathers like him.

WE'VE BEEN TUCKED AWAY in the barn for what feels like forever until finally I hear footsteps entering. I slowly grab my handgun from my side getting ready for whatever comes our way. Drake tenses up again holding onto me with a death grip. The shadow of two men covers the barn wall as they come closer.

"Caruso, it's just us man," I hear Johnny yell out.

I exhale relieved. "We're over here!" I call back over Drake's head. "Everything's going to be okay, bud. It's time to go see your mom."

He nods still holding onto me for dear life. Johhny hands me a jacket, I cover Drake's head as we walk out of the barn. I can't risk him witnessing anything more than he already has. Bodies are covering the ground, and the wounded are being worked on by ambulance. I look over my shoulder to my right before heading to the truck, noticing Antonio's body lying still on the ground. I knew he had no chance once he walked out but I'm just glad it wasn't me that had to take him down. That's not the way I wanted to do it. And I don't want that on my conscience when having to look at Drake every day.

"Cam, where is she?" I ask as I jump into the back of the SUV.

"We have her down the street, she refused to leave and go to the hospital," Cam notifies me. "You want me to drive you up there?"

"Nah, man. They need you here. Jake here will drive me over there."

I SEE Skylar pleading with a cop, I'm assuming she's trying to get back to Drake. Her bruised face is filled with fear, determination, and exhaustion. I rub Drake on his back. "Hey, we're here. You ready to go see your mom?" I ask.

He nods after finally calming down some and no longer shaking. He still has a death grip on me, but he's a strong little boy who has so much courage. With lots of love and comfort, I know he's going to be okay. Skylar will make sure of it.

I open the door still carrying him with me. Skylar finally notices us and starts running toward us from afar.

She slams into us, wrapping her arms around us both bawling her eyes out. "Oh my God! Thank God you are both okay!" she says as she looks Drake over before taking him from me.

I watch as they embrace each other with tears streaming down their faces. I'm not one to ever shed a tear but watching this moment and after a long night with the worrying of losing them finally has me succumbing to my emotions. I stand back giving them some time for themselves before going in for another hug.

I lift her chin so I can get a good look at her swollen face. I rub my thumb gently over her bottom lip being careful not to touch her cut. My insides begin to boil. *That fucking sick bastard,* I think to myself looking down seeing the dried blood on her shirt, but then a serene calm spreads over me as I remember that this is now over for her. She's finally free from him, from Ray, and from it all.

"Did they hurt him, Neal?" she asks worried as she kisses his head still holding onto him tight.

I shake my head. "No, he was so brave," I tell her. She exhales nodding her head with relief. "Did they hurt you anywhere else?" I ask her, hoping what I can see is all of it.

"No, your guys rescued me before that could happen. I'm still in shock, I think. These past couple of hours feel like a nightmare that I haven't woken up from yet. What about James? Is he okay?"

I nod. "He's going to be okay. He tried his best to protect you all these years and in the end, it paid off," I inform her. She nods with a satisfied smile. Once things have calmed down, I'll tell her more about his heroism.

I wrap my arms around them again kissing her forehead. My world is finally right again. Everything is going to be okay. I still have yet to tell her about Ray and Antonio, but I think right now isn't the time to go over everything that went down after she was knocked out.

She looks up at me. "Thank you, Neal. Thank you for keeping your word in protecting us, I love you," she tells me.

My smile grows from ear to ear. Just hearing these words turns my insides into goo. She fucking loves me. This woman that I adore and am so damn in love with loves me back. I heard these words from Missy, but I never got this euphoric high after I heard them. I didn't feel as though I was floating on cloud nine and could take on the world because she loved me. But hearing these words from Skylar is just so much more.

"I love you too, Sky. I love you both so much."

EPILOGUE

SKYLAR

*I*t's been about a month since that awful night. Drake's nightmares finally subsided again, and we've all fallen into a normal routine called life. God, I never thought I would ever say that. It sounds so surreal coming from myself. No more running or looking over my shoulder. No more having to wake up in the middle of night to check on Drake, even though it became a habit and I continue to do it out of enjoying watching him sleep now instead of being frightened. No more being alone; friendless and loveless. I finally have connections and people who I can depend on.

Ray and Antonio's sister, Helen, left town and went back to Miami where she buried her two brothers. Only time will tell if she's going to become a problem in the future, but for now Neal will be keeping an eye on her. Drake now understands who Antonio was and sadly he looked relieved when I told him he was never going to bother us again. Our nightmare is finally over, and dreams of the future now lie in its wake.

Emily has been a great support system for Drake at school, advocating for him and making sure he has had someone great to talk to that deals with child trauma. She's totally stepped up to the plate as a friend, and we've become closer than ever. She now feels like a sister to me, and the fact that she's dating Neal's best friend, Johnny, means the four of us are always together. We've created our own little family filled with friends.

I still carry the guilt with me every day of choosing the wrong father for Drake, but little by little we're both healing and I'm slowly beginning to forgive myself. Some days are harder than others, but Neal has been a huge supporter in helping me navigate through my emotions during the hard times.

The cop that followed me home went missing. No one has seen or heard from him, so we're assuming that's how Antonio found me so fast. They used James as a pawn all these years but in the end he won. He's now become Uncle James to Drake and is a big part of our lives after he risked his life for him. I'm just so glad to have him back in my life again.

"Hey, whatcha thinking about?" Neal asks, knocking me out of my deep thoughts, bringing me closer to him as I continue to look off into the distance.

We continue to glide slowly on the front porch swing while watching Drake run around with Benny in the front yard. "Just thinking about the past year while trying to picture our new life with this new baby," I explain while placing my hand on my growing belly.

Neal kisses my cheek, then places his hand over the top of mine. "Our life is already perfect and will just get better with this new little dude in the mix."

I exhale. "Do you think Drake is really going to be okay with all the new changes? I'm nervous he may think he's going to be replaced," I admit worried.

Neal grabs my chin gently so I'm now gazing into his eyes. "Sky, you have raised such an amazingly kind little guy. I already know he's going to love this baby and be the best big brother one can have. You're an incredible mother, I'm so proud to have you as the mother of my child, and I can't wait until this baby is born so I can call you my wife too."

He always knows just how to make me tear up, and now that I'm pregnant, it's even worse. I smack his chest with the back of my hand. "Stop making me cry, Neal Caruso," I say sniffling.

"Can we just go elope already and say fuck the damn wedding so I can finally call you my wife?" he tries to joke, but I know deep down he's truly serious.

I roll my eyes. He knows how I feel about this. I've missed so many things and experiences these last couple of years because of Antonio, I just want to be selfish in having this forever memory of marrying my best friend. Neal has become my rock over these past couple of months, something I never thought I would have allowed – *ever*. But the ability to heal from just merely being loved is the greatest gift on earth and he gave this to me.

"Now, now, you know the best things are worth waiting for, Mr. Caruso," I tease him with a quick kiss.

He brushes his nose against mine. "I feel as though I have waited a lifetime for you, and I would wait a million more if I had to. I love you, Miss Skylar soon-to-be Caruso."

"I love you too, Neal. Thank you for putting my shattered pieces together again."

THE END

ACKNOWLEDGMENTS

This book took me years to write and I almost didn't finish, but I am so happy I did! This book wouldn't have come to life if it wasn't for multiple people helping me along the way.

First, I'd like to thank my editor, Virginia Carey. You have made me feel at ease and comfortable with sharing my writing after being out of the industry so long. So, thank you. Also, Michele Ficht, who did a quick and thorough job of proofreading, helped me with the finishing touches of making this book perfect.

Second, I'd like to thank Sommer Stein for my beautiful book cover – you always knock it out of the park! Paige Jenkins, my formatter, for making the inside beautiful, and The Next Step PR for all the great promotions over the weeks before publication. You guys are all amazing at what you do!

Third, to my family for putting up with my craziness while writing and cheering me on along the way. You all are my biggest supporters.

And last, thank you to the readers who took a chance on me again. I will be forever grateful.

ABOUT THE AUTHOR

Shevaun DeLucia lives in upstate New York with her husband, and two boys while also enjoying spending time with her two grown children who have already left the nest. As a stay-at-home mom while her children were young, she fell in love with reading. She indulged in the small moments that took her away from the reality of her loud, overly rambunctious household, bringing her into a world of fantasy. When reading wasn't enough to satisfy her, she turned to writing, determined to create the perfect ending of her own.

Visit her on her website at: https://shevaundelucia. com/

f facebook.com/AuthorShevaunDeLucia

www.ingramcontent.com/pod-product-compliance
Lightning Source LLC
Chambersburg PA
CBHW071542110726
47908CB00007B/1962